Death on the Danube

A fast-paced psychological thriller

D.J. Maughan

Hulyeseg Inc

Dedication

For you, Luke. A better friend a guy couldn't have. From the time we were kids, playing games like hanging eggs or throwing them at each other, to working out together almost daily as adults, you've been a loyal friend and support. Thank you for your friendship. I hope you enjoy this one!

Summary of cruise characters

Sue Kingsbury – Cruise passenger and wife to Phil.

Phil Kingsbury – Cruise passenger and husband to Sue.

Dave Silva – Cruise dining hall server.

Brianna Murphy – Cruise passenger and wife to Derek.

Derek Murphy – Cruise passenger and husband to Brianna.

Arpad Balazs – Cruise dining hall server.

Edit Fehér – Cruise cabin maid.

Albert Wagner – Cruise director.

Captain Arany Bence – Cruise captain.

Marko Novak – Cruise hospitality director.

Naomi Costa – Cruise passenger and wife to Jacob.

Jacob Costa – Cruise passenger and husband to Naomi.

Melody Jones – Cruise passenger and wife to Theo.

Theo Jones – Cruise passenger and husband to Melody.

Chapter 1
Sue Kingsbury

Cruise Day 7 - Budapest, Hungary, October 2001

My husband leans forward and picks up his wineglass, and I see the almost imperceptible flinch and quick intake of breath as he raises it to his lips. My focus stays on him, even as the old woman across the table, seated next to her daughter, drones on about who knows what. When will she ever shut up?

Tonight's the last night of our cruise. Tomorrow, we'll endure a long day of flights and layovers as we return home to Denver. The next day, we'll be back at work, jet-lagged and unsure of what time it is as our bodies try to assimilate to home. I'll be back at the hospital, and Phil will go to his office. He's a sales manager, and although his job is far from physically taxing, I wonder how much longer he'll be able to continue working. Will this be our last vacation together? What will the long hours on the plane do to him?

"What about you, Sue?"

The sound of my name brings my attention back to the pair of women across the table. The daughter has spoken, but they're both staring at me expectantly. We've sat with these women every night of the cruise. They're sweet people, but I'm ready to have new dinner companions, or none at all. Phil has tried to convince me to move to a different table, but I can't do it. I'd just feel too bad.

"What was that?" I ask.

The old woman—what's her name again? Janice? Tries to help her daughter out by repeating the question. "What was your favorite part of the city today?"

Before I can answer, I sense a familiar man approaching our table. He's wearing a crisp white shirt, dark vest, dark trousers, and a gold-colored name badge. I haven't looked at the name since our first night on board. He's been excellent, and I'll truly miss his hospitality and kindness. I look up at him and smile. Tonight, he's wearing his dark-rimmed glasses, and although they look stylish, I prefer seeing his eyes directly.

"Sorry to interrupt, but we're concluding our service for the evening. Is there anything else I can get you?"

I shake my head and smile, along with the two other women, but Phil reaches across the table and picks up the wine bottle.

"How 'bout one more?" Phil says, handing the bottle to Dave.

I reach out and put a hand on Phil's shoulder. "Honey, don't you think you've had enough?"

Phil's eyes flash to mine, and I see the clench of his jaw and fire in his eyes. When he speaks, his voice is heavy with irritation. "No, Sue." He draws out my name. "I think I'd like one more." He stares at me, challenging me with his eyes.

I know better than to say anything more. It's not worth the fight. I look at Dave and nod, and he takes the bottle, promising to return.

Phil continues to watch me as I turn my attention back to our companions. The younger woman is looking down as she slowly folds the white napkin she's removed from her lap. The old woman glares at Phil. I know what she's thinking; she made her view of men clear during our first meal, and she's repeated it every dinner since. She might think she knows Phil, but she doesn't. Not like I do. I need to divert her attention.

"It's hard to choose," I say, putting my fingers to my lips and pretending the interaction never happened. "For me, Budapest has been the most beautiful city on the trip, and I don't think it's even close. The views from the castle area were breathtaking."

Becky, the younger woman, about my same age, drops her napkin to the table and looks back up. Pleased to hear we've returned to our prior conversation. "Oh, me too," she says. "Did you see that view from the fisherman's place?" She looks at her elderly mother and raises her hands to form a peak. "What was that place called right by the white church? Fisherman something." She turns and points out the window across the river.

"Bastion," Phil says, staring down at his empty wineglass. I didn't think he was paying any attention to the conversation.

"Right," she says, crinkling up the skin on her forehead. "What does that mean?"

"Bastion?" I ask.

She nods.

"Didn't you hear our tour guide?" her mother asks.

Becky frowns. "Oh, did she talk about it?"

The old woman nods.

"What did she say?"

Her mother looks at her, then at me, before a sheepish grin spreads across her face. She raises her palms and chuckles while shaking her head. "Beats me. Who could understand anything with that accent? I was lucky if I got half of what she said."

I smile and glance at Phil. He's staring at his glass, his mind elsewhere. He notices me watching him and straightens. Again, I see him wince in pain as he stretches back, trying to loosen his joints.

Dave returns, and our conversation halts as he opens the bottle and offers to refill Phil's glass.

"Dave," I say while he pours.

"Yes, Sue?"

"We'd love to have a picture with you. Could one of your colleagues come and take it?"

"Of course."

He crosses the room and asks a young woman I've seen every night, but I don't know her name. Phil and I stand and gather around Janice and Becky while Dave joins us, and the young woman takes several pictures with my camera. We thank her, then hug Dave, and he walks away.

Once we're seated again, I see Janice as Phil raises his glass. She discreetly bumps her daughter with her elbow. They look at each other, then at me.

"I think we'll turn in. That was a lot of walking," the old woman says, pushing away from the table and struggling to stand.

I smile and nod, and Phil stands as we wish them a good night and offer each other safe travels back home. They walk away, and Phil sits again, palming his glass and draining it. He notices me watching him as he lowers it. "You could join me, you know?" he says, reaching for the bottle. Has he forgotten my glass is still full?

I shake my head, and his hand falls to the table. I see the disappointment in his eyes. He's always liked drinking more than I have. That's nothing new. But since his back problems started, he's turned to the bottle more than ever. When I've broached the subject, he's reacted as he did tonight. I know what he wants. He wants company. He wants me to drink with him.

"How's your back?" I ask, reaching over and placing my hand on his.

He shifts from side to side, grimacing the whole time. "They say walking is supposed to help. Tonight, it feels worse than ever."

I rub the skin on his knuckles with my thumb and give him a sympathetic look.

He stares back at me with glassy eyes.

"You've got to go see a specialist when we get home."

He shakes his head. "They can't help me," he says and picks up his glass. "Have you ever known anyone who's had a back surgery and actually recovered?"

I watch him. He's right. Serious back pain seems to be a lifelong affliction. I look down at the table and stare at my cup, then look away out the window. Our boat is docked beside one of Budapest's many bridges. Night has fallen over the city, and lights illuminate the bridge. It's a beautiful sight, and I don't want it to end. At least, not yet. I stare out the window for several seconds, then get an idea.

I stand from the table, reaching for the wine bottle. I pick it up and walk away, Phil calling after me in frustration.

"Hey," he says. "I wasn't done with that."

I turn back and wink, giving him a sly smile. "If you want more, you're going to have to come with me."

He frowns. "Where are you going?"

I shrug and point at my glass as he stands. "Get mine."

He gives me a curious look but eagerly complies as I turn away from him and walk out of the dining hall. I stop in front of the elevator, and he catches up to me. He looks down at me, searching for an explanation, but I only smile as the elevator arrives. We ride it to the top deck and step out into the night. The air is fresh and much cooler than at midday. It's October, but today was hot until the sun went down.

I put my arm through his as we walk along the carpeted path on the top deck. It's a gorgeous night with a slight breeze. There's energy in this city, and a car horn blares from the street several hundred meters away. We're nearly alone on the top deck, and we reach a small table with two chairs, and I pull him to it. I fill the rest of my cup and take several big gulps before sitting down.

"What's gotten into you?" he says, watching me.

I smile and stretch my hands, demonstrating all around us. "Look at this. Look at where we are. Haven't we always dreamed of being in Europe? Isn't this just as you've always imagined it?" I motion to the other side of the river. "Look at the castle over there." I look up the river. "Look at those bridges. All of the sparkling lights. This is our last night. Let's enjoy it. Let's make it memorable."

He smiles and reaches for my hand as we sit looking at the majestic city. For several minutes, we say nothing, enjoying each other's presence and taking in all the sights and sounds while music softly plays below. It sounds like it's coming from the lounge. I don't recognize the song. I think it might be a Hungarian folk song. I noticed in our program that Hungarian singers and dancers would perform in the lounge. I considered asking Phil if we could go but knew what the answer would be. I look at him, and another idea forms. I stand, take a couple of steps toward him, then force his legs open with my knees and hold out my hands.

"What?" he asks.

"Dance with me," I say, looking down at him.

He stares at me for several seconds, then sighs and puts his glass on the table, letting me pull him. He takes me in his arms, and I put my head on his chest as we embrace. I feel his warm breath on my neck as he nuzzles in close. The music plays as he slowly turns me. I gaze up the river at the large government building that sits on the edge of the water. The domes at the top look like a king's crown. I can't believe we're here. I could stand here and stare at this city all night.

When the music ends, he stops turning me, and I look up at him. He leans down and presses his lips to mine. Soft at first, then more firmly. It takes my breath away and forces me to step back. As our lips part and he straightens, he takes a sharp intake of breath.

"Your back?" I ask.

He nods, and I lead him back to the table and force him back into the chair.

"I'm sorry," I say, standing over him.

He gives me a half-smile and shrugs.

I gaze at him sympathetically, then step away and approach the ship's rail. I look out at the castle up on the hill, then further north at the spire of the church and the bastion in front. Lights decorate every location. I close my eyes, savoring the moment. I just turned sixty-two years old, but tonight, I feel thirty years younger. I don't remember a time I've felt more alive. I wish I could stay here forever.

With my hands still on the railing, I turn back to look at Phil. A sound of water splashes below me, and I turn back, looking down into the dark water. Something is moving. I lean out further and squint, trying to see better in the dark as my eyes adjust. It's the shape of a body. The body rotates, and the face stares up at me, wide-eyed and lifeless. My heart drops as I watch the face submerge. It's a face I recognize. A face of another passenger I've seen many times over the last week on this cruise.

There's been a death on the Danube.

Chapter 2
Brianna Murphy

Cruise Day 1 – Munich, Germany, October 2001

The pilot announces he's begun our descent into Munich, and we should be on the ground in fifteen minutes. I lift the screen on the window and look out, bubbling with excitement. I'm expecting to see something very German—seismic snowcapped mountains with men wearing leather pants and drinking huge mugs of beer. Women with floral dresses and long blond braids. Instead, I see clouds. Our elevation is too high for anything else.

I frown but keep the shade raised and watch the clouds rush by below. I've never been to Europe. In fact, I've never really been outside the United States, unless you count Mexico, and I don't. Sure, if it was *real* Mexico, like Mexico City. But it was one time at an all-inclusive resort in Cancun. We were surrounded by Americans, not Mexicans. Everyone spoke English. We could even drink the water because it was filtered.

I look back at my husband and then return to window gazing. Derek and I always talked about crossing the pond and visiting his old country, but between kids and life, we could never swing it. Now our dreams are finally being realized, and I can barely contain my excitement. The clouds part, and in the distance, I can just make out mountain peaks. I turn back to Derek and almost bump him awake but stop. His eyes are closed, and his chin rests on the neck roll I gave him. How can he still be asleep? Isn't he excited?

I watch him, wanting so badly for him to wake and share this moment with me. I study his face for any sign of life. How can I be angry with him? He's so gorgeous. He's older but even more attractive now than the first time I saw him. If that's possible. We were just kids, really. He was a junior at ASU, and I was in my second semester. My friend Anna was dating his bestie, Jon, and Derek came along on a visit to our dorm. At the time, Anna and Jon claimed they weren't trying to set us up, but we knew better. Anna said they were only coming to watch TV since they didn't have one. I knew what that meant. It meant Anna would be with Jon, and Derek would be paired with me. I'd be forced to sit with him and pretend to be interested. No thank you. I told her in no uncertain terms that I wasn't interested in being set up, and I was going to stay in my room the whole time until they left. And I intended to until my curiosity got the better of me. I snuck over to the door and silently cracked it, trying to see him. He and Jon were sitting on the couch while Anna was making popcorn in the kitchen. I couldn't see anything but the top of his head, which told me nothing, because he was wearing a royal-blue surf-shop hat.

"Do you guys want anything to drink?" Anna asked from the kitchen, getting both boys to turn their heads. I still wonder if she knew I was watching and helped me out.

"Got any beer?" Jon asked.

I didn't even register the words. I was transfixed. Derek was nothing short of gorgeous. His features were perfect, his light eyes offset by his dark hair, and that jawline...yum. Never had I seen a face like that so close, and my breath caught in my chest.

Jon stood from the couch and went into the kitchen while Derek turned back to the black-and-white TV. I closed the door and felt a rush of inadequacy. He couldn't see me like this. Immediately, I set to work remedying the situation. I wasn't going to let this opportunity pass me by. I was going out there. After changing my outfit three times, reapplying my makeup, and brushing my hair until it gleamed, I took a deep breath and strode out with more confidence than I felt. The show, *Charlie's Angels*, had already started, but I made enough noise that the three of them turned and looked at me. Like a Charlie's Angel, I walked right over and took my place beside Derek. I haven't moved since. I'm still beside him now.

I can't stand it anymore and reach out and tickle the side of his face. He doesn't even stir. He's been asleep forever! He fell asleep shortly after they fed us dinner when leaving Atlanta and hasn't woken since. I've watched two movies, read a couple hundred pages in my romance novel, and dozed twice while he's just slumbered away, oblivious to the world around him. I just don't understand how he can sleep this much. Isn't he excited?

The flight attendant comes by and looks us over, checking our seat belts. Derek's is on, but his seat is reclined, and the attendant gives me a disapproving look. She acts as if he's my child, and I should know better. Before she can, I reach over and press the button on his armrest. His seatback comes up, and she nods before walking away, seeking her next victim. I've never understood why a slight incline in a seatback endangers passengers. We're already packed in here like sardines.

The overhead lights come on, and that finally does it. Derek stirs, but his eyes still don't open. I watch him, wondering if I should nudge him, then his eyelids flutter. He straightens and looks over at me before yawning and closing his eyes again.

I nudge him with my elbow. "Time to wake up, sleepyhead. You've slept enough."

"Are we landing?" he asks with a grumble, keeping his eyes shut and yawning.

I grip his bicep and point out the window. "That, my dear, is Germany. Or, at least, it better be."

He opens his eyes, looks at my extended finger, then smiles. I look back out the window and slide my hand down his arm to his hand. We've dropped below the clouds, and I scan the horizon, looking for a city. I've heard Munich is one of the largest in Germany, and I'd love to see that Glockenspiel clock. It's supposed to be the largest cuckoo clock in the world. Maybe if we aren't too far from the city, we could go see it before they take us to the boat. But I don't see the city. In fact, all I see are scattered houses among emerald farmlands. It looks just as I thought it would, and I squeeze his hand with anticipation. This is going to be such an adventure!

The runway becomes visible, and within a minute, we're on the ground, taxiing to the gate.

"How did you do that?" I ask Derek.

"Do what?"

"Sleep the whole flight."

He smiles and chuckles, his Adam's apple bobbing. "I was tired."

I shake my head and start gathering my things before we reach the gate. We're near the back of the plane, and even though there are two open exits, it takes several minutes before it's our turn. When we're finally off, we're funneled through baggage claim and customs. We exit the restricted area and see a man holding a sign with our names on it. We make eye contact as we approach.

"Murphy?" he asks with a foreign accent.

We nod, and he extends his hand. "I'm Arpad."

I smile and take it. "I'm Brianna."

"Brianna," he says, then turns to Derek and extends his hand.

"Derek *vagyok*," my husband says in perfect Hungarian.

Shock registers on Arpad's face, and he starts rattling off something in Hungarian. Derek replies, and I watch my husband with both amazement and jealousy. Since we've been married, I've only heard him speak Hungarian a few times. He joked as we were preparing for this trip that he might not even remember how. Now, he speaks effortlessly. I hear something that sounds like my name, and they both look at me.

"What?" I ask.

Both men smile, and Arpad directs us to a group of people waiting with their luggage. Pretty much all of them are Americans, and I feel a little relief. I love hearing Derek speak Hungarian, but I don't think I could handle it the whole time. I'm glad to see I'm not alone.

Arpad directs the large group to follow him, and we walk out of the airport and reach a bus. Arpad and the driver load our bags while we find seats inside.

I nudge my husband. "How was that?"

He grins. "Like riding a bike."

"Did you think you'd forget?"

He shakes his head. "But I didn't know if it would feel natural."

"But it did?"

He nods. "Arpad said he's the only Hungarian here picking up passengers. All the others are from Austria and other European countries."

"Hmm," I say, smiling and looking away from him. I can feel his eyes on me.

"What?"

"Nothing."

"Bri?"

I turn and wink at him. "It's just another sign. Even if you don't think so, I know it. We were meant to come on this trip."

Chapter 3
Derek Murphy

Cruise Day 1 – Passau, Germany

After an hour bus ride, we arrive in Passau and are welcomed onto the ship by a jovial, rotund, bald man wearing a red jacket. He points us to the registration desk, and a trim woman with exceptionally curly hair greets us and offers to check us in.

"Welcome aboard," she says with a distinct accent. I know it's Eastern European, but beyond that, I can't place it. All I know is it's not Hungarian. I can see her name tag. She has a Slavic name, maybe Czech. "Can I have your names, please?"

"We're the Murphys," Brianna says, beaming. "I'm Brianna, and this is Derek."

My wife's enthusiasm makes me smile. I'm so glad we can do this, despite my reservations. The woman smiles, revealing a slight crowding of her lower teeth, and types several strokes on the computer. "Oh, yes. You will be in room 327. How many bags do you have?" I hold up one finger and Brianna two. "Okay, so three total." She types on her machine again and then frowns. "I'm sorry, but your room is not ready. It shouldn't be too much longer. You're welcome to wait in our lounge. We have drinks and snacks." She points up the stairs to the level above us. "Or you can go to the top deck. We have a golf putt game and shuffleboard. The day is beautiful."

We thank her, and I take Brianna's hand in mine, and we turn to leave, but then my wife stops and turns around. "What about our luggage?"

"Did you put tags on them? The ones we provided with your names?"

"Yes."

"Then you have no problems. They will be delivered to your room when it is ready."

"Thank you."

We step away, and I look down at Bri. I sense some anxiety beneath her enthusiasm. Is it because of me? Because of what I said about this vacation? I shouldn't have said anything. I need to distract her. "What do you want to do?"

She doesn't look at me. "I don't care."

"Do you want to go to the lounge?"

"Okay." We start toward the stairs, but she grabs my arm. "How about let's go to the top? She's right. It is a beautiful day."

"You aren't hungry or thirsty?"

She shakes her head. "Are you?"

I am, but I shake my head. I don't know what it is about me, but I rarely express my true desires. Especially with her. Maybe subconsciously, I think it's easier to do what she wants. I'm more accommodating.

I follow Bri up the stairs and out onto the top deck of the ship. I've never been on a cruise ship, but I've seen plenty advertised on TV. I imagine this one is very different from the ones on the ocean. The ships in the commercials have waterslides, casinos, and multiple restaurants. This one doesn't appear to have any of that. It's much smaller, for one. I can see only four levels in total. The top of the boat is basic, with a running track along the outside and chairs with umbrellas scattered in different locations. Maybe it's because we haven't started yet, but the vibe on the boat seems much slower and more relaxed than on the ocean cruises. Neither of us wants to sit, so we stand along the railing and look out over the water and the city.

"Is that Passau?" Bri asks, pointing.

I shrug. "I assume." I've never been to Germany, but that doesn't stop her from asking me questions about it.

We gaze at the city, and I don't know if it's the architecture or the signs with different languages, but European cities look so much different from those in the US. I've grown accustomed to the US, and now Europe is foreign.

"Is this what you imagined?" I ask as I turn and look across the river at the castle on the hill.

"What do you mean?"

"Is this what Europe looked like in your mind?"

She frowns. "I don't know."

"No?" I say, turning back to her.

She's looking out over the water, and she scrunches up her nose. She's everything I've ever wanted, and I can't help but reach out and take her in my arms.

"What?" she asks, looking up at me and grinning.

I smile down at her. It's been twenty-five years since she became my wife, and I love her more each day. There's nobody I'd rather be with at this moment. I love and trust her, but that doesn't mean I can always tell her everything. There are things she's better off not knowing. Things she just wouldn't understand.

"Happy anniversary," I say.

She grins. "Happy anniversary."

We stay up on the deck for another thirty minutes, playing miniature golf and looking out over the beautiful landscape, then go downstairs and check on our room. It's available, and the concierge walks us down the hall until we stop at number 327. She gives us each a key, then reminds us that dinner will be ready in two hours, and before that, there will be a cruise orientation in the lounge.

She leaves, and we walk into the room. It's small, but why do we need a large room? We will not spend much time in here anyway. And if we do, it's going to be in the bed. There's a balcony with a sliding door leading out. There's a bottle of sparkling water on the counter with a note from the maid welcoming us. The maid's name catches my attention, and I stare at it, thinking. Bri enters the bathroom when there's a knock at the door. I answer it, finding an attractive woman with long dark hair and light-hazel eyes standing before me. She wears a different uniform from the staff we have met thus far but has the same name tag.

"Hello," she says with a heavy accent. "Is this," she looks down at the paper in her hand, "Murphy room?"

I look at the name on her tag, then respond in our shared native language. "*Igen*." (Yes)

Surprise registers on her face, and she studies me for a full second but sticks with English rather than Hungarian. "I have your bags."

I thank her and reach out, rolling the bags into the room.

She extends her hand. "If you need anything, my name is Edit."

"Thank you, Edit," I say, taking her hand.

She leaves, and I shut the door.

"Who was that?" Bri calls through the closed bathroom door.

"The maid. She brought our luggage."

The toilet flushes, and the sink water runs. Then Bri joins me as we unpack and get settled before heading to the lounge for the orientation.

When we arrive, all the tables and cushioned seats are occupied. The only remaining spots are a couple of rows of folding chairs directly in front of the screen and microphone. I scan the other passengers and notice we're at least ten years younger than anyone else. Most of the heads are silver, white, or bald. We take seats on the folding chairs just as a man with a dark vest and white shirt asks us if we'd like something to drink. I order a beer while Brianna asks for a soda. He leaves, and the man with the protruding belly, who greeted us as we boarded the ship, walks to the microphone and introduces himself.

"Welcome aboard. I'm your cruise director, Albert Wagner. We're delighted to have you with us." He paces as he speaks. "I have the best job on the cruise. Do you know why?" He pauses, and nobody answers. "Because I'm in charge of all the fun." He smiles and looks around, and his eyes fall on us when he says, "Out of curiosity, how many of you have been on a river cruise in Europe before? Show me your hands."

Hands go up all around, but not ours.

"Wonderful! What about this cruise? Has anyone been on this cruise before?"

Only a couple of hands raise.

He smiles, turning his attention to them. "We welcome you back. You're going to know the answer to most of these questions, but try not to spoil it for the others," he says, winking. "Give them a chance."

He turns his attention back to the entire group. "This cruise we affectionately call the Danube Waltz in honor of the famous composer Johann Strauss, who named one of his works *An der schönen blauen Donau*, which translated to English means *On the Beautiful Blue Danube*. Can anyone tell me where the great Johann Strauss was from?"

I expect hands to raise, but they don't. After a second or two, I raise my hand, and he calls on me. "He was Austrian."

"Correct," he says, pointing to me with excitement. "Now, can anyone guess where I am from?"

The woman at the table to our right calls out a tentative "Austria."

He snaps his fingers. "Also correct. One more question: can anyone tell me what country we'll be in tomorrow?"

The same woman who responded before is more confident this time. "Austria."

"Once again, correct. Boy, do we have a sharp group," he says and walks to the other side of the screen projector. "Tonight, we'll spend the night docked here in Passau. We'll have dinner, and several of you have excursions into the city, then tomorrow all of you are welcome to join our walking tour, which begins at eleven, lasts for an hour and a half, then affords you another two hours of free time for shopping and stuff like that before we require you to return to the boat." The screen changes, and he points to it. "We ask that everyone be back on board by four p.m. Now, you must be back by four. We need to keep to our schedule. Captain Arany, who I will introduce in a moment, is a stickler for time. And you don't want to get on the captain's bad side. Or you might spend time in the brig." He laughs. "Tomorrow, perhaps more than any other day, it is particularly important, because we have several locks we will pass through on our way to Linz. Those locks are scheduled because of the traffic on the river, and if we don't arrive in time, we are forced to wait until an opening in the schedule. So please make sure you are back by four p.m. tomorrow."

For the next fifteen minutes, he summarizes each of the stops, including Passau, Linz, Krems, and Vienna in Austria, Bratislava in Slovakia; and Budapest in Hungary. When he finishes, he introduces us to the captain. The captain isn't a tall man, maybe five feet eight inches. But he's powerfully built with broad shoulders and thick forearms. He speaks with a heavy Hungarian accent, and I wonder what part of Hungary he's from. His remarks are brief, focusing primarily on safety and rules of the voyage.

When he finishes, he introduces the director of hospitality, Novak. Mr. Novak is a tall man with black hair and a bulbous nose. His English is also heavily accented, but he's not from Hungary or Austria. He's from Slovenia, a neighbor to both countries. His speech is longer than the captain's but still brief. He focuses on the dining experience and the comfort of our rooms. At the end of his speech, he introduces tonight's dinner menu and invites us to go down one level to the dining room, where the chef has prepared an authentic German meal.

The room clears, and Bri and I follow two women who look like they may be mother and daughter. The mother is quite old, considering the daughter has long white hair. When we enter the dining hall, servers stand on either side, greeting guests. All wear the uniform of black vests, trousers, and crisp white shirts. They answer questions and point out seating options, reminding us that no tables are reserved. We can sit wherever we like.

"Where should we sit?" Bri whispers.

I shrug and look around. We don't know anyone on this ship.

"How about over there?" she asks, pointing to the table where the mother and daughter we followed sit. The location looks as good as any next to the window. I shrug and tell her I'll follow.

When we reach the table, Bri asks if we can join them, leaving two more empty seats.

"Of course," the mother says with a slight domestic accent. It sounds like she might be from the south.

"I'm Brianna," my wife says as we sit. "This is my husband, Derek."

I wave.

"I'm Janice, and this is my daughter, Becky."

"Nice to meet you both," Bri says.

"Where y'all from?" Janice asks.

"Phoenix," Bri says. "You?"

"I'm originally from Little Rock, but we've been living in St. Louis for the last thirty years, so I guess that's home."

I sense movement on my right and turn to see another couple approaching the table.

"Do you mind if we sit in these seats?" a woman with brown hair to her shoulders asks. She appears to be in her early sixties. Her husband stands beside her, smiling.

"Of course. The more the merrier," Janice says.

The man sits beside me and reaches out a hand. "Phil Kingsbury," he says as I take his hand.

"Derek Murphy."

"Nice to meet you, Derek."

"We were all just getting acquainted," Janice says. "Where y'all from?"

"I'm Sue, and this is Phil, and we're from Denver."

"Denver. Well, I'll be," Janice says. "I've been out to Denver a time or two. Beautiful mountains out that way."

Our server, a man of average height and build and with black hair, stands beside the table. "Welcome to the dining room. My name is Dave, and I'll be your server tonight. Maurice will also be by to assist me. Can I get anyone a drink?" he says as he distributes menus.

Janice and Rachel each order cocktails while I get a beer. Brianna, Phil, and Sue all ask for wine. When he leaves, we examine our menus.

"German food," Phil says to nobody in particular. "What's that all about?"

"A lot of sour cabbage and meat," Janice says with a chuckle.

Phil lowers his menu and looks at her. "Have you been to Germany before?"

She shakes her head. "First time."

"We've been," Sue says and looks over at Bri.

"I've never been," Bri says.

"Has anyone been anywhere in Europe?" Becky asks.

Bri shakes her head, but Sue and Phil nod.

"We've been twice. We did a cruise like this one last year. It was along the Rhine."

"How was it?" Bri asks.

"Wonderful," Sue says. "And we did another one before that."

Phil nods while looking at his menu.

"What was that one?" Becky asks.

Sue looks at Phil, then at Becky. "Paris to Prague."

"Ooh," Bri coos. "How was that?"

Sue looks at Phil, and he gives a less-than-enthusiastic smile. "It was fine."

We all wait, sensing more to the story as Phil lowers his menu.

"Well, they claimed it was a river cruise. But there isn't a river that runs from Paris to Prague. A bus cruise would have been a more accurate description," he says with a chuckle.

Dave, our server, returns, and we place our orders. When he leaves, Phil raises his glass and offers a toast. We all clink glasses, and an awkward pause falls on the table.

"So, nobody has been to any of the stops we have on this cruise?"

Sue smacks his arm and shakes her head. "They said they've never been to Europe, remember?"

"Oh, that's right," Phil says.

"Derek has," Bri says. I look at her but say nothing. They all watch us, and when she sees I'm not going to respond, she puts a hand on my arm and says, "Derek's from Hungary."

I give her a look, then acknowledge it to the rest of the table.

"Wow," Sue says. "I couldn't even tell. You sound American."

"I am," I say. "I left Hungary when I was a kid. I haven't been back since."

"This will be your first time back in Budapest?" Phil asks.

I nod.

"How does that feel? You know, to go back to your home?" Becky asks.

I look at her and answer as honestly as I know how. "I don't know yet."

Chapter 4
Naomi Costa

Cruise Day 2 – Passau, Germany

I *hate* my husband. There, I said it. I know I shouldn't. I feel nasty saying it. I don't want to feel this way. But I do. Oh, how I do. Sometimes, at times like these, when it's just the two of us, I imagine how I might kill him. I don't think it would be violent. I don't have it in me. I've never shot a gun, and I worry about a knife. What if something went wrong? What if he fought back? He's too strong. He'd overpower me. I'd have to sneak up from behind. Surprise him.

Poison seems more likely. I could slip it into his drink. His precious Diet Coke. He wouldn't know the difference. He thinks he would, but he wouldn't. I've given him the real stuff, nondiet, on trips like these plenty of times without him knowing. Gasp. It's a game, one of my only enjoyments. I buy two Cokes, a diet and a regular. I pour out the diet and fill it with the regular one and give it to him. Occasionally, he makes a comment like, "Boy, these drinks sure taste different in other countries." I smile and nod. He's too dumb to figure it out.

As if he hears me, he picks up his Diet Coke and takes a drink as I look away. I roll my eyes and look out the window. It's unfair, really. I used to like Diet Coke. Now I detest the sight of it. My eyes return to him as I watch him read his novel. Who brings a book with them to the dining hall of a cruise at breakfast? My husband, Jacob Costa, that's who. He sips his Diet Coke, reads his action thrillers, and is completely oblivious to the woman sitting across the table, imagining his untimely demise.

He glances up from his book as he turns the page and gives me a courteous smile as I unwrap a blueberry muffin and break off a piece. I put it in my mouth, chewing slowly. His eyes are already back in his book. With his other hand, he palms the Diet Coke and takes a swig, his eyes never leaving the page. I clear my throat in disgust and pick up another chunk of muffin. Sometimes I argue with myself about what it is. Why does his Diet Coke obsession bother me so much? I think it's the "diet." There's this sense that somehow it's healthier. Tell that to the mound of fat that hangs over his belt loops every time he takes off his shirt. How's that "diet" working out?

I turn away and look back out the window. It's a beautiful morning. The sun's rays are gleaming off the water. The city stands behind it, welcoming our exploration, with its old buildings and elevation changes. I should be excited. It's our first full day of a seven-day European river cruise that other people would kill to experience. But I'm dreading it. Not because of the place. Because of him. I shake my head and tell myself to stop it. We have Theo and Melody here too. Our friends are with us, and I'm so grateful. There's no way I would have come if they weren't along with us. They should be here now, except they slept in like normal people. Jacob made me come and see the sunrise. He couldn't go alone. And what's so funny is that as soon as the sun was up, his nose was back in the book.

I haven't always felt this way about him. There was once a time I actually loved him, as hard as that is to imagine. It feels like so long ago that I can barely remember it. We met in our midtwenties. It was a blind date, of all things. We were both graduates from the U of A and were getting started with our careers. We were dating other people, but maybe sensing our dissatisfaction, our friends matched us up. They thought we would hit it off, and we agreed to go.

It was nothing special—dinner and a movie. He's not the type of man who makes a woman look twice, but he's also not ugly. At least, he wasn't. It wasn't his looks that attracted me. It was his confidence and determination. He already had a good job in the mortgage industry and was going places. He wasn't shy about his dreams and plans, and I found that intoxicating. I craved a man who would make me feel safe and comfortable. I didn't care that we didn't have amazing sexual chemistry. He was someone I could trust and build a life with.

We got married a year later, and it wasn't long before I was pregnant with our first. Now we've been married for twenty-eight years, and he's the father of my three children. He's been everything I thought he would be. A devoted father and a wonderful provider. My kids have never wanted for anything. We've lived a comfortable life. There's absolutely no reason for me to hate him. But I do.

Things changed seven years ago. When our kids were young, we were so busy in their lives that we barely paid attention to our own.

We were just trying to keep our heads above water. But then, our kids grew up and began leaving the house for college, and we found we were alone more and more. Then Jacob's father died, and his mother was forced to move in with us. For me, it was a blessing. It gave me something to occupy my time. I wasn't alone with him. But, unfortunately, that didn't last long. Within a couple of years, she was dead, and we were completely alone in the house. They say distance makes the heart grow fonder. What they don't say is that the opposite can also be true. Too much time with your husband makes you despise him.

I finish the muffin and fold the paper, preparing to stand when a couple enters the room and grabs my attention. They're young. I mean, relative to all the other passengers on the boat. They can't even be fifty yet. I thought we were the young ones because we haven't reached sixty. Apparently not. I watch as they approach the breakfast bar hand in hand and order omelets. Their energy fascinates me, and to my surprise, they sit at the vacant table beside us. They sit close, their arms touching as they eat. The happiness is evident in their eyes. They love each other. They want to be together.

I glance at Jacob, wondering if he's seen it. Of course, he hasn't. His head is still in the book. Reading about life instead of experiencing it.

"Do you feel the humidity?" I hear her say. She has a sweet, lilting voice. "How does my hair look? Is it frizzy?"

"You look great," he says. "Gorgeous, as always."

She smiles and leans over to him, and he kisses her. The server arrives and asks them if they'd like anything to drink, and they order tea, which I find strange. They don't sound British. They sound American. I thought only the British drank tea?

"What temperature is it going to be today?" she asks.

He examines the information sheet we all had under our doors this morning when we woke. He brought it with him. He must be the planner. "It looks like it'll be in the high seventies or low eighties. Perfect weather."

She smiles. "What temperature do you think it is back home?"

His response surprises me.

He chuckles. "Probably a hundred and fifteen."

She laughs. "Maybe we should stay here. Live here instead."

He grins. "Maybe. But we might be getting ahead of ourselves."

I glance away from them and notice Jacob is watching me. The book is closed and resting on the table. "Should we go?" he asks.

I nod and stand, moving past them. As we walk down the hall toward our room, I can't stop thinking about them. Are they from Arizona too? What are the chances? I've got to meet them. Maybe they can be our new friends. Wouldn't that be fun?

Chapter 5

Jacob Costa

Cruise Day 2 – Passau, Germany

Naomi, Theo, Melody, and I stand outside the ship behind the woman holding the 3A lollipop-shaped sign with our ship's logo on it. She's a small woman with a reasonable accent, and I question how we're all going to hear and understand her if the group is larger than just us. As if sensing my thoughts, the cruise director walks past and pulls out a set of earpieces and radios. He motions to the tour guide, and she pulls a microphone from the bag she's holding and instructs us all to switch our devices to channel twenty-two. We comply, and I hear her clearly through the earpiece.

"Okay, we are just waiting for two more people, then we should have our entire group, and we can start walking. While we wait, let me introduce myself. My name is Katrina. I'm originally from Innsbruck in Austria, but I am now here in Passau for more than ten years. My first husband was American, and I lived in the US for twenty years but returned to Austria after he died. I met a German man not long after and, unfortunately, let him talk me into marrying him. I moved with him here to Passau. I love Passau, but it turns out, American husbands are better than German ones."

She laughs, and Theo and I give each other a look.

"Okay, I see a couple coming off the boat. Maybe they belong to us."

I look and see a man and wife walking down the boat ramp. He's wearing an LA Dodgers hat and holds his wife's hand. I've noticed them before. They stand out because of their age. Life hasn't beaten them down yet. The man says something to his wife and points to our group as they angle toward us. When they arrive, our tour guide hands them earpieces and waits several seconds for them to turn them on.

"Can you hear me?" she asks into the microphone. Both nod, and she turns her attention back to the entire group. "Okay, are we ready to go?"

We all nod, and she walks away from the river while sharing a brief history of the city. Our first stop is a cobblestone street that you would only see in Europe. The buildings on either side are ancient, and the city allows nothing other than pedestrian traffic on the street. Our guide tells us about the road and how every year the river floods and often submerges the street and halfway up the buildings. She points to the corner of one building, and I see lines and years painted on it. They represent the meters reached by the floods. She explains that annually, they know a flood is coming, they just don't know when. It changes every year. Because of this, they rent the bottom two floors of the buildings at a much lower rate. The shops have minimal furniture, and the apartments are primarily occupied by students. Only those who can leave in a hurry choose to rent here.

As she speaks, I notice Naomi isn't paying much attention. Her eyes are fixed on the couple that joined us late. Her focus is so occupied by them that I'm afraid someone is going to notice. Embarrassed, I bump her arm, causing her to break her trance and look up at me.

"Stop staring at them," I whisper.

"I'm not," she says, looking annoyed.

I scoff and whisper, "Yes, you are. It's obvious."

We continue walking, and I focus back on our guide. The small city is charming, and I find myself increasingly caught up in its mystique. There's a large fountain near the river that they use to pump beer rather than water during celebrations. Every alley seems to have at least one arch, which we learn prevents the buildings from collapsing into each other. There's a beautiful church up on the hill and a gorgeous municipal building. When we near the end of the tour, we travel down several stairs that lead us back to the river. I'm surprised, considering we're on the opposite side of the city.

"Does anyone know the name of this river?" our guide asks when we're all grouped along the riverbank.

I frown. Why is she asking this? Our cruise is along the Danube. She would expect us to answer with that. This must be a trick question.

"Danube?" Melody says, raising her hand.

The tour guide shakes her head. "No. Anyone else?"

We all remain silent, not wanting to be wrong.

"Passau is often referred to as 'the city of three rivers.' The Danube is one. But there are two more. This river is the Inn River." She turns and points. "At the end of the peninsula, you can view the joining of the rivers. You'll notice one is much dirtier than the other. The third river is the Ilz. That one is visible from the side of the castle. If you have time and can handle a small hike, I encourage you to go up there. It has a lovely view of the city and the rivers."

I look at Theo and can see he's thinking the same thing as me. She tells us several more interesting facts about the Inn River, then walks us back up to the top of the hill in the middle of the peninsula before wishing us well and reminding us to return to the ship in two hours. I walk over and hand her some cash, and she leaves. The group separates, and Naomi, Theo, Melody, and I congregate to talk about where we might go.

"Well, that was interesting," Melody says.

"It was," Theo says.

"I'd like to see what she was talking about with the three rivers converging," I say, looking at them.

"Sounds good," both say, and I look over at Naomi. She isn't listening. There's that transfixed look again. Her eyes are following something on the other side of the courtyard. We all look, curious to see what has her so intrigued. I'm not sure if Theo or Melody sees it, but I do. It's the couple again. She's watching them.

"Hey," I say, bumping her arm. She looks at me, and I can see I finally have her attention. "We were thinking we'd go see the castle across the river where the three rivers meet."

"Isn't that a hike?"

"Yeah, but only thirty minutes."

She shakes her head and frowns, looking at Melody. "Do you want to do that?"

Melody shrugs. "Sure."

Naomi scrunches her face. "I might want to do some shopping. You guys can go."

"Oh, come on," Melody says. "Let's at least go look at it. If the hike is too much, we'll let these boys do it while we go shopping."

Naomi considers, then turns back to me. "Which way is the castle?"

I point across the courtyard toward the younger couple. They've almost cleared the area and are about to leave our sight.

"Okay," Naomi says. "Let's go," and starts walking quickly.

We all fall into step beside her, crossing the courtyard and descending the hill as we draw closer to the river. We pass a cuckoo clock shop, and I can't believe my wife doesn't stop. She's been talking about getting a clock ever since we planned this vacation. I wonder whether she even noticed.

When we reach the bottom of the hill, we find a bridge that connects the peninsula to the other side of the river, where the castle is.

"Up there," I say to Naomi, pointing to the top of the hill on the other side. "See that castle?"

She nods.

"That's not high," Theo says. "I bet it takes twenty minutes, tops."

"Let's go," Naomi says before we can even discuss it further and starts walking across the bridge.

Again, we're all hustling to catch up. When we reach the other side, we cross the street and start climbing when I see the couple that was in our group. So, this is why she's so eager to hike now. She must know them somehow.

The couple stops to take pictures. It's a beautiful setting with Passau behind them. Naomi slows, obviously wanting to talk to them, and I worry that they have no plans to go any higher. I get an idea and approach them.

"Hey, could you take our picture?" I ask the guy with the Dodgers hat.

"Sure," he says, and I hand him my camera.

The four of us line up with the bridge, river, and Passau behind us, and he takes a couple of photos before handing back my camera.

"We were thinking we'd walk to the top. Do you guys want to go?" I ask.

He looks at his wife, and she shrugs. "Sure."

"Great. I'm Jacob," I say, extending my hand.

He takes it. "Derek. This is my wife, Brianna."

I nod at her and then introduce Naomi, Theo, and Melody, and we start climbing the steps up the hill.

"You're a Dodgers fan, I see," I say.

"Yeah, my stepfather was a big fan. He grew up in Southern California. I went to games when I was younger. I guess you could say I was kinda indoctrinated from an early age," he says, chuckling.

"I'm a Dodgers fan too. I was there when Kirk Gibson hit that walk-off home run in the World Series."

"No way."

"Way," I say, nodding. "Are you from LA then?"

"No. His parents lived there, but we never did."

"Where are you from?" Naomi jumps in but asks Brianna.

"Phoenix," she says.

"Oh my gosh," Naomi says. "So are all of us. What part?"

"Gilbert," Derek says.

"We're from Scottsdale," Naomi says, then points at Theo and Melody. "They're from Chandler."

Melody and Theo nod as they walk behind us.

"Wow," Brianna says. "What are the odds?"

"Right?" Naomi says.

"Did you grow up in Arizona?" I ask Derek.

He hesitates. "Kinda. I've been in the Phoenix area for a long time. I even went to ASU."

"Hmm," I say and look back at Theo. "I don't think we can be friends with him."

He looks at us and smiles. "U of A fans, huh?"

"You know it," I say. "Theo played basketball there."

"Really?" Derek says. "That's cool. They've always been good at basketball. Maybe I saw you play."

"I doubt it," Theo says.

"Why do you say that?" Derek asks.

"I was only on the scout team. Never played in any games. Unless you were at practice, you'd never know I was on the team."

We've reached a spot near the top and stop to take pictures. We get someone else to take a few so we can all be together in the photos. After reaching the top and looking around for a few minutes, I look down at my watch.

"We'd better head back."

Everyone agrees, and I remain with Derek on the way back down. There's more distance between us now, and Naomi and Brianna talk while Melody and Theo walk together.

"What do you do, Derek?"

"I work in sales. Software. What about you?"

"Real estate. Primarily mortgages."

"Nice."

We chat about the real estate industry and changes in the types of loans in recent years. When we reach the bottom and cross the street, Theo falls back a few steps to hang with us while Melody joins the women up in front.

"What do you do, Theo?" Derek asks.

"I'm a vice president with a mortgage company."

Derek looks at him and then at me. "Do you two work together?"

I shake my head. "We used to. Not anymore. We work at different companies. I guess you could say we're competitors," I say while smiling.

Theo grins, then looks at Derek. "Do you golf?"

"Not well," Derek says, chuckling. "You guys?"

They both nod.

Theo says, "I love golfing, but I'm not great. Jacob is the true golfer among us."

I shake my head but don't argue. It's true. I am better than Theo. I look up and see we've reached the boat. We walk down the ramp and back inside, then make plans to all sit together in an hour for dinner. When we separate and head back to our rooms, I finally have time to ask Naomi what I've been wondering for hours.

"What is it with you and them?" I say as I unlock the door to our room.

She frowns. "What do you mean?"

"I mean, you clearly wanted to talk to them. What is it?"

She enters the room and sits down on the bed, taking off her shoes. I stand looking down at her. I want an answer. She looks up at me, then lies back and puts her hands behind her head. "I overheard them in the dining room this morning. I knew they were from Phoenix."

"So?"

"So," she fires back at me.

"So what? Who cares if they're from Phoenix?"

"We're from Phoenix."

"Yeah, along with millions of other people. What do you care?"

She shrugs. "I just thought it was neat that we'd meet other people from Phoenix on a cruise halfway around the world."

She stands as I sit on the bed. She leaves and enters the bathroom. I watch her close the door through the mirror on the closet, then pick up my book and lie back on the bed. My eyes scan the words, but I'm not focused on them. There's more to the story. Something she's not telling me, and I want to know what it is.

Chapter 6
Melody Jones

Cruise Day 2 – Between Passau, Germany and Linz, Austria

"Are you ready to go?" I ask Theo as he lies on the bed with his head propped up on two pillows. He's watching *The Sound of Music* on TV.

"Yeah," he says.

"Don't you think you should wear shoes?" He isn't looking at me. He's not paying any attention. "Theo," I say more emphatically. "Come on. We're late. Let's go."

"Fine," he says, turning off the TV and walking over to put on his shoes.

I stand at the door waiting for him.

"Let me go to the bathroom first," he says, squeezing past me.

I sigh and shake my head. He always does this. After the toilet flushes and he washes his hands, we exit the room and walk down the hall. When we reach the dining room, we see Naomi and Jacob sitting at our usual table. There's no assigned seating, but we've sat at the same table each meal and likely will the rest of the vacation.

"Hey, guys," Naomi says, greeting us.

Jacob looks up, smiles, and puts down his book.

"Where are our new friends?" I ask.

"I haven't seen them yet," Naomi says.

I sit beside her while Theo sits on the opposite side of the table beside Jacob.

"Oh, there they are," Naomi says, pointing.

They've changed clothes. Derek no longer has a hat on, and Brianna is wearing a beautiful dress. I never realized Derek was bald.

Naomi waves to them, and they smile and come over.

"Hi, guys," Naomi says as they sit down in the two remaining chairs at the table.

Our server, Arpad, comes over and greets us. He has a thick accent that sounds a little like Dracula. Most of the time, we understand him just fine. But occasionally...

"Good evening. It looks like we have a bigger group tonight," he says, smiling and nodding at Derek and Brianna. "Welcome. What can I get everyone to drink?"

We order as he passes out menus. When he's gone, we turn our attention to our menus, and Derek looks at Theo and Jacob. "What are you guys going to get?"

Jacob shakes his head. "I'm not sure. You?"

"I can't decide. I think I want more than one entrée."

"So do it," Theo says. "That's what I might do."

"Can you get more than one entrée on a cruise?" Derek asks.

"Of course," Jacob says. "I do it all the time. Get your money's worth."

We discuss some of the menu options, and after a few minutes, Arpad returns with our drinks and takes our orders. When it's my turn, I ask, "What is this wiener schnitzel? What's that like?"

Arpad looks at my menu, where I'm pointing, and looks up at the ceiling. "Well, it is breaded. It is fried."

"What kind of meat is it?"

He looks at me, and I can see he's struggling. "I can't remember the word in English," he says, and then he says something in what I can only guess is his language.

"Veal," Derek says, not taking his eyes off his menu.

Arpad turns and looks at him, then says something in his language, and Derek responds in the same language. I look over at him, but he doesn't look at me, and Brianna sits smiling. We finish our orders, and when Arpad walks away, I ask what all of us are wondering.

"Uh, Derek?"

"Yes?"

"What language was that?"

Derek looks at me as he picks up his drink and takes a gulp. "Hungarian."

"Hungarian?" Jacob asks with astonishment.

Derek nods.

"Derek speaks fluent Hungarian," Brianna says.

"What? How?" Theo asks. "Isn't that a really hard language? How did you learn it?"

"He's from there," Brianna says.

Derek shifts in his seat, and I can see he's uncomfortable with this conversation.

"Are you from Budapest?" Theo asks.

Derek shakes his head. "I'm from a little town outside Budapest called Vác."

"But you've been to Budapest before?" Jacob asks.

"Yes, many times."

"Isn't that the last spot on our cruise?" Naomi asks.

We all nod as Derek takes another drink, then looks away from us out the window. He's clearly uncomfortable with this conversation, and I decide to take pity on him, even though I'm dying to know more about how he got to the US and how he sounds American. "So, how many kids do you guys have?" I ask Brianna.

"Four," she says with a smile.

"Wow, four?"

"Yep. All girls."

I smile and look over at Derek. "I bet you were hoping for a boy, huh?"

He shrugs and smiles, obviously much more engaged in the conversation. "We kept trying."

Theo bumps him with his elbow. "Too bad we didn't know each other sooner. I could have given you some pointers."

I sigh and roll my eyes as everyone laughs.

We go on talking about our kids and family as we eat. When the meal is over, we separate, retiring to our own rooms and pledging to spend the day together tomorrow in Linz. When Theo and I get back to our room, I'm dying to know if he saw what I saw.

"That was a surprise learning Derek is from Hungary, huh?" I say.

Theo lies down on the bed and turns on the TV while taking off his shoes. "What?" he asks as he fiddles with the remote.

"Derek, weren't you surprised to hear he's from Hungary?"

Theo shrugs. "Yeah, I guess."

"He didn't seem like he wanted to talk about it, did he?"

Theo frowns at the remote, and I don't think he's heard me.

"Theo?"

He looks at me. "What?"

"I said, it didn't seem like Derek wanted to talk about Hungary."

"It did?"

"You didn't notice?"

"Notice what?"

I groan. "Never mind," I say, walking into the bathroom and shutting the door. I strip off my clothes and get in the shower, letting the warm water run down my body as I think about Derek and Brianna. Brianna was so eager to tell us Derek was from Hungary, but Derek acted like he was being tortured when we asked him questions. Why? If I were from the country we're visiting and could speak the language, I'd be proud of it. Why isn't he? What is it he doesn't want us to know?

Chapter 7
Theo Jones

Cruise Day 2 – Passau, Germany to Linz, Austria

There's a knock on our cabin door, and I roll off the bed and answer it. Jacob stands in the hallway holding a book.

"Naomi and I were thinking we might hang out on the top deck for a little while. Apparently, we're going through a beautiful canyon. The cruise director recommended we check it out."

I look down the hall and see Naomi is watching our conversation, and I get the sense she sent Jacob to ask us to come, and it's not just because she has a pleading look on her face and motioning with her hand.

"Okay. I think Melody is taking a quick nap."

"No," I hear her call from inside the room. "I'm awake."

"I guess she's awake," I say, shrugging. I call out to her. "You want to join them on the top deck?"

"Sure."

I turn back to Jacob. "We'll be right behind you."

When we reach the top level, we see Derek and Brianna have also joined and are sitting beside Naomi and Jacob. They've already pulled two more chairs to form a circle, and we take our places, looking around.

"This is beautiful," I say.

We all remain quiet for several minutes, watching the surrounding landscape. Forest covers the hills on both sides. There's an occasional village with a church in the center of town where bells play. The sun is low in the sky, but it's still quite warm and very comfortable. Especially when compared to an October day in Arizona.

"Where are the umbrellas?" I ask, looking around.

It seems nobody else noticed they're missing, and we all look around for them. Jacob, his nose back in his book, looks up. "Oh, they took them down."

"What? Why? Do they do that in the evening?"

"I don't know. The captain made an announcement and said that because of the height of some bridges we're going to pass under, they can't leave them up."

"Hmm," Melody says, and I look over at her. She points to the captain's station in the middle of the boat. "Won't that be too tall also?"

She's got a point. The captain's station is at least nine feet tall. It's likely taller than any of the umbrellas that were shading the tables.

"Looks like we're reaching a low bridge now," Naomi says, and we all turn back to watch the front of the boat.

A couple members of the crew walk around, reminding us all to stay seated, and a siren blasts. At the same time, I notice movement out of the corner of my eye and see that the captain's station is shrinking. The walls are actually lowering, and it's causing the entire structure to become shorter. When it stops, it's only half the height it was previously. As we pass under the bridge, the temptation is too great, and I stand out of my chair and reach my hand up to touch the bridge. As soon as I do, a crew member blows a whistle and calls to me to sit back down. I comply but smile at my companions.

"Leave it to Theo," Melody says.

"What's that supposed to mean?" I ask.

"You know what it means," she says with a teasing smile.

"You like it when I'm a little wild. At least, you did last night."

She rolls her eyes and looks away, and Derek bursts out laughing. I smile at him and notice Brianna is blushing. She might be a little too innocent for me.

For the next thirty minutes, we sit around talking as we pass through the beautiful canyon. Along the way, we pass through several locks where they have to raise or lower the water level to allow the boat to pass through. I find the whole thing fascinating, and when Melody and Naomi say they are going to get a drink in the lounge, I tell them I'm going to stay. After five minutes, Jacob says he has to make a phone call, and I'm left alone with our new friends, Derek and Brianna.

"So," Derek says, leaning back in his chair and watching the passing forest, "how did you get started in the mortgage industry?"

I look at him and Brianna. She's holding Derek's hand, and I can tell even with her sunglasses on, she's fallen asleep.

"I actually have Jacob to thank for that."

"Oh, yeah?"

"Yep. After college, he got me a job. In a lot of ways, I've got Jacob to thank for my entire career."

"Why do you say that?"

A server comes by and offers to get us drinks, and we both order something.

"When I was finishing college, I didn't have any job offers. I was getting pretty nervous that I wouldn't find anything. And, to tell you the truth, I didn't know what I wanted to do anyway."

"What was your major?"

The siren blasts again, and I see a low bridge in the distance. This time I stay seated.

"Business management. I knew I wanted to go into business, but I didn't really have experience in anything."

He smiles. "You should have gone to ASU. You would have had all kinds of suitors."

I roll my eyes. "I thought ASU was only known as a party school. Do you actually have any academics?"

He smiles and shakes his head.

"Anyway, Jacob had finished college before me and already had a great job with a national mortgage company. He pretty much got me the job. The interview was a formality."

"You said you guys only worked together for a while?"

"Yeah, he stayed for a couple years, then got recruited away to another firm. I stayed put and kept climbing the ranks."

"What's your title now?"

"I'm a vice president."

He nods. "That's right."

"Yeah, I've loved the company, and they've been really good to me. We had a tough family situation several years ago, and they were really flexible and supportive."

He frowns. "What happened?"

"Our daughter was born with a heart defect. We knew it was a long shot for her to live, and she made it until she was three. The last year of her life, she spent in the hospital. It was a trying time for our family and our marriage."

"I'm sorry," Derek says.

"Thank you."

"She didn't make it?"

I shake my head. "No. She died. We were waiting for a heart transplant, but it didn't come through in time. Jacob and Naomi did so much for our family. Jacob was back working with me at the time and stepped in and handled many of my accounts. If not for him…" I stop and look down. "He's a great friend. I'd do anything for him. Her illness put a major strain on our marriage. Melody was depressed and distant. I couldn't reach her. I don't know how, but Jacob helped her come back to me. I'll be forever grateful."

"How long have you guys known each other?"

"Since we were kids."

"Wow."

"Yeah, his parents actually took me in when we were in high school. I lived with them."

"Really? Why?"

I look behind me and see Melody and Naomi have returned. They're only a few paces away. "I grew up in a house with addicts for parents. Jacob's dad found out and invited me to live with them. He even paid for my basketball camps and helped me get into college. I'll forever be grateful to the Costas," I say and stand up, moving over to my wife.

"We're thinking of calling it a night," she says.

"Sounds good. I'll join you."

"See you tomorrow," I say, turning back and waving to Derek and Brianna, then walking away with Melody and Naomi.

Chapter 8
Brianna Murphy

Cruise Day 3 – Linz, Austria

After breakfast, we went on another walking tour, this time in Linz. It lasted about two hours and took us all around the city. I didn't know it before the tour, but apparently Linz was considered Hitler's hometown. He lived here from 1898 to 1907. Many movies, including *The Sound of Music*, portray Austria as having been taken over by the Nazis. But according to our tour guide, this wasn't true at all. Austria wanted to be part of Germany under Hitler, and Hitler had big plans for Linz. He renamed the city Führerstadt (the Führer city) and planned to turn it into a major industrial and cultural hub.

Along the tour, we stopped in front of the Linz City Hall, where Hitler had famously announced the annexation of Austria into Nazi Germany in 1939. It was there that he said his homeland was entering the German Reich.

When the tour finished, we separated from our friends and the rest of the group. Our friends had previously booked a separate tour visiting the Mauthausen concentration camp on the outskirts of the city and needed to get back to the boat to catch the tour. We stayed in the city, walking around and doing some shopping. I love shopping, and Derek hates it, but he's being a good husband and indulging me.

We stop in front of a shop where dresses hang from a mobile rack. "These are cute," I say, picking one off and holding it up to my body. "What do you think?"

He looks at me and yawns, then shrugs and tells me it's "cute." I've noticed he uses that phrase more and more in our twenty-five years of marriage. Probably because I do. He's learning.

"Do you think it would look good on me?" I ask.

He nods and gives me an enthusiastic smile, and I know it's probably because he's thinking, the sooner I find something to buy, the sooner we can leave.

"I'm going to try it on," I say, and carry it into the store.

The blond woman behind the counter greets me in German, and I ask if she speaks English.

"Of course," she says. "How can I help you?"

"I'd like to try this on."

"Very good. Come with me."

She leads me up a set of stairs, and I look back and see Derek standing in the store, looking like a little boy who's lost and doesn't know where to go.

"I'll be right back," I tell him and follow her the rest of the way up the stairs.

Five minutes later, when I come back down, I find him sitting on the bottom step. He hears me coming and stands, and I go to him, reaching for his hand as I turn back to the shop clerk. "Thank you for your help."

"You're welcome. *Auf wiedersehen.*"

"Goodbye."

We walk out of the store and continue down the street, which is where the tram runs down the middle.

"You didn't like it?" Derek asks.

I shake my head. "My boobs are too big. I couldn't even button it at the top."

He winks at me. "I think they're just right."

I smile at him. "I know you do."

We continue up the street, stopping at different shops, but I don't find anything I love. We turn back in the direction we came, and when we reach the main square, we stop and get an ice cream cone at the place our tour guide had suggested, then decide to return to the ship. As we walk, I look up at him and ask something that's been on my mind.

"So, last night," I begin.

He looks at me warily. "Yeah."

"Why were you being so vague with them?"

He sighs. "I wasn't being vague."

I guffaw. "Whatever. You didn't even want to tell them you were Hungarian. Why?"

He shakes his head and then pulls my hand to speed up as we cross the street. "You know why."

"What? Because of your past? They don't know anything about that."

"They're from Arizona."

"So?"

He looks away from me as we walk along the river beside the cultural museum. "So, they might know somebody who knew me. Maybe someone who was hurt by it."

I shake my head. "You're being ridiculous."

He doesn't reply, but I can see from his face that he's not happy.

I stop walking and keep hold of his hand, forcing him to stop. He won't look at me. "Derek, you've got to forgive yourself. You made a mistake, but it was many years ago. People have moved on. You need to move on too."

He shakes his head, and his hazel eyes come back to me. "You know, one reason I was really looking forward to this vacation was I thought it would be so far from home that nobody would know me. There wouldn't be any awkward situation where I might go out and see someone that reminds me of my past." He looks down. "I just couldn't believe my luck that someone on our boat would be from back home. And not only that, two couples."

I squeeze his hand. "Do you want to stay clear of them? We don't have to hang out with them anymore. Would that be better?"

He looks up at me, and I can still see the pain in his eyes. "No, you're right. I need to get over it. There's almost no chance they know who I was or what I did. I'll try and be more relaxed and open."

I step closer and go up on my tiptoes to kiss him. "I love you," I say, looking in his eyes.

"I love you too."

We begin walking again, silent, lost in our own thoughts. I wonder what he's thinking about. Beyond wanting to celebrate our anniversary, I scheduled this trip to grow closer to him. See if he would fully open up to me. I wanted to see if I could get him to admit he's been hiding money and what he planned to do with it.

Chapter 9
Derek Murphy

Cruise Day 3 – Between Linz, Austria and Krems, Austria

There's a knock on our cabin door, and I look at Brianna and see she's asleep. Rather than call out and risk waking her, I roll off the bed and make my way to the door. When we came back from our tour of Linz, we had lunch, then spent some time relaxing on the top deck before deciding to come back to our cabin. I could tell she was sleepy and knew she wouldn't last long.

I open the door and see Edit, our maid, standing in the hallway.

"Oh, sorry. I didn't know you came back."

"It's no problem," I say in Hungarian.

She looks at me curiously and speaks to me in our native tongue. "How do you know Hungarian?"

"I'm Hungarian. I moved to America as a teenager."

"Really?"

"Yes."

"From Budapest?"

I shake my head. "Vác."

She jostles her head back and forth. "That's pretty much the same thing."

I nod in acknowledgement.

"Do you come back to Hungary often?"

I shake my head. "First time since I left."

"I bet you're excited to come back home."

I nod, and she looks at me curiously, as if wondering if I'll say anything else.

When I don't, she says, "Do you need anything else in your room? Is everything to your liking?"

"Everything is great."

She smiles and turns, taking a couple of steps away from me, then turns back. "Where are you from in the United States?

"Phoenix."

She frowns. "Is that close to Arizona?"

I smile. "Phoenix is in Arizona. Arizona is the state or territory. Phoenix is the capital city of the state of Arizona."

Her eyes go wide, and her hand comes up to cover her mouth. "You're from Arizona?"

I nod.

She frowns. "Are there many Hungarians in Arizona?"

I shake my head. "No. I know only a few."

She nods and, while still looking perplexed, waves and continues down the hall. I watch her go, then reenter the room.

Brianna is sitting on the edge of the bed. She's changed clothes and is putting on her shoes.

"Who was that?"

"Edit. Our maid."

"What did she want?"

"She thought the room was empty. She asked if there was anything we needed. Do you need anything?"

Brianna stands and comes over to me, giving me a kiss and smiling up at me. "I've got everything I need. Now get ready. We need to get to dinner." I shrug and tell her I'm ready, but she shakes her head and goes to the closet and pulls out a new shirt. "How about you wear this?" It's the green shirt I don't remember packing, but somehow appeared in my luggage.

"Fine," I say, taking it from her and turning toward the bathroom.

She grabs me by the arm. "Where are you going?"

I frown. "To change."

She gives me a sly smile. "I'll help you."

Twenty minutes later, we leave our room and head for the dining hall. We're late for dinner, but I'm not complaining. When we walk in, we see our friends sitting at our table, and we go over to join them. Arpad, our server, is taking their drink orders and hands us menus. After we've all ordered, he leaves, and we talk about our day. Most of the conversation revolves around their visit to Mauthausen. Their descriptions of the museum are both educational and heartbreaking, and I'm torn on whether I wish we had gone.

As dinner winds down and desserts are served, Naomi asks Arpad about the sauce on Theo's plate, and I can tell he doesn't understand the question. Before he can ask for clarification, I whisper the question in Hungarian. He looks at me gratefully, then answers her question. When he returns a few minutes later to remove the plates, he speaks to me in Hungarian.

"How do you speak Hungarian?" he asks.

"It's my native tongue."

"You're Hungarian?"

I nod.

"When did you go to Arizona, in America?"

"When I was a teenager. I was fifteen."

He holds all the plates in his hands, and everyone else at the table is watching us talk but doesn't know what we're saying. He frowns and gets a confused look on his face. "But your name is Derek Murphy. Murphy isn't a Hungarian name."

His statement gives me pause, and I nearly repeat the same lie I repeat whenever this question comes up back home. But then I think about my conversation with Brianna as we walked back to the ship and decide I need to stop being so paranoid.

"Derek Murphy is a name I took when I moved to America. My Hungarian name is Dominik."

He stares at me as if not comprehending. "What?"

I frown. "Dominik. That's my real name."

"Oh," he says and smiles. "That's a true Hungarian name. Where were you from?"

"Vác."

He nods. "Well, welcome back home. We'll talk more. Have a good night."

"Thank you," I say in English.

Everyone else joins in, and he says goodbye to all of us and walks away.

"We were thinking we'd all go upstairs to the lounge. I guess they're doing some kind of music-trivia game."

"Sounds good," I say.

We all stand and exit.

As we climb the stairs, Jacob puts his arm around me. "That is so cool you can speak Hungarian like that."

I smile. "You think?"

"Oh yeah. My family is Italian, but I don't speak a lick of it."

We reach the lounge and find a seat where we can all be together. The cruise director takes the microphone and explains the game with considerable enthusiasm. The DJ plays different songs, and we all try to guess the name of the band and the song title. It's fun, although the song choices skew old. We do pretty well but don't end up winning. Eventually, we all retire to our rooms, and after Brianna and I turn off the lights, I lie in bed looking up at the ceiling. There's one thing Arpad said that I can't get out of my mind. He mentioned Arizona. He knew I was from Arizona. How? I'm positive I never told him that. Either he's been looking into me, or he's been talking about me with someone else.

Chapter 10
Naomi Costa

Cruise Day 4 – Krems, Austria

For the first time, our included tour wasn't a walking tour of the town. Instead, we were taken on buses to visit the Göttweig Abbey. The abbey was up on the hill, visible from Krems but still about a fifteen-minute drive. We toured the apricot orchard, walked around the abbey, and went inside to admire the artwork and cathedral. At the end, we exited through a shop where we could try alcoholic beverages made from the apricots. I took a sip but put my sample cup back unfinished.

On the way to the abbey, I sat next to Jacob. But this time, I'm determined to sit by Melody. Jacob started a new book this morning and didn't look up once during the bus ride. As we exit the shop and walk toward the buses, I grab Melody by the arm to walk with her.

"What did you think of that?" I ask her.

"Meh," she says.

"Right?" Brianna says, stepping up to join us. "Wasn't that supposed to be a Christian church?"

"Yeah," I say, confused by what she means.

"It was Christian," Melody says, frowning.

"Could have fooled me," Brianna says as we reach the bus.

"What do you mean?" I ask.

"Did you see a single picture of Christ anywhere inside that church? There were all these pictures of monks but nothing of Christ. It looked like they worshipped monks."

Melody and I stare at her as we reach the bus, then look at each other.

"That's true," Melody says. "I can't think of a single one."

I shake my head. "No, what about the painting on the ceiling? You know, on that staircase?"

"The one with the angels?" Brianna says.

"Yeah," I say.

She shakes her head. "There were angels, but Christ wasn't anywhere in it."

I think back as I step onto the bus and climb the stairs. She's right. How odd. I pick a row halfway down the aisle and sit while pulling Melody to sit next to me. I pat the row in front and tell Brianna to sit there. She does.

"I think I should sit with Theo," Melody says as we see our husbands enter the bus. Theo glances at her with a questioning look.

"Oh, let the boys sit together for once," I say. "Stop trying to control your husband so much. You don't need to be with Theo everywhere we go."

Melody looks at me, and I can see I've broken through. She stays seated as Theo approaches and tells him she's going to stay by me. The men look at us and then find seats on the other side of the aisle.

We watch as they sit together and continue their conversation about football.

"See," I say, bumping Melody with my elbow. "They're just fine on their own." I lean forward in my seat as the bus driver closes the door and pulls away. "Hey, Brianna. I've got a question for you."

She turns around and looks at me.

"Does Derek know Budapest really well?"

She nods. "He hasn't been there for about thirty years. He was a kid when he left. But, yeah, you've seen how well he speaks Hungarian. And he's been on the internet every night at home studying the city."

"Right. What are you guys going to do in Budapest?"

"The first day, we're going to go to all the tourist spots. Fisherman's Bastion, Stephen's Basilica, the Chain Bridge, and Parliament. After that, we're going to go up and see his hometown. We're going to stay a few extra days."

"You aren't going home on Monday?" Melody asks.

She shakes her head. "Not until Thursday."

"Did you guys get a hotel?" I ask.

She nods. "It's up by the castle on the Buda side of the river."

I look at Melody and then back at her. "I've got a question. And you can tell me if you don't want us to, but I was wondering if we could hang out with you guys on our day in Budapest. Maybe Derek could be our tour guide? We have nothing planned other than the provided walking tour. It might be fun for him to guide us."

Brianna smiles. "That would be great."

"You're sure it wouldn't be intruding?"

She shakes her head. "Not at all. Honestly, I've been a little worried about the Budapest part of the trip."

"Why?" Melody asks, frowning.

She drops her voice, even though the boys aren't listening. "Because I worry he'll speak Hungarian to all these people, and I won't know what's going on. He'll blend in, and I'll be the dumb American who can't speak Hungarian and won't know where I'm going. If you guys are there, I won't be alone."

I reach over and rub her shoulder. "We're happy to be dumb right along with you." I turn and look at Melody. "Oh, I'm excited. Are you?"

She nods.

"I think Budapest is going to be my favorite city of all."

Chapter 11
Jacob Costa

Cruise Day 4 – Krems, Austria

After arriving back on the boat following the trip to the abbey, Naomi reminds Melody, Theo, and me that we have a food tour of Krems scheduled with a local guide. We separate from Derek and Brianna, promising to see them at dinner, and find our tour guide, who's parked in a shuttle in a parking lot beside the river. The group is small with only two other couples besides us. We take a short drive to the center of town and exit the shuttle. Our guide, an Austrian with flawless English, shows us around the town and arranges food and wine sampling at various shops. Nothing is too spectacular, but after a couple of hours, he gives us some free time before we need to head back to the boat. We're on the pedestrian-only road below a large archway, and Naomi says she wants to do some shopping. She pulls Melody along, and Theo and I hang back, seeing an ice cream shop. We each buy cones with a couple of scoops and find a spot to sit and people watch.

Since the day began, I've been looking for an opportunity to talk with Theo alone. I thought the bus ride could be my chance when the girls were on the other side, but Derek was there.

I lick my ice cream and watch two old ladies walk by arguing about something in German. With my eyes on them, I ask him my question. "Could you understand anything Derek was saying to our server last night?"

From the corner of my eye, I see Theo take a bite of his ice cream, his arm resting on the back of the bench. He chuckles. "Yeah, right. That language is nothing like I've ever heard. I stopped paying attention after a few seconds."

I nod. "Naomi told me she asked Brianna if Derek would be our guide when we visit Budapest."

"Oh, yeah? That would be cool. I'm sure he'll be better than anyone we could hire."

"Yeah, I'm not sure. He lived in Hungary when he was a kid. He hasn't been there since. That was back in the communist days. I bet it's changed a lot."

"Sure, but he speaks better English than any other guide we've had."

I nod and take a bite of my ice cream. "True. But our guide today spoke great English."

He leans forward to take another bite of his ice cream but stops and looks at me. "Are you saying you don't want him to be our guide?"

I shrug.

"Why? You don't like Derek?"

I turn away from the street and look him in the eye. "Something's not right about him."

He frowns. "Not right about him? What do you mean?"

"Do you remember how I told you I hired that private investigator to find the guy who killed my dad?"

"That guy didn't kill your dad."

I grit my teeth. "Maybe he didn't pull the trigger. But he was responsible."

Theo sighs. He knows I'm right.

"I think he's Derek. Derek's the man I was looking for."

Theo blows out his breath and shakes his head. "No way. You're crazy."

I lean over and grab his arm, looking into his eyes. "Am I? Do you remember the name the private investigator gave me? The guy who disappeared?"

Theo looks up and shakes his head.

"Dominik Meszaros."

"So?"

"So, Derek's real name is Dominik."

He frowns, and for the first time, I can see he's considering it. "You know that?"

I nod.

"How?"

"I was listening to Derek talk last night. I heard him say *Dominik*."

The skepticism is back in his eyes, and he shakes his head, grinning. "No way. There's no way. You heard him wrong. He could have said anything, and you wouldn't have known. The Hungarian vocabulary is totally different than English or even Spanish. You don't speak Hungarian."

"No, I don't. But I heard him say that name."

He shakes his head. "Jacob, no way you heard that. And even if you did, the chances of him being that guy are like a million to one."

"So you're tellin' me there's a chance," I say and smile.

He looks at me strangely.

"That's what Jim Carrey said in *Dumb and Dumber*. Remember? When Lauren Holly said he had a one-in-a-million chance of getting together with her."

Theo shakes his head. "Man, I don't understand your obsession with that movie."

"It's a great movie. I don't understand how you can't see it."

He stands and wipes his face with his napkin, then throws it away and sits back down. "So why don't you ask Derek?"

"What do you mean? Ask him if he knows a Dominik?"

"Yeah. Say you were listening to the Hungarian last night, and you heard him say Dominik."

I shake my head. "If he's that guy, I don't want him to know that I know. I've got to find out without him suspecting anything."

I look away and lick my ice cream. I've got to speed up. It's starting to melt and get on my hands. I see Naomi and Melody exit a shop down the street, and they see us. I'm running out of time. "Listen," I say, looking at him. "I'm telling you, I can feel it. He's the guy I've been looking for. I need you to help me find out. So will you?"

He looks at me for a long second, then nods. "What dc you want me to do?"

Chapter 12
Melody Jones

Cruise Day 4 – Krems, Austria

During dinner, the six of us talk a little more about the abbey, our food tour, and Derek and Brianna's day. They went to a carnival in the city center and seemed to have a good time, although nobody at the place they had lunch spoke English, which became an adventure.

"I think it gave me a level of empathy," Derek says.

"How so?" Theo asks.

"Well," Derek says, leaning back in his chair and palming his drink. He looks over at Brianna. "Since Bri and I decided to come on this vacation, I've wondered what Hungary would be like for her. Aside from knowing a word or two, she really doesn't know any Hungarian."

"So?" Brianna says.

He reaches over and touches her arm. "No, I'm just saying, I worried it might impact how you'd like it. Maybe Budapest wouldn't be your favorite place because I'd be able to speak but you wouldn't."

She nods, accepting his explanation.

"How old were you when you came to America?" Jacob asks.

"Fifteen."

"Did you speak English then?"

Derek shakes his head.

"Then I don't understand your point. You've been through it before. Why was today any different?"

Derek pauses and looks up. "Recency, I guess. It's been so long since I went through it I kinda forgot. Being there today made me see more of what it will be like for her."

"And what did it show you?" I ask.

He looks over at Brianna again. "I had a lot of fun. It didn't matter that I didn't speak German. But I also think it helped that we were in it together. Neither of us could speak. It was an obstacle we faced together. That's why I'm so happy to hear you all will hang out with us in Budapest for a day."

"Brianna told you, then?" Naomi says.

"I think it's a great idea," Derek says.

"Oh, good," Naomi says.

"But, keep in mind, I haven't been to Budapest for a long, long time. When I lived in Hungary, I was a kid during communism. I've done studying, and I should be fine. But I won't be perfect."

Theo laughs. "Well, if you're not, you aren't getting a tip."

We all laugh, and Arpad, our server, returns and offers to bring us coffee or tea as he cleans up the dessert plates.

After he leaves, Derek looks at me. "So, I know Jacob and Theo work in the real estate industry."

"Me too," Naomi says.

"Oh," he says. "What do you do?"

"Realtor," Naomi says.

"Oh, right, I think you mentioned that when you were telling us how you and Jacob met."

She nods, and he looks back at me. "But what about you, Melody? Do you work?"

I nod. "I have my own cookie-baking-and-decorating business."

"Really?"

"They're so good," Naomi says.

"I wouldn't know," Theo says, and I look over at him and slap his arm. He exaggerates his pain. "What? I wouldn't. You never let me eat them."

I roll my eyes and shake my head.

"For real?" Derek asks.

Theo nods.

"That's not true," I say.

"Yeah, it is," Theo says. "Since you've been doing this, you never want to bake for the family."

I look at him questioningly, but he seems serious.

"Well, it looks like you aren't wasting away," I say, poking his stomach.

"Oh, a fat joke. Nice." He turns away from me and looks at Derek. "I get my cookies from another supplier."

I smile and slap his arm, and once again, he gets as dramatic as a Broadway actor.

"Anyway...," Derek says. "So, how long have you had the cookie business?"

"About ten years," I say.

"Wow! Do you have a place where you bake them? A store with employees?"

I shake my head. "All from my house."

"But don't let that fool you," Naomi says, leaning toward me and putting a hand on the table. "They are so well done. Very professional."

"How did you get started?" Brianna asks.

"I've always been artistic. I would make special cookies for my kids' birthday parties and stuff like that. Other parents would see them and start asking me where I bought them from."

"That was back when I was allowed to eat them," Theo says.

I get a pouty face as I look at him. "Oh, poor you."

"Poor me is right," he says.

I roll my eyes.

"So, then you started making them for friends and neighbors?" Derek asks.

"A little bit here and there. But then Jenny was born, and I didn't have time."

"That was your daughter that passed?" Brianna says quietly.

I nod. "Taking care of her was a full-time job. And then when she was in the hospital..."

I look down, and Theo reaches over and takes my hand.

"After Jenny passed away, I encouraged her to start baking more. Turn it into a business," Theo says.

I look at him. "See, it was your fault. You've got no room to complain."

He smiles at me and winks.

"Why?" Derek asks.

"Why what?" Theo asks.

"Why did you encourage her to get into baking?"

I look up and see that Theo is watching me, but he speaks to Derek. "She needed something. Like she said, she's always been so artistic. She was dealing with so much, I knew she needed an outlet. Something that would give her purpose."

I squeeze his hand and look at all of them. "I was in a bad place when Jenny was sick and after she passed away."

"I imagine," Derek says.

I shake my head. "I didn't like who I'd become. I wasn't myself anymore. My thoughts weren't my own."

"What do you mean?" Jacob asks.

"Do you believe in God?" I ask. Not to anyone in particular but to the table as a whole.

Nobody answers, just looking around.

"I do," Brianna finally says.

"I did too," I say. "But when you have a child die..." I look down. "It makes you question everything. When you watch your child suffer, and there's nothing you can do about it," I look back up and lock eyes with Brianna, "your perspective changes. I started changing who I was. I did things I never would have done before. My whole moral code was different."

The table is silent for several seconds.

"I get that," Jacob says.

I look around, and everyone is nodding.

"I'm not saying I went through what you went through," Jacob says. "But when my dad died…I saw the world a lot differently."

We all look at him, but it's clear he has nothing else he wants to say.

"What about now?" Brianna asks me.

I frown at her. "What do you mean?"

"Do you believe in God now?"

I chuckle. "Depends on the day."

"How many cookies you sell?" Derek asks with a smile.

I shake my head. "No, I already have to turn people away."

"Why haven't you hired employees? Gone big with it?" Derek asks.

I shrug. "I'm a perfectionist. Every cookie has to be perfect. Other people don't care like I do."

He nods. "Better that way anyway. Owning your own business isn't all it's cracked up to be."

He says no more, and we don't push him, but I see the same questions in Theo and Jacob's eyes. What business did he own? And what happened to it?

Chapter 13
Theo Jones

Cruise Day 5 – Vienna, Austria

"Are you ready to go?" Melody asks, knocking on the bathroom door.

I don't understand the rush. Do we have to eat every meal with Jacob and Naomi? Can't we have just one by ourselves?

"Yeah," I say. "Let me just finish combing my hair."

I hear her annoyance in her sigh, and it makes me smile. It's funny for two reasons. One, I don't have any hair to comb. Two, because I wear a hat all day when we're on these tours. Unless I'm combing my chest hair, it makes no sense.

I finish stalling and come out of the bathroom.

She's standing at the door, giving me a look. "About time," she says.

"Beauty takes work," I say, slipping past her and picking up my hat from the bed. I put it on and hear her open the outside door as I sit on the bed.

"What are you doing?" she says, holding the door open.

"What? I can't go to breakfast in just my socks," I say, reaching under the bed for my shoes. "If it really matters that much, just go. I'll be along in a minute."

She looks at her watch.

"Go," I tell her. "I'll be right behind you."

"Fine," she says, letting the door close and leaving me in peace.

It's not that I don't want her around. I love her. I've always loved her. But I get tired of being rushed around. Especially to appease Naomi and her plans. She's the one who dictates everything. She's the one who schedules the excursions, calls Melody, telling us when we should go to meals. It feels like I'm on Naomi's cruise, and I can't help the desire to rebel a little bit.

I take my time putting on my shoes and lie back on the bed, savoring the quiet, when I hear a knock at the door. I wonder if it's Melody coming back to get me and sit up. I can't let her catch me lying on the bed. The doorknob turns, and I duck behind the wall so she can't see me.

This is ridiculous. I'm a grown man in my fifties. What am I afraid of?

The door opens, and I hear a female voice say, "Hello? Anyone here?"

I think it's the maid, and I clear my throat before I step around the corner.

"Oh, I'm sorry," she says, looking up at me. She's dragging a cart behind her. "I thought you already go."

"It's okay," I say, holding up my hands. "I was just leaving. Come in, please."

She hesitates, stepping toward the door.

"No, no. Please, come in. I'm leaving to go to breakfast."

I motion for her to enter, and she eyes me, then pulls her cart into the room so I can pass.

"I'm Theo," I say, extending a hand.

She takes it, saying, "Teo." She can't seem to make the sound of a *th*.

"What's your name?"

"Edit," she says, looking up at me. She's a lovely woman with bright hazel eyes and dark hair.

"Where are you from?"

"Hungary."

"Budapest?"

"Yes."

"Nice. I'm excited to go there soon."

"Me too," she says, smiling.

I look down at my watch. I'm late.

"Well, I'll get out of your hair. I'm going to breakfast."

She frowns at me, looking confused. "Okay. Enjoy."

I step past her cart and head down the hall. As I walk through the lobby to the dining hall, I wonder how many Hungarians work on the ship. I know of Edit, Arpad (our server), and the captain. Is that it? Or are there more?

I enter the dining hall and see Jacob, Naomi, and Melody are all just getting up. They're already done. Melody sees me approach.

"Well, I guess you're going to be hungry."

I look past her to the breakfast area. The staff is cleaning up.

"I'll meet you in the front," I tell them and walk to the service area. Arpad is one of the servers, and I go to him. "Hey, Arpad, can I grab a muffin and some fruit?"

He looks over, and I can't see any still on the counter.

"What kind?" he asks.

I shrug. "I don't care. Whatever you've got."

He holds up a finger and walks away while the other staff members continue cleaning up. He enters the kitchen and comes back two minutes later carrying a plate with a couple of muffins, strawberries, pineapple, and an orange.

"Here you go," he says, putting them down on the table nearest me. "I'll get you silverware." He turns away, then looks back. "Do you want coffee?"

"Sure."

He nods, and I sit down, stuffing my face with the muffin. He returns with a cup of coffee and the silverware.

"Thanks, Arpad."

"You're welcome," he says, but before he can turn away, I stop him.

"Hey, can I ask you something?"

"Yes."

I look around to make sure nobody is close enough to hear us. I drop my voice. "You know Derek? The guy we eat dinner with. The guy who speaks Hungarian."

"Yes."

"You were talking to him the other day. What were you guys saying?"

"When we were talking Hungarian?"

"Yeah." I nod and start shoveling pineapple into my mouth.

"I asked where he was from in Hungary and when he left. Stuff like that."

I take a drink of coffee. "Is Derek a Hungarian name?"

He frowns. "No."

"So, he changed his name in America?"

Arpad looks at me curiously. "That's what he said."

"Did he say what his name was in Hungary?"

Arpad frowns and gets hesitant. "I don't..."

I hold up my hands. "Listen, I'm just curious. I thought he said the name Dominik. I was feeling kind of good, thinking I understood Hungarian for a second there. Did he say that?"

Arpad nods, and I stand up smiling. "See? I knew it. Thanks for the food, Arpad. I better get out to the tour, or my wife is going to kill me."

As I walk out of the dining hall and off the boat, I see Jacob, Naomi, Melody, Brianna, and Derek waiting beside the bus that will take us into Vienna. Melody sees me and waves, and as I walk over, I look at both Jacob and Derek. I greet them all when I arrive, and we climb onto the bus. We put on our earpieces so we can listen to our guide while we drive through the city. It's a beautiful city, and I should pay more attention, but I can't. My eyes steal over to Derek. Could he really be *that* Dominik? And if he is, does he know? Does he know who Jacob is? Does he know he's on the cruise with the son of the man he's responsible for killing?

Chapter 14
Brianna Murphy

Cruise Day 5 – Vienna, Austria

After we got on the buses, they drove us into the heart of Vienna and dropped us off right beside the enormous statue of Maria Theresa, Queen of Austria. The six of us posed for pictures in front of the fountain and art museum and then followed our tour guide as he walked us through the city, pointing out a Habsburg palace where Elisabeth, the wife of Franz Josef and the empress they called Sisi, lived.

"Can we go inside there?" I ask the tour guide after raising my hand until he saw me.

"What?"

"Inside the palace? Can we go in?"

He nods. "You have to get a ticket. There are a couple of museums. One is about Empress Elisabeth."

"Elisabeth? About her?" I say excitedly.

He nods.

"Where do we get those tickets?"

He points and then continues the tour as I look at Derek. He winks, seeing my eagerness. I don't have to tell him that's exactly where I want to go after the tour ends. Several years ago, I read a book about Elisabeth, and I've been slightly obsessed ever since. Something about her life and the struggles she endured spoke to me. Derek saw me reading about her and asked who she was. I was shocked he didn't know. He's Hungarian, and she was his queen. Even a bridge is named after her in Budapest.

The guide takes us down a swanky shopping street called Kohlmarkt. It's supposed to rival other famous places like Fifth Avenue in New York or the Champs-Élysées in Paris. Shop signs include all the luxury brands like Chanel, Hermes, and Cartier. I love to shop, and I love jewelry, but I don't care about expensive brands. I don't care if a necklace costs ten dollars or ten thousand. I care only about the look. If I had a thousand dollars, I'd be walking away with multiple necklaces, not just one.

After a couple more blocks, the tour ends in front of a large Gothic cathedral in the center of the city called St. Stephen's. Built in the twelfth and thirteenth centuries, the beautiful cathedral stands out against the backdrop of a modern city. Our guide finishes the tour by recommending the cathedral and reminding us we have two hours before the buses leave the city and return to the boat. We must be at the Maria Teresa statue by 12:00 p.m. or be forced to find our own way back.

When he stops talking, the six of us congregate together.

"What do you guys want to do?" Naomi asks.

"I want to go into the church," Theo says.

"I need a Diet Coke," Jacob says.

Naomi glares at him.

He doesn't see it, and I wonder if it's an act. "I'll head to the shop over there. Anyone else?" He looks at Theo, who doesn't respond.

"We'd like to go into the church," Derek says, looking at me for confirmation. I nod.

"Let's go," Melody says and grabs me by the arm while also pulling Theo.

Naomi looks up at Jacob. "I'm going to go with them into the church."

"Fine," he says, seeing he's alone in his desire for carbonated caffeine. He walks away, and the rest of us head toward the cathedral. I look back and wonder about him. Something's different. He doesn't seem the same as when we first met him. There's a tension growing, and I think it's between him and Naomi. Did something happen?

Throngs of people mill around the outside of the cathedral, and we have to push our way past them as we enter. Our eyes are drawn to the ceiling, but the entire thing is lovely with a ton of hard-carved art pieces. We take thirty minutes to fight the crowd and see every part. When we exit, Jacob is nowhere to be seen.

"What do you want to do?" Melody asks Naomi, clearly wondering about Jacob.

Naomi sighs. "He'll be fine on his own. He's a big boy. He can make it back to the bus stop. Let's go back to the Golden U and look around."

Theo frowns. "Maybe I should go find him. Let him know where you'll be."

"Theo...," Melody says.

He reaches out a hand and touches her shoulder. "It'll be fine. I can make it back to the bus. You girls go shop." He looks at Derek. "Do you want to come with me?"

Before Derek can respond, I look at Naomi. "Don't you guys have an excursion planned, riding bikes along the river?"

Naomi nods.

"We don't have anything formally scheduled for today." I look up at Derek. "We were going to stick around the city for several hours. We might part with you now. The museums sound like they're pretty big."

"Oh," Naomi says with a frown. "You don't want to shop?"

I give her a shy smile. "Not really. I'm afraid Derek will kill me if I spend too much more money." I laugh and grab Derek by the hand and pull him. "We'll see you guys back at the boat."

"How will you get back?" Melody calls after us.

"We'll ride the subway," Derek says, extending his arms. "It'll be an adventure."

We walk away, and I squeeze his hand. I'm so grateful we've met our friends on the cruise, but I'm excited to be alone with Derek. As a little girl, I always wondered how a woman could ever feel comfortable being around and talking to a man, not to mention anything physical. Before I met him, there were boys I found attractive. But none of them fit. I always found myself pretending to be someone else when I was around them. Never with Derek. I look down and see his hand in mine and cuddle closer to him as we walk. We were made for each other. I've always believed that. I just worry that after learning what I have about him, he doesn't feel the same.

We follow the same path the guide had shown us and return to the Habsburgs' palace and stop at the ticket office for the Elisabeth Museum. We ask for tickets and are informed that nothing is available for several hours. Apparently, the demand is too great for some of the narrow passageways.

After buying the tickets, we step back from the ticket window and look at the tickets. We can't enter for another three hours.

"What do you want to do?" Derek asks, looking at me.

I look around the courtyard, then out of the archway that leads to the large open area with enormous statues. "I don't care. I wanted to come to this. You choose."

Derek reaches up and wipes a bead of sweat that's rolled down the side of his face. It's a warm day. The hottest of the voyage. "How about the art museum? I think it has a couple famous pieces, including *The Tower of Babel* by Bruegel."

I laugh. "Who?"

He grins. "Bruegel."

I look up at him warily. "Are you making that up?"

He chuckles. "I'm serious."

Derek has always been more interested in art than me. When I first met him in college, he was considering majoring in art history. I think it might have been me who convinced him not to. I didn't do it on purpose, but my question about career options for an art major seemed to give him pause. The next thing I knew, he was a finance major.

I smile at him. "I've always wanted to see *The Tower of Babel* in person. Looks like today is my lucky day."

He grins, and we walk back to where the tour started and enter the museum. We spend a couple of hours exploring the exhibits and viewing the sculptures and paintings. As it gets closer to our time to return to the Elisabeth Museum, he looks at me and asks if I'm hungry. I nod, and we visit the restaurant inside the art museum.

After we're seated and place our order, I lean my elbow on the table and put my palm to my cheek. "What were you thinking about when you looked at some of that art?"

"What do you mean?"

As we explored the museum, I waited for him time and time again. It was like the paintings were completely different for him than they were for me. He saw a message that I couldn't see.

"I mean," I reach out and take his hand, wondering how I might phrase my question, "what paintings did you like the most?"

He shrugs. "I thought it would be the Babel painting, but it was actually *The Peasant Dance.*"

I look at him, and he can see my confusion.

"It was another of Bruegel's paintings."

"Oh, right," I say, pretending to remember the art piece. "What did you like so much about that one?"

Our server returns with our drinks, and he takes a sip of his and shakes his head. "So much. Did you notice the faces of the peasants?"

I nod, but I'm lying. I can't even remember the painting.

"Each one was so unique. You could feel their individual personalities. Each person has their own history, pain they've experienced, joy, thoughts, and desires. We're all so different, and I think he captured that uniqueness so well in that painting. You can tell so much about a person by studying their face."

He's right, and I guess I've never really thought about it that way. Our food comes, and we continue to discuss the museum, then hurry out and walk back to the Habsburgs' palace. It's the warmest part of the day when we climb the stairs and begin exploring the exhibits, and even though I've been dying to see this museum, the heat pushes me forward a little faster than I'd like. After less than two hours, we're done and welcome the fresh air as we follow directions to the subway entrance. Other than a quick visit to a chocolate shop, we go straight there. We ride several stops and exit, walking along the river to our boat.

"Well," Derek says, "is that what you imagined in your book?"

"Imagined?" I ask as we walk hand in hand.

"Yeah. I would think you had a picture in your mind about Elisabeth and her life while you read her book. Was it what you imagined? Did the palace and her clothing look like you thought it would?"

I look out over the river and consider his question before finally nodding. "Pretty much. What did you think of it?"

"I didn't know she had been stabbed."

"Oh, no?"

He shakes his head. "She had a tough life. She didn't seem happy. Her son's death and her not-so-great marriage didn't help."

I nod and see we're getting closer to the boat and feel my nerve slipping away. Inside the museum, learning about how Elisabeth had locked out her husband, I made a resolution. I was going to confront Derek with something I've wanted to know for years, and I was going to do it before we reached the boat. I stop walking and turn to look up at him. I study his face, thinking about what he said about the peasant dance, how you can read so much about someone through their face.

He stops and gives me a curious look. "Are you okay?"

I nod. "Derek." I take a deep breath. "There's been something I've wanted to ask you for a long time."

He frowns, sensing how serious I've become. "Okay."

"I want you to be honest with me."

He swallows. "Okay."

"Will you promise to be honest with me?"

He frowns. "I, I don't know…"

I shake my head. "Do you trust me?"

He looks at me but doesn't answer.

"Do you believe I love you?"

He pauses. "Yes."

I nod. "Do you believe I want nothing but the best for you?"

He nods.

"Then why," I stop and have to fight back the tears, "why did you make plans to leave me?"

He frowns. "What?"

"After the business failed. Were you going to run away? Were you going to leave me and the girls?"

He looks at me, and I can see the uncertainty in his eyes.

"Derek, why?"

He can't hold my gaze and looks away. I want to push him but hold back and wait.

After several seconds, his eyes return to me. "I was so ashamed."

"I know. But I love you. The girls love you. Why would you want to throw that love away?"

I've seen my husband cry only once. It was the day our oldest, Allison, was born. Tears well up in his eyes. He tries to speak, but he can't, and I can see the pain he's holding. I put my hand on his chest and inch closer to him.

"You and I were meant to be together. No matter what happens, I'll always love you. Do you believe that?"

He looks at me and nods.

I hold out my pinkie finger. "Then make me a promise."

He watches me and grins.

"Promise me that, no matter what, we'll always stay together. That no matter what happens, our love will mean more."

He stares at me for several seconds and finally reaches up and intertwines his smallest finger with mine. "I promise."

Chapter 15
Derek Murphy

Cruise Day 5 – Vienna, Austria

I lie in bed staring at the ceiling, listening to the rhythmic breathing of my wife. Bri fell asleep almost immediately after we returned to the cabin after dinner. I'm not so lucky. I can't stop thinking about our conversation as we returned from Vienna and walked along the river. How did she know? How long has she known? What else does she know?

I turn and look at her in the dark. I can barely make out her face as she sleeps beside me. Gently, I lift the blankets and slip a leg off the bed. I quietly dress, grab my wallet, and exit the room, holding the door so it doesn't slam as I enter the hall. The lights are dim, and I walk toward the lounge, hoping it's still open. Beyond our conversation, I know what's bothering me. I'm closer and closer to being home. It's the first time since leaving thirty years ago. I thought I was only leaving for a couple of weeks, but I never returned.

It was two years after my father's death, and my mother and I traveled to the United States to visit my aunt and cousins. It was 1970, the peak of the Cold War, and looking back, I can't believe my mother got us permission to leave. She says she worked on it for a full year and had to perform certain favors to high-ranking communist officials to earn the opportunity to travel. She never told me what those *favors* were, and I never asked. They tried to force her to leave me at home, but somehow she was able to bring me along. We were supposed to stay in America for three weeks and then return. When we landed in the United States, she told me we were never going back.

I was heartbroken. I was in a country I didn't know. I had left behind a girlfriend I thought I loved. Hungary was flawed, but it was home. I grew up sharing a house with my grandparents. Life was difficult, but family was everything. After my father's unexpected death, my grandfather took on that role. He loved me through it. He was my best friend, not just my closest male relative. I loved him, and my heart ached at the prospect of never seeing him again. My mother assured me that something would change in the future. It wouldn't be goodbye. Four years later, the letter came telling us he had died of a heart attack.

I climb the stairs in the main lobby and see lights on in the lounge. The automatic glass door opens as I approach and enter. The tables surrounding the bar are empty, but the bar still has a couple of patrons. Only men occupy the barstools, and it's just two at that. I pick the seat furthest from them and look at the bartender.

"What can I get you?" he asks with a slight accent.

He's a tall man in his late twenties with dark hair and thick eyebrows. I can see a five-o'clock shadow covering his cheeks and jaw.

He places a paper napkin on the bar before me, dark hair covering the skin on the back of his hands.

"I'll have a beer."

"What kind?"

"I don't care," I tell him.

He places a glass on the paper napkin and reaches for a bottle beneath him, pulling out an Austrian beer, Stiegl, opening it, and pouring it into the glass. A thick layer of foam sits at the top when he finishes.

"Thank you," I say.

"You're welcome," he says, and steps away.

I pick up the glass and take a gulp, then put it back on the bar and wipe the foam off my mouth with the back of my hand.

"You could have asked for a Hungarian beer," a male voice says from beside me in Hungarian. I notice the man for the first time. He's our ship captain. Captain Arany. I stare at him, wondering how he knows I'm Hungarian. Word must have gotten out among the staff.

I respond in Hungarian. "Is that what you have there?"

He shakes his head. "No. Tonight I needed something stronger."

I look at his glass as he raises it to his lips. It's a tumbler of whiskey.

"Should I be worried?" I ask as he lowers the glass.

He looks at it, then back to me. "Why? Because of this?"

I nod.

He smiles. "The first mate is on duty. I'm done for the night."

I nod and take another gulp of beer. "I guess the crew talks."

He looks at me with a glassy-eyed expression and shrugs. "It's not every day a fellow Hungarian from America joins us on board." He runs his finger along the top of his cup. "First time back?"

I nod.

"How long's it been?"

"Thirty years."

He lets out a low whistle and then looks up, and I can see he's calculating.

"You were young."

"Fifteen."

He nods. "From Budapest?"

I shake my head. "Vác."

He fixes me with an intense expression. "Really?"

I nod, curious about his reaction.

"I grew up in Vác."

"You're kidding?"

He shakes his head.

"Small world," I say.

"What's your name?"

"My Hungarian name?"

He nods.

"Dominik."

He rubs his chin. "Family name?"

I hesitate. I haven't shared this information in ten years. "Meszaros."

He watches me, continuing to rub his chin. "You're forty-five?"

"Forty-six."

He continues rubbing his beard, then shakes his head. "I don't remember any Meszaroses. Did you have any siblings? Maybe anyone younger?"

I shake my head.

His eyes soften, and he shrugs. "Well, I guess I don't know you then."

As we finish our drinks, we talk about jobs and family. Nothing too significant. He sticks around for ten more minutes and then wishes me a good night and leaves. I consider getting one more beer but finally feel sleepy and walk back to my room. As I undress and climb back into bed, I think about his eyes. It might be my imagination, but I swear I saw a change when I mentioned my name. He tried to hide it, but it had some significance for him.

Chapter 16
Naomi Costa

Cruise Day 6 – Bratislava, Slovakia

We ate breakfast alone again. Jacob focused on his book while I ate two croissants. It's been several days since I dreamed of killing him, but this morning my thoughts were more violent than ever. I imagined my hands around his throat, squeezing until his face turned purple and he keeled over. The daydream was so vivid that I hadn't noticed when he stood up and spoke to me. It wasn't until he bumped my shoulder that I came out of my trance.

That was thirty minutes ago, and now we're walking around with our group and tour guide. She's a woman in her midfifties with a thick accent. She speaks too fast, and everyone in the group struggles to understand her. She gets way more questions for clarification than any tour guide before.

The contrast between Vienna and Bratislava is stark. This is my first time in a former Soviet country, and its influence can be felt everywhere. Anything constructed in the last forty years is square with no curves or shape, lacking any artistic style. Many of the buildings are in ill repair, and the people have a repressed feel to them with their down-turned expressions and slow stumbles. They look at us like unwanted guests, scowling and grumbling when we get in their way.

We exit the main church, St. Martin's Cathedral, which, compared to St. Stephen's Cathedral in Vienna, is plain and forgettable. She walks us down a cobblestone street to a square and gives us a history lesson about the city. Bratislava has belonged to several different kingdoms and recently became the capital of Slovakia after the Slovaks separated from the Czechs in 1993. Long before that, Bratislava was once the capital and coronation city of Hungary. She points out several buildings that existed way back then, which include writing in three different languages: German, Slovak, and Hungarian.

There's no doubt I liked Vienna more. But I do find the history of this city fascinating, and having grown up during the Cold War, I can't help feeling a little awed by being in a town that was once behind the Iron Curtain.

"I'm going to go get a Diet Coke," Jacob says, leaning toward me.

"Now?" I whisper, trying to keep my voice down but feeling my temper flare.

"Yeah," he says, frowning at me.

"She's not even done talking yet," I hiss. My whisper was louder than intended, and I see Melody turn and look at us. "She'll be done in five minutes. Just wait."

"Eh, I'm done with her. Sorry," he says, pulls the headphone from his ear, and turns off the radio.

I grab his arm. "You left last time," I say even louder, no longer worrying about pretenses. I'm sick of this, and he needs to hear it.

"What?" he says, freeing his arm from my grasp.

"In Vienna." I'm shouting now. I can feel my hands trembling with rage. I point to Theo as everyone in the group is watching us, including our guide. "Theo had to separate from us to go find you. He didn't want to do that. It's not fair to him. Stop thinking of only yourself all the time."

He looks around. Our entire group, even the tour guide, is watching us. His cheeks flush with embarrassment, then turn hard. His jaw clenches and looks back to me. He takes a step closer, and his voice drops to a fierce whisper as he raises his hand and points a finger at me. "Did you ask me even once? One time what excursions I'd like to do on this trip? Did you care?" He demonstrates to the group with his hand. "Everyone, including me, Melody, and Theo. Hell, even Brianna and Derek do what you want when you want it. Don't lecture me about selfishness, Naomi. You're the most selfish of all."

I stare at him in shock. His words sting, but that's not why I'm surprised. This isn't him. I'm the one with the temper. Making a scene in public isn't a common practice of mine, but it's not unheard of. He has never talked to me like this. He always backs down. What is going on?

He's fuming. Waiting for me to reply. But I don't. And when he sees I have nothing left to say, he spins away, walking fast.

I call after him. "Jacob, come back here."

He ignores me and rounds the corner, disappearing. I look back at the group. All eyes are on me, but slowly, one by one, they stop staring and return their gaze to our guide.

"Well," she says. "Where was I?"

She fumbles with her words as she tries to regain her composure, and members of the group flash glances at me. I feel a hand take mine, then a reassuring rub of my shoulder. I turn, expecting to see Melody, but instead, it's Brianna. I look at her through cloudy eyes, and she winks and continues to rub my arm. I look down and cry as the tour guide finishes her speech and then separates.

My eyes are still down, but I can sense my friends surrounding me. I pull myself together and look up into their faces. Brianna and Melody are watching me while Theo and Derek look away.

"We've got an hour before we need to be back at the boat for lunch," Theo says, checking his watch. "Why don't we look around for a few minutes?"

"Good idea," Melody says. "What do you think, Naomi?"

I don't trust myself to speak and only nod while wiping my eyes. Brianna squeezes me, then releases her grip. We walk back down the cobblestone street—Theo in front with Brianna and Melody on either side of me. When we enter the first shop, I notice Derek is no longer with us.

"Where did Derek go?" I ask Brianna as she examines a package of licorice.

We're in a candy shop. There are large wooden barrels throughout, overflowing with sweets, and I wonder if they are all really full or if filler is in the bottom.

She shakes her head. "Oh, he said he forgot something on the boat. He needed to go get it."

I look at her and wonder if she's lying, but she doesn't make eye contact.

"Sorry about that back there," I say.

She puts the licorice package back down. "About what?"

"Jacob and I."

She waves a hand. "Couples fight. Especially when they're stressed. You should have seen me and Derek ten years ago."

I look at her curiously. "What happened ten years ago?"

She walks over to a barrel of chocolate candies and examines it. "Derek had a business that failed. We were broke, and he wasn't in a good place. I didn't know how to help him, and the stress put a serious burden on our marriage." She looks at me and shrugs. "We got through it."

"What kind of business?"

"Telecommunications. He had this idea and got investors. He was going to make millions, but then the bottom fell out. He lost a patent case, and suddenly the company was worthless. All of his investors lost their money. They were angry with him and sued him. It was really rough."

I stare at her. "Derek owned the company?"

She nods.

"What was it called?"

Rather than answer, she comes forward and puts a hand on my shoulder. "I know this might seem weird, but I'd rather not say."

"Oh."

She shakes her head. "I know. It's just...it's a part of our life we're trying to put behind us."

I reach out and embrace her. "I get it. It's okay. I'm sorry you went through that."

She waves a hand. "It's strange to say, but I'm not. I mean, when we were going through it, it royally sucked. But it helped us grow. And our love has never been stronger." She nods at me encouragingly. "Whatever you and Jacob are going through, just work together. You might just learn to love him more."

She steps to another barrel of candy, and I watch her as my mind races. The man who ran the business my father-in-law invested in and lost everything was from someplace in Europe. Was it Hungary? Could Dominik be Derek? Is that why Jacob reacted like that to me? Is that why he left? Could the man he's been searching for all these years actually be our new friend?

Chapter 17
Jacob Costa

Cruise Day 6 – Bratislava, Slovakia

I round the corner and look behind me, checking to see if I'm being followed. I half expect Theo to be there, coming after me, but he's not. I walk along beside the shops with umbrellas in front and duck into one of them. A convenience store with a picture of a polar bear drinking a Coca-Cola on the window. I buy my Diet Coke, struggling to understand how much money to give the attendant. I eventually show him bills and let him point to the correct one. With my Diet Coke in hand, I walk to the door and check the window before exiting. I don't see Theo or Naomi, but I do see Derek. He's several doors down, walking slowly, looking into the shop windows. He's on the other side, so I act quickly, stepping out of the shop and nearly running up the street before turning a corner into a small alley. I slow to a common pace and move through the alley to emerge on the other side. I open my drink and take a swig while resuming my path back to the boat.

As I walk, I think about Naomi. How could she attack me like that in front of everyone? I was only going to get a drink. Things are getting worse with her. Our troubles aren't anything new, but that attack was. Normally, she berates me in private. Not public. She's been different toward me for years, ever since Dad died. She never understood my obsession with finding Dominik. And she especially didn't like the amount of money I paid that private investigator, only to fail. I know she thought it was a wild-goose chase, and she was right. But it wasn't a total loss.

I gave it up after thousands of dollars, but our relationship still hasn't recovered. Maybe it's gotten worse. Now, we're nothing but roommates. I can't even remember the last time we had sex. Hell, I don't remember the last time she kissed me. The love is gone, if it was ever really there. And if I'm being honest, I'm not sure how I feel about her. How much longer can I go on like this?

I walk down the ramp onto the boat and am greeted by a young staff woman. I give her my name, and she marks me returned. I consider going down the hall to our room but figure that's most likely where Naomi will find me if she comes looking. It's a beautiful day, and I decide to go to the top deck and sit under an umbrella while drinking my Diet Coke. I turn my chair toward the city, figuring I'd like to know when the rest of the group returns. I look at my watch and see I have another hour before lunch. After lunch, we have another excursion. Something Naomi planned, of course.

I take a drink and look around. I'm alone on the top deck. Everyone else is ashore exploring the city. I don't even see any crew members, except one, and he's down on the other side of the boat smoking a cigarette. I sit back in my chair, close my eyes, and consider going back to the room to get my book but decide against it. I don't think I could read right now, even if I wanted to. There's too much going on in my head. I can't get over the irony of this week. I hired a private investigator to look for Dominik Meszaros for over a year without any luck. I gave up, thinking he'd disappeared. I never would have guessed I'd take a cruise with him several years later. His name is Derek Murphy now, but I know it's him.

After my father's death, I had to find him. I always wondered what I'd do if I found him. Would I really extract my revenge? Could I really kill him? Or at least make him suffer? He's a father, after all. He has children. But what about *my* father?

An image of my dad comes to mind. His head lying on his home office desk. A gunshot wound in his temple. So much blood. The gun lying beside him. The investigators said it was self-inflicted. That he had killed himself. But I knew the truth. Dominik had done everything but pull the trigger.

"Nice weather," I hear an accented voice say beside me.

I open my eyes and squint against the sun. A man with black trousers and a crisp white shirt stands above me. It's the ship's captain.

"Yes," I say, leaning forward and grabbing my Diet Coke. He talks to me as I unscrew it.

"You did not like Bratislava?"

I gulp Diet Coke, then shake my head. "No, it's not that. I got separated from my group and came back here to wait for them."

He nods and looks away from me, back to the city. "I don't like it," he says.

I don't know what to say.

"You know, it used to be part of Hungary."

I nod. Is he bored? Why is he telling me this? I've barely said two words to this man since getting on board six days ago. Now he acts as if we're friends.

"I'm Hungarian," the captain says. He pulls a chair over and sits beside me. "You are friends with Derek Murphy." It's a statement, not a question. "Good friends?"

Hmm, he knows who I am. And he knows Derek.

I shake my head. "I never met him before the cruise."

"But you are from Arizona. He is from Arizona."

I frown. How does he know that? Did Derek tell him? "Yes, but I didn't know him before."

He nods. "What about his wife? Did you know her?"

That's an odd question. What is this all about? I shake my head.

"But you know Mr. and Mrs. Jones? They are from Arizona."

"Yes, Theo and I have been friends since we were kids. We came on this cruise with them."

The captain leans back in his chair and rubs his short beard. "I want to tell you something."

"Okay."

"When I was a boy, my older sister liked a boy in our village."

What is this? What is he talking about? Is he confused? Does he think I'm somebody else?

"That boy went to America."

He stops and stares at me.

"Okay?"

His eyes smolder. "That boy raped my sister."

I frown.

"He went to Arizona in United States. His name was Dominik."

Chapter 18
Melody Jones

Cruise Day 6 – Bratislava, Slovakia

After stopping at several souvenir shops in Bratislava, we walk back to the boat. We go up the ramp and give our names to the young woman checking passengers back in.

"Lunch?" Theo says, motioning with his head toward the dining hall.

Naomi looks down at her watch. "Yes. We have only an hour before we're supposed to be back here for the excursion."

We enter the dining room but notice the tables are empty. Arpad, our server, sees us and comes over. "Sorry, we only serve food in the lounge today for lunch."

Derek says something to him in Hungarian, and they jabber back and forth before Arpad smiles and tells us he will see us tonight and walks away.

"What did he say?" Brianna asks.

Derek shrugs. "I guess they only serve lunch on the Bratislava day in the lounge because so many people stay and eat in the city."

"Why is that?" I ask.

"Probably because it's so cheap," Derek says, pulling Brianna by the arm.

We walk back out to the main foyer and up the stairs to the lounge.

"Are you guys coming with us on the excursion?" Naomi asks Brianna.

She nods happily. "We were able to get added. They had some extra spots."

"Great!" Naomi says as we all sit at a table at the back of the boat under an umbrella.

I look around, hoping to see Jacob, but he's nowhere in sight. Theo and I make eye contact, and he motions with his eyes. I frown, not knowing what he's trying to tell me.

"Can I get you anything to drink?" a man with dark-rimmed glasses asks as he approaches the table and offers us menus.

Everyone asks for water, and Theo orders a lemonade.

After the server leaves, Theo stands from the table. "I'm going to head to the bathroom. I'll be right back." As he leaves the table, he gives me another look, and I think I get it. He wants to find Jacob. I watch him leave, then turn my attention back to Brianna and Naomi. They're talking about the excursion we're going on later today. It's a Habsburg palace that's apparently back in Austria but only thirty minutes from here by bus. Derek's attention is on the menu, and when I look back to where Theo left, I see him. He's hiding behind the corner, out of sight of the rest of the table. He locks eyes with me and motions with his hand. I frown, and he mouths, "Come here."

Confused, I stand and excuse myself, telling them I also need to visit the bathroom. When I come around the corner, Theo grabs my hand and pulls me with him as we walk out of the lounge. There's a small seating area just outside the doors, and we sit down on the couch. Theo looks around, then leans closer to me, his voice barely above a whisper.

"I have something I need to tell you."

"Okay."

"You remember Jacob's dad? Leo?"

I look at him, confused, and nod. I'm holding my breath. Does he know? Does he know what I did?

"You remember how he invested in that business and lost all his money?"

I nod. "Yes."

He looks back, then leans forward and whispers in my ear. "Derek is Dominik."

I stare at him, shocked. I was preparing a response, a way to defend myself. But this news has caught me off guard. I never saw it coming.

"What? How?"

"Do you remember the night when Derek was speaking Hungarian with Arpad?"

"Yes."

"Derek said the name Dominik while talking to him."

"So?" I shake my head. "He was speaking Hungarian."

Theo nods.

"And you heard him say Dominik?"

He shakes his head. "Jacob did. He told me."

I blow out a breath and shake my head. "No way. Jacob heard him wrong. You've heard that language. You can't even make out the words."

He puts a hand on my knee. "That's what I thought too. So, I asked Arpad."

My mouth drops. "You what?"

Theo nods. "I asked Arpad. He confirmed Derek's Hungarian name is Dominik."

I look away and think for a second, then shake my head. "No, it's too big a coincidence. Plus, Dominik wasn't Hungarian."

Theo raises an eyebrow. "How do you know that?"

I frown. "Wasn't he from the Dominican Republic or something?"

Theo chuckles. "Why? Because his name is Dominik?"

I raise my hand to my mouth. I just assumed that. Why did I assume that?

"Look," Theo says. "We know he was from a country in Europe. We just didn't know which." I shake my head, but Theo presses on, raising each of his fingers as he ticks off a list. "Mel, he was foreign, from Europe, and had the name Dominik. His age matches. Jacob is convinced it's him."

So that's why Jacob's acting this way. That's why he can't stand being with the group. He doesn't want to be anywhere near Derek. Oh, wow. What must Jacob be going through?

The door opens behind us, and Naomi comes out looking around. She sees us, and we stand to greet her.

"Hey, we need to order. Our excursion starts in less than thirty minutes."

"Sorry," Theo says and grabs me by the hand as we walk into the lounge, trailing her. When we reach the table, we see the server standing patiently, waiting to take our order. As Theo orders, I can't help glancing at Derek. Could he really be Dominik? I don't believe it. I need to prove it isn't him.

Chapter 19
Theo Jones

Cruise Day 6 – Bratislava, Slovakia

After lunch, we exit the lounge and descend the stairs to see Jacob standing by the exit doors, waiting for us. He waves, and we all wave back and join him.

"Good to have you back," I say, and Melody and Brianna smile at him.

"The group wouldn't be complete without you," Brianna says.

"Thank you," Jacob says without looking at Naomi.

She's looking down, not making eye contact with him.

We exit the boat, following the instructions of the crew member, and board the bus outside. As we walk, I notice Jacob angles over to be beside Derek. Curious to see what he's up to, I stay close, holding Melody's hand. Brianna and Naomi hang back, caught up in a conversation about something they saw in a shop in Bratislava.

"Hey, sorry about all that before," Jacob says to Derek.

"All what?" Derek asks.

"Me and Naomi..."

Derek waves a hand. "Oh, don't apologize. Sometimes you're just having a bad day."

"Yeah, but I hate to fight in front of you guys. That's pretty embarrassing."

"Don't worry about it," Derek says and smiles. "We'll make it up to you by fighting sometime in front of you."

We reach the bus, and I see Jacob stop and turn back. "I forgot to get a water bottle."

"I've got an extra one," Derek says. "It's in my backpack."

He starts to swing it off his shoulders, but Jacob reaches out and stops him. "I can get it. Which compartment is it in?" He steps behind Derek to access the backpack.

"The big one."

Jacob looks at the rest of us and waves us forward. "You guys go ahead and get on the bus. Theo, save me a seat, would you? I'd like to talk to you."

"Sure," I say, and we follow Brianna and Naomi as they get on.

We walk down the aisle of seats, and Naomi turns back to me. "Thanks for sitting with him. We still need some time."

I nod. "Happy to."

Naomi looks around. "Well, who wants to sit with me?"

"I will," Melody says with a smile. "I guess I'll take one for the team."

Naomi laughs and sits against the window in the middle of the bus while Melody joins her. Brianna sits on the same row but on the opposite side by the window, and knowing Jacob wants to talk to me, I go back several more rows and take another window seat.

After a few seconds, Derek and Jacob walk on, and Derek sits beside Brianna while Jacob joins me.

"What was that all about?" I whisper.

Jacob looks at me and raises an eyebrow but doesn't respond.

After several more passengers join, our guide gets on the bus and tells us to put on our headphones. We do, and the bus pulls out while he gives us a brief overview of our tour. The ride is about thirty minutes, and he tells us he'll come back on when we get closer to the palace.

As we cross over a bridge, Jacob pulls something from his back pocket. It's a wallet, and when he opens it, I see it's not his.

"What are you doing?" I ask as he flips through it.

"You know what I'm doing."

I look up a few rows to Derek. He's conversing with Brianna.

"You stole it from him?"

"I borrowed it."

He removes Derek's ID and examines it, then pulls out several credit cards. Finally, he removes a couple of pictures from the plastic holders. There's a family photo of Derek, Brianna, and their four girls. The other is a black-and-white photo with folds and creases. It's a boy with two older people. They look like they might be his grandparents. The house behind is small, and the driveway is dirt. It looks rural or maybe taken in a foreign country.

Jacob shows it to me. "Do you think that's Derek?"

I look at the boy and can see a resemblance. I think it is. Jacob puts the rest of the items back into the wallet but keeps the photo and puts it inside his own wallet.

"What are you doing?" I ask.

"I want to show this to someone," he whispers.

"Who?"

"The ship captain."

"Why?"

He tells me about his conversation with the captain. About the boy, Dominik, who raped the captain's sister.

"Maybe he'll recognize him."

I look over at Derek. "He raped her?"

Jacob looks at me gravely and nods. "That's what it sounds like." He turns so he can watch Derek. "You'd never guess it, right?"

"What?"

He looks back at me. "You never know who someone really is."

I hold his gaze for a moment and then look out the window at the green fields surrounding us. "I told Melody."

"What?" Jacob says, glaring at me and then looking several rows in front to where Melody sits beside Naomi.

"She should know. So should Naomi."

"No. You should have told me you were going to tell her."

"I would have, but you were gone."

He shakes his head and glares at me. "He can't know that we know."

"They aren't going to tell him."

He grabs my arm. "That's not what I'm afraid of."

"What, then?"

"How do you know they aren't going to tell Brianna?"

I begin a retort but stop. That's true. After the palace, I need to talk to Melody and warn her not to tell Brianna.

Chapter 20
Melody Jones

Cruise Day 6 – Bratislava, Slovakia

I'm sitting on the bus beside Naomi. Derek and Brianna are across the aisle from us, and Theo and Jacob are several rows back. We must be getting close to the Habsburg's palace because our tour guide has come back on the microphone and is speaking to us through our earpieces. I look over and see Brianna and Derek are listening and bump Naomi with my elbow. She frowns, and I pull my earpiece from my ear and motion for her to do the same. Confused, she complies, and I lean closer so I'm speaking directly into her ear. "There's something I need to tell you."

She looks confused but waits for me to go on. I check Derek and Brianna one more time, then whisper in her ear, "Derek is Dominik."

She frowns, then her eyes go wide, and she stares at me as I slowly nod, allowing the information to sink in. "*That* Dominik?"

I nod.

She looks across at Derek and Brianna, then leans closer to me. "What are you talking about? Why do you say that?" she whispers.

I look her in the eye and quickly recount what Theo had told me before lunch. She keeps her attention forward as I whisper in her ear. When I finish, the bus slows down, preparing to stop, and Naomi leans into my ear. "That doesn't prove it's him."

I shrug. "It doesn't mean it's not. You've got to admit, it seems pretty likely."

She stares at me, her mind working. "We need to find out."

I nod and watch her. Her face is flushed. She's still processing what I told her. I'm still unsure about it myself. The bus stops, and we let Derek and Brianna go first, then exit after them. Jacob and Theo follow. When we're all out of the bus, our guide gathers us. We're a small group of no more than twenty.

"Welcome to Schloss Hof," she says. She's a woman in her late forties with graying blonde hair pulled back in a bow. She speaks good English with only a slight accent. "We have a short five-minute walk to the ticket office. There, you can use the bathroom, if you need. The tour is all on foot. We'll begin by touring the grounds, then enter the palace and visit several rooms. The entire tour should last about two hours. At the end, I'll give you thirty minutes of personal time, then we'll meet back here at the bus." She scans our faces. "Any questions before we begin?"

Nobody speaks, and she motions for us to follow.

I remain with Naomi while Jacob and Theo lag behind. Derek and Brianna are at the front near the guide.

"How long has Jacob known?" Naomi whispers without looking at me.

"I don't know. Only a couple days, I think."

She gazes up from looking down at her feet as we walk along the dirt path. "That's why he blew up at me this morning. That's why he separated from the group in Vienna and Bratislava."

I nod, assuming she's right.

"He never said anything to me," she breathes. She's still working it out in her mind.

We reach the ticket office, and there's a small shop and horse barn, along with restrooms. Theo and Jacob visit the bathroom while Naomi and I enter the shop, and Derek and Brianna find a shaded spot as a respite from the heat. Inside the shop, Naomi and I walk down an aisle, and then she turns to me. "We've got to talk to Brianna."

I frown. "What? We can't talk to her."

"We've got to find out if he's Dominik."

I shake my head. "You can't just ask her if her husband is a killer."

She glares at me. "Of course not. But we could find out more. She told me Derek had a failed business. We need to find out more."

"What kind of business?"

Someone interrupts us. "Excuse me," a woman says. She's standing behind the cash register in the corner. "I think your guide is waiting for you." She points out the window.

We turn and see our group gathered around our guide. We walk out, and our guide sees us coming and waves us over. She waits to speak until we join the group.

"There's a wedding happening inside the schloss today. So, the courtyard is off limits to us. But we can see the rest of the castle. Is everyone ready to go?"

We all nod and follow as she guides us to the back of the castle. It's a hot day, and we look for shade anywhere we can find it while listening to the guide. She stops at the back gates and gives us a brief history of the ownership of the castle. In the distance, we can see mountains, and below, there's a beautiful, large fountain with a statue of a woman sitting on a lion as it lies its head back and sprays water from its mouth. I've seen pictures of famous European palaces, and this one doesn't disappoint. The gardens are in great condition, and the landscape in the surrounding countryside is emerald green.

"How old is this castle?" a woman in the group asks as we stroll through the back gate along the pebble path to the rear of the palace.

"Schloss Hof was built in the sixteen hundreds and added to in the seventeen hundreds. The style is Baroque, which was typical for that time period. Have you all been to Vienna yet?"

We all nod.

"You likely saw and heard about the Habsburg Empire and Empress Maria Theresa."

"Yes," Brianna says excitedly.

We've reached the back door of the castle now, where several wedding guests are exiting.

"Maria Theresa purchased the palace, and it became one of the imperial estates of the Habsburgs. Did you visit the large estate, Schönbrunn Palace, in Vienna?"

A couple of women nod.

"That was one of the others."

"Did Sisi ever come here?" Brianna asks.

"Queen Elisabeth?"

"Yes."

Our guide shakes her head. "Not to my knowledge. She and her mother-in-law didn't always have the happiest relationship." She holds up a finger. "I'll be right back. I'm just going to go in and make sure we're allowed to enter. Wait here."

She goes in, and we all stand around, turning away and admiring the gardens. After a couple of minutes, she returns and tells us we can enter and visit the ceremonial rooms, but we'll need to come in on the side.

She walks us around the building, and we enter the palace and visit several gorgeous rooms with high ceilings and white walls. She tells us that the palace has been restored to what it looked like when Maria Theresa owned it.

We visit many more beautiful rooms and even see Maria Theresa's bedroom with an ensuite bathroom, which was a novelty in those days. Before the tour ends, we're allowed to sample some locally made champagne and cider.

As we sip our drinks, Naomi whispers to me. "You need to find out more about Derek's business."

"Me? Why me?"

"I'll get Derek away from her. You need to talk to her."

"When?"

"Just pay attention."

We stay for another minute, then exit the palace and take several pictures in front before returning to the ticket office and shop. Our guide answers our remaining questions, then tells us to meet back at the bus in thirty minutes, reminding us we can go anywhere on the grounds or to the shop. She leaves, and the six of us congregate.

"Derek," Theo says. "Jacob and I were going to go look around the front of the palace a bit more. Want to come? The girls will probably want to shop."

He looks at Brianna.

"Go," she says, pushing him. "Just leave me your wallet."

"Naomi will buy anything you want. Our treat," Jacob says as Derek pulls his backpack off his shoulders and opens it up.

Naomi looks at Jacob, then puts a hand on Derek's shoulder. "I'd love that. It can be payment for your guide services in Budapest tomorrow."

Derek looks at her but continues searching his bag. He opens it wider, then looks at Brianna. "Did you see my wallet anywhere?"

She shakes her head. "No. Did you leave it back on the boat?"

He frowns and opens every compartment.

"I'm sure you left it on the boat. Don't worry. We've got you covered if you need anything," Theo says.

I see the concern on Derek's face, but what troubles me more is the look on my husband's face. Theo is nervous. Naomi sees it too. What did they do?

"Come on," I say to Brianna and Naomi, grabbing each and pulling them along with me. "Let's go see what we can buy."

We walk away and enter the shop. It's full of all kinds of Schloss Hof merchandise. Little ceramic replicas, shirts, hats, pictures, and paintings. Even the champagne and cider we sampled earlier. We stroll around, picking up everything and looking at it. There's a pair of earrings Brianna seems most interested in.

"Those would look so pretty on you," Naomi says.

"You think so?"

I nod. "What about this locket?" I pick it off the rack and hold it up to her. "I love that. It's perfect for your coloring."

Brianna smiles, and we talk her into letting us buy it. I purchase the necklace while Naomi buys the earrings.

"We'll take these," I say to the store clerk.

"Sounds good. Where are you all from?"

The store clerk is a nice-looking woman in her midthirties with dark, curly hair.

"Arizona."

"Okay. Well, welcome to Austria."

She tells me the cost, and I hand her the money.

"Your English is very good," I say as she gives me my change. "I don't even hear an accent."

She laughs. "It should be. I'm American."

"Oh," I say, embarrassed. "Where are you from?"

"Seattle."

"What are you doing here?"

"Long story. I needed a change after a divorce."

Before I can ask anything more, another woman approaches and asks a question. I return to Naomi and Brianna, and we look around for a few more minutes, then exit and don't see the men waiting for us.

"Where do you think they are?" Brianna asks.

"Probably back at the bus," Naomi says. "We're supposed to meet there anyway. Let's walk back."

Brianna looks around, clearly uncomfortable with leaving Derek, but we encourage her, and she reluctantly walks with us.

"I don't remember," Naomi says as we walk. "Do you work back home?" she says to Brianna.

"Only part-time. I work at a golf course."

"What do you do there?" I ask.

Naomi is on one side of her, and I'm on the other. It feels a little like we're jackals closing in on our kill.

"Oh, I work in the café. It gives me some spending money," she says and laughs.

"And what does Derek do?" I ask.

She smiles. "Can I admit something to you? I don't really know. Is that bad?" She looks at each of us, and we shake our heads. "He does something with software. Sells it and manages a bunch of people. He's told me before, but I don't really remember. Maybe I just don't care," she says with a chuckle.

"It's boring anyway. Right?" Naomi says and laughs.

"Exactly," Brianna says, smiling.

"Has Derek always done that?" I ask.

She shakes her head. "He owned his own company before."

I make eye contact with Naomi but keep pushing. "Oh, yeah? What kind of company? Software?"

"No. It was telecommunications. He had this great idea for a business, and it was going to be huge."

"So, what happened?" I ask.

"I don't know. Something with patents. Anyway, he lost this court case and, just like that, the business was gone."

"Oh, I'm sorry," Naomi says. "I bet those were tough times."

She nods. "Really tough. It was bad there for a while. But Derek's resilient. He picked himself up, and now things are good."

"I bet it was hard on your marriage," Naomi says.

"It was. But if you stay together and trust each other, you can get through and grow closer." She gives Naomi an encouraging smile.

"What was the name of the business?" I ask.

We're getting to the end of the path by the trees. We don't have much time before we reach the bus.

"Tela-Earth."

I shake my head and lie. "I've never heard of it. Did he have investors? Maybe partners?"

She nods. "There were a few people who invested in it."

"What happened to their money?" Naomi asks.

Brianna shakes her head and frowns. "They lost it."

I put an arm around her as she looks down, and I lock eyes with Naomi. It's him. He's Dominik.

Chapter 21
Derek Murphy

Cruise Day 6 – Bratislava, Slovakia

I never found my wallet. I looked through my bag, even turned it upside down and shook it, but it never came out. I know I had it earlier in the day when we bought some candy in Bratislava. I remember putting it at the bottom of my backpack, below the water bottle. The bag was with me the whole day. Someone must have stolen it.

After we got back to the bus and returned to Bratislava, I went to our room and searched it. Nothing. I couldn't find it. I've got money in the safe. That's the only thing keeping me from losing my mind right now. I think I've still got enough cash to get through the trip. But what do I do about my credit cards and debit cards? They were in that wallet. Did someone steal them and use them? Should I call and cancel them? I don't want to do that until I'm sure.

At dinner, everyone talked about the palace and our day in Bratislava, but I hardly said a word. I couldn't get my mind off the wallet. I'm not even sure how I'd call the banks. I don't have a cell phone over here. I wonder if the cruise company could help.

As dinner ends, we make plans to participate in the provided walking tour in Budapest, then go off on our own. I'll be the guide for the rest of the day. Brianna and I will be staying an extra week and will have plenty of time to see the more remote aspects of the city. Plus, I plan to take her up to Vác, where we can see my childhood home where my grandparents lived. I wonder if it's still there.

I let the other two couples go in front as we leave the dining hall, and as they walk down the hall to their rooms, Brianna and I stop at the concierge desk in the lobby. The woman with curly hair and thin glasses greets us.

"Good evening. What can I help you with?"

"Hi," I say. "I've got a problem. I think I've lost my wallet."

Her eyes widen in surprise. "Oh, that's not good. I'm so sorry to hear it."

I release Brianna's hand and rub mine together. "I might need to call and cancel my credit cards. Would you be able to look up the phone numbers I need to call?"

She nods. "Certainly. This computer doesn't have access to the internet. Only our office computer. If you can write who you need to contact, I'll find the numbers and bring the information to your room."

"Thank you."

"You're welcome."

I retake Brianna's hand, and we walk down the hall to our room. When I open the door, she says, "Let's look one more time. Check everywhere. It's got to be in the room."

"It's not," I say, letting my frustration show.

"Let's just try."

"Okay," I say, without any confidence. "You check. I've already looked."

I go to the bed while she looks around the room. She opens the closet and pulls out our luggage, going through it. It seems pointless. It's not like I've done anything with the luggage since we arrived. I turn on the TV and start flipping through the channels.

Next, she goes into the bathroom, and I can hear her moving things around. *Mission Impossible*, with Tom Cruise, is on the TV, and I get lost in watching it. A while later, I see her hold something up out of the corner of my eye. I turn as she clears her throat. It's my wallet. I jump off the bed and go to her, grabbing it and looking through it. The money is still inside. Nothing changed. All the cards are still there.

She looks at me and grins.

"Where did you find it?"

"It was in your backpack."

I look over and see the backpack on the ground. I go and pick it up.

"It was in the big pocket," she says.

I shake my head. "No way."

"Way."

I grab her and kiss her hard, and she laughs. I shake my head and return to the bed, lying down and watching the movie with the wallet in my hands. "I can't believe it. I was so worried. I couldn't think of anything else."

"Let me see it," she says, sitting at the end of the bed.

"Why?"

"Just let me see it?"

I toss it to her.

"What's the code to the safe?" she asks.

"Why?"

"Just tell me."

"Why? Are you going to put it in there?"

She shakes her head. "No, but I think we should leave everything we don't absolutely need. Maybe a credit card or two in the safe, just to be sure."

I see the wisdom in that and tell her the code. She opens the safe, but there's a knock at the door. She goes and answers it, and I can hear it's the concierge. She's brought the phone numbers. Their conversation is brief, then Brianna closes the door and hands me the paper. "I guess you don't need that now."

"You never know," I say, grinning.

"Don't say that."

She returns to the safe in the closet, and I can see the money is still inside. She pulls all my cards from my wallet, and I get a little nervous but push it down. She won't notice. She's had my wallet plenty of times and never noticed. But instead of watching the movie, I keep my eyes on her. She starts putting cards in the safe, then stops and stares at one, and my heart stops.

"What's this?" she asks and holds it up. It's a blue debit card. It's the card I didn't want her to see.

I shrug and act like I'm invested in the movie. "Just another credit card."

She shakes her head. "No, this is a debit card. It says it right across the top. I don't recognize the bank. What account does it belong to?"

Oh no…

"It's nothing. It's an account I set up a long time ago. It's not even active."

She stares at it, and I can see her face is getting hot. When she looks at me, her eyes are smoldering. "The expiration date is two years from now. It's current. Are you keeping money from me?"

I shake my head, but she's not buying it. "Look, it's not what you think."

"Oh, really? It's not what I think, huh?" she says and throws the debit card at me. It flutters to the bed.

"No," I say, holding up my hands.

"How much money is in the account?"

"None."

She balls up her fist. "Stop lying to me, Derek."

"I'm not lying."

"Oh, yeah, right. You have a secret bank account with no money in it? Then why do you have the debit card?"

"I know, it seems weird. But no money ever stays in the account."

Tears roll down her cheeks. "Are you planning to run away again?"

I frown. "Again? I never ran away."

"You were planning to."

My hand comes up, and I wipe my forehead with my palm. "Look, I make deposits into that account, but there isn't any money in there. Deposits go in, and they leave."

She shakes her head. "You're a liar," she yells and throws the nearly empty wallet at me.

I jump up off the bed and grab her before she can reach the door. She's fighting against me.

"Listen to me," I yell. "I've been making deposits into that account to pay back my investors."

She stops fighting, but I still have her by the wrists. She looks up at me in surprise. "What?"

I nod and then shake my head. "I've been paying money back to my investors. It's not much. They only get a couple hundred dollars a month. I set up that account so they wouldn't know where the money was coming from."

She looks at me, confused. "I don't understand."

I let go and sit back on the edge of the bed. "When my business failed, it tore me up. You know that. Then, when I found out what happened to Leo, Jacob's father, I just had to do something. My conscience wouldn't allow it. Any extra money I've had went into that account."

She looks at me, still skeptical.

I can feel the repressed emotion start to bubble up, but I'm powerless to stop it. "When he killed himself...I don't know. It broke me. I thought about doing the same thing." I put my head in my hands, and for the first time in years, I cry in front of my wife.

After a minute, I feel her hands on mine. She pulls my hands away from my face. She's kneeling before me. "You've been giving them money?"

I nod and wipe the tears from my cheeks.

"You knew Jacob's father was your investor?"

I nod. "I wasn't sure, but then I heard his last name. When I learned his father had died ten years ago, I knew it was him."

"Does he know who you are?" she asks.

"I'm not sure. I thought maybe that's why he blew up at Naomi this morning. That's why I went to try and find him. I was going to confess."

"But you couldn't find him."

I shake my head.

"You should talk to him. Tell him who you are."

I stare at her, then look away and shake my head. "I can't."

"Dominik," she says, and it's as if she's slapped me. Ten years ago, we agreed she wouldn't use my real name ever again. She's held to that promise until today. "It's time for you to let go. You've been doing everything you can do. You've been an amazing father and husband. You've been saving money and paying it to your investors, even when you don't have to. He'll understand. Trust him. Tell him."

We stare at each other, then she does something I can't believe. She holds my hands in hers and kisses them. It's too much, and I cry that much harder.

Chapter 22
Naomi Costa

Cruise Day 7 – Budapest, Hungary

We're at breakfast again, and Jacob has his book, but it sits on the crisp white tablecloth. Unopened. He's looking out the window as he eats his omelet and sips on his Diet Coke. I watch him, wondering what he's thinking. What he's planning. This morning, we'll be arriving in our final port, Budapest, Hungary.

"Why did you do it?" I ask, breaking the silence.

He turns away from the window, his eyes searching mine. "Do what?"

"Steal Derek's wallet."

His eyes narrow, and he picks up his Diet Coke and takes a drink. "I don't know what you're talking about."

I smile and break off a piece of my bran muffin. Don't ask me why I chose bran today. I can't remember the last time I ate a bran muffin. Bran muffins remind me of my grandmother. Oh, am I becoming her? "I know who he is, Jacob. Melody told me."

"Who is?"

"You know who."

He watches me.

"Derek is Dominik. So, why? Why did you take it? Was it to get more evidence? Prove you were right? Steal his money? Or do you have another motive?"

He leans back in his chair. "Like what?"

I roll my eyes. He knows exactly 'like what.' For a tourist visiting foreign countries, there's no greater fear than losing your wallet. Okay, maybe your passport. But your wallet is right up there. We both saw his face.

"Did you give it back?"

He shrugs.

"How?"

"How what?"

"How'd you give it back to him without him knowing it was you?"

He looks away from me, back out the window. The landscape is changing. There are more signs of human life. More housing and roads. We're getting closer to a big city.

"Yesterday, when I came back from our fight in Bratislava, I sat up on the top deck. The captain came and visited me."

"The ship captain?"

He nods. "He's Hungarian, you know."

I did, but I don't remember how I knew it. Maybe something Derek said earlier.

"He told me a story about his sister. He grew up in a city called Vác. His sister was raped by a boy in their town." He turns back to me. "Do you know the name of the boy?"

"Dominik?"

He nods. "After that, I had to know for certain if Derek is the same Dominik." He slides his book across the table. "Open to page one hundred."

I stare at him, then pick up the book and flip through the pages. Page one hundred opens easily. There's something stuck between the pages. I pick it up and examine it.

"I took that from the wallet. Do you recognize the face of the little boy?"

I bring the old photograph closer, studying the boy's features. He's much younger, but I can see it in the shape of his nose and jaw.

"I showed it to the captain."

"And?"

"He didn't recognize the boy. But he recognized the grandparents."

My eyes shift to the old people standing on either side of the boy.

There's an overhead announcement through the speaker system, telling us we're about to enter Budapest. But I don't look away from the photograph. Finally, I put it back in the book and return it to Jacob.

He picks up the book and looks at the photograph.

"Now what?" I ask.

His eyes darken, and he closes the book and slowly shakes his head. "I don't know yet. All I know is that the man who killed my father was a rapist before that, and he's traveling around Europe having a great ol' time, and I'm pretending to be his friend."

The boat slows, and we look out the window, seeing we're about to cross below a bridge. I look around the dining room and see we're alone, other than the staff. The cruise director, Albert, enters the room and sees us sitting at the table.

"Have you been to Budapest before?" he asks as he approaches.

We shake our heads.

"This is not something to be missed. Get upstairs onto the top deck."

He motions for us to follow, and we comply. When we reach the top, every passenger seems to be there. We see Derek and Brianna with Theo and Melody, but we don't join them. We stay back, out of their view.

"That side is Buda," Albert says, pointing. "And this side is Pest."

We follow his finger. He points out bridges, famous buildings like the Parliament and the castle on the hill. It's by far the most captivating of the cities we've seen on this trip. Everywhere I look could be a picture. But I'm not appreciating it like I should. I feel sick. I'm filled with a terrible sense of foreboding. My life is going to change forever in this city, and I'm not sure it's good.

Chapter 23

Jacob Costa

Cruise Day 7 – Budapest, Hungary

After reaching the dock in Budapest, north of the Liberty Bridge on the Pest side of the river, we return to our room to gather our things to prepare for a day of sightseeing. Naomi and I meet up with the rest of our group in the ship's foyer and walk up the ramp. Our guide, a small Hungarian woman in her fifties, greets us. She's pleasant, and although her accent is thick, I don't struggle to understand her. Maybe I've grown more accustomed to accents over the last week. I watch Derek, wondering if he'll say anything to her in Hungarian, but he doesn't. She has no idea he's Hungarian.

We follow as she guides us down a pathway and up several stairs to the street level. There, a large bus awaits. We file in, sitting in couples, and our guide gets on the microphone. The bus tour begins on the Pest side of the city. We pass the St. Stephen's Basilica, New York Café, and the Opera House before eventually turning east and driving down Andrassy Street. At the end of the street, there's a large limestone square with a tower in the center and the archangel Gabriel atop, holding the Holy Crown of Hungary and the apostolic double cross. Behind him, there are left and right colonnades of statues depicting famous Hungarians from history.

We turn and circle the square, and she points out the buildings on either side. One is the Museum of Fine Arts, and the other is the Palace of Art. Behind the square to the east is City Park, where a fairy-tale-like castle, fashioned after the Corvin Castle in Transylvania, stands.

I lean forward to ask Derek a question. He and Brianna sit in the row in front.

"Why Transylvania?" I ask.

He looks back at me over the seat. "Transylvania used to be part of Hungary. Over a million native Hungarians live there."

"Was Dracula Hungarian?" Naomi asks, also leaning over the seat.

Derek shrugs. "It's hard to say. Neither the Hungarians nor the Romanians want to claim him." He points beyond where we're looking. "Do you see those domes on that building in the park?"

Naomi and I nod.

"Have you heard of the thermal baths here?"

I nod.

"That's where the most famous ones are. They're called the Széchenyi baths."

"Have you ever been there?" Brianna asks.

Derek shakes his head. "I've been to one when I was little. But I don't remember which. I went with my grandparents. There are lots of thermal baths around here."

The bus turns west, and after several minutes, we pass over the Margaret Bridge. There's an island in the river to our right. When we reach the other side, we're in Buda. We sit in traffic for several minutes as the bus makes its way behind Castle Hill and parks near the top. We all get out, and our guide gathers us near a public restroom. After giving everyone an opportunity to use the facilities, we walk south to the castle.

It's a large building with a green domed roof and plenty of statues adorning every corner. We start in the back and the courtyard, then make our way to the front. Our guide has definitely saved the best for the end. The view is incredible with the Chain Bridge down below and Pest on the other side. As I look up and down the river, I count five bridges, all with unique architecture.

After plenty of time for pictures, our guide gathers us and takes us north two blocks. We reach a large white Gothic-style church, and she gathers us again. She gives us a brief introduction to the church. It's named after a Hungarian king, not the biblical apostle, as I would have guessed. We enter after our guide buys us tickets and sit in the pews while she talks to us about the church and the Hungarian people. At the end of her speech, she releases us to tour the rest of the castle district, and we all look to Derek. He's at the end of our pew and stands and walks up a row so he can be seen and heard by all of us.

"I was thinking we'd check out the views from Fisherman's Bastion, then walk back down to the castle and ride the cable car to the bottom of the hill. From there, we can walk across the Chain Bridge and then see St. Stephen's Basilica. Then, depending on time, we can walk down Váci Utca to the large indoor market, which isn't far from our ship. What do you all think?"

"Sounds great to me," Theo says.

"You're in charge," Melody agrees.

"Great," he says. "We can look around for a few more minutes here, then go out."

We mill around for several more minutes, admiring the church's arched ceilings, carved sculptures, and stained-glass windows, then exit. The sun is extraordinarily bright, so we all put on our sunglasses.

"We should take a picture," Brianna says. "Something with all of us in front of the church."

"Let's do it," I say, and look around for someone to take it.

Derek beats me to it and finds our tour guide sitting on a bench beside a light pole. He approaches, and she recognizes him. I can't hear what they're saying, but I can see from the excitement in her expression that he's speaking Hungarian. He guides her over to us, and we line up with our backs to the church and the gigantic statue of the horseman. We stand in couples, Naomi and I on the left, Theo and Melody on the right, and Brianna and Derek in the middle.

She snaps several pictures and hands the camera back to Derek while we thank her, and she goes back to her bench.

"Who's the horseman?" I ask Derek.

"He's King Stephen, the first Christian king of Hungary. The Hungarians came from somewhere near modern-day Mongolia about a thousand years ago and conquered their way down into this area of Europe. Stephen, knowing he was surrounded by Christian countries, embraced Christianity, and the pope ordained him the first king."

We circle the statue while waiting our turn to take pictures in front of it. When we're done, we walk to the structure behind it.

"This is Fisherman's Bastion," Derek says, pointing to the white structure that looks something like a castle's walls. "I read the points or towers represent the different Hungarian tribes that were with them when they migrated here."

We approach the throng of people taking pictures around it. This might be the most popular spot we've seen on the cruise to this point. I look through one opening and see why. There's a direct view of the Parliament building across the river. I find myself mesmerized by it and can't look away. With the Margaret Bridge to the north and the yellow tram running along it, this city is like nothing I've ever seen.

After milling around and taking pictures for about twenty minutes, Derek gathers us, and we walk along the cobblestone road back toward the castle. We stop at a small convenience store and get drinks, and I find myself fascinated by all the different brands and food items. When we're back on the street, I make sure I'm beside Derek as we walk.

"So, how is it?" I ask.

"How's what?"

"How's being back in your home country? Is it different?"

He chuckles. "So different."

"How so?"

"Well, I was a kid when I was here last. And at that time, we were part of the Eastern Bloc. Like going in that store back there. There were products that we didn't have. It's really amazing to see how much the country has progressed since the fall of communism."

I nod. "I've been wondering. How did you leave back then?"

He looks at me. I can't see his eyes through his dark sunglasses. "I didn't know we were leaving. My mother got us on a plane to America, and we never came back. She knew but didn't tell me. I thought we were only going on a big vacation."

"How'd she do it?"

He frowns. "What do you mean?"

"Well, I mean, my impression of people behind the Iron Curtain is that they couldn't leave, except in very rare circumstances."

Derek nods. "That's true."

"So how did she get you guys out?"

Derek shakes his head. "I'm not really sure. I'd asked her a couple years before she died. She didn't really tell me, but I get the impression she did a couple favors for some men in prominent positions."

I don't miss his emphasis on the word *favors*.

"Did you leave anyone behind?"

He nods. "My grandparents. My grandfather was like a father to me after my own father died."

"Anyone else?"

He shrugs. "Distant family members. Nobody I knew well."

"You didn't have a girlfriend or anything?"

He looks at me, and I wonder what he's thinking, but he shakes his head.

We're back at the castle now, and he leads us to an area with a gate and a large statue of a bird with what looks like a sword in its claws. There's a small ticket booth near a cable car track. Derek purchases the tickets, and we stand around, waiting and looking out at the views. Finally, the cable car arrives, and we enter. Derek and I sit at the top, while Naomi and Brianna sit below us, and Theo and Melody sit on the bottom level. Although it's fairly quiet inside the car, I'm grateful the others are talking and aren't paying attention to our conversation. With my eyes watching the river and the view below, I ask Derek a question.

"I guess you were really close to your mother, huh?"

He nods.

"Do you think about those men? Those men who made her do what she did to get you out of Hungary?"

I see the tightness in his jaw.

I nod. "I sure would. I was really close to my father. He was my hero and idol. Someone did something to him. Something awful. I think about it every day."

His attention was focused on the bridge below, but now he turns to look at me. His expression is unreadable under those dark glasses, but I don't care. I'm going to say what I want to say. "Someday I'm going to make that guy pay for what he did to my father. He thinks he's gotten away with it, but he hasn't."

The cable car stops, and I open the door and exit before Derek can respond.

Chapter 24
Melody Jones

Cruise Day 7 – Budapest, Hungary

Today, after separating from the rest of our tour group, we went with Derek across the Chain Bridge, walked along Váci Street to the large indoor market, and visited St. Stephen's Basilica, where we saw the thousand-year-old hand of King Stephen. It's held in a box in the church. We also rode the elevator to the top and had a tremendous view of the city. The basilica is tied for the tallest building in the city, along with the Parliament building further north.

As we stood at the top, taking pictures, it started to rain. After riding the elevator back down and exiting the church, a downpour began. Not having any other choice, we ducked into a café and waited out the worst of it. It almost seemed silly; we were already soaked. We considered going back to the boat, but none of us wanted that. Especially those of us who were scheduled to fly back home tomorrow.

When the rain finally died down after thirty minutes, Derek suggested we ride the two tram north to the Parliament. It was perfect and gave us a magnificent view along the river. When we exited the tram, I stood and stared at the Parliament building for several seconds. What an iconic building that is, with its crown-shaped dome and pink hue. I've seen nothing like it. We tried to enter, but the tickets were sold out for the day. We were disappointed but still able to visit several small exhibits that surrounded the building.

Finally, as dinner approached, we all agreed to return to the boat. There was so much more to see, but we were exhausted. We separated once on board, and now Theo and I lie on the bed, not moving but also not sleeping. I know I should get up and get ready for dinner, but I don't want to move. If I don't say it now, I might never tell him.

"Theo?"

He turns and looks at me.

"There's something I need to tell you."

He frowns, seeing the look on my face. "Okay."

I take a deep breath and look away from him, back up at the ceiling. "You know that year when Jenny was sick? When she was in the hospital waiting for the transplant?"

He doesn't respond and I turn back to him. He's not looking at me now. His eyes are on the bedsheets.

"There was something going on that I never told you about."

He looks back up into my eyes, waiting for me to go on.

"I..." Tears come to my eyes.

He shakes his head and reaches out to me. "I already know."

I brush at the tears but stop. "You do?"

He nods, and I give him my hand. "Leo told me."

I frown. Leo told him?

Theo shakes his head, seeing my expression. "I thought something else was going on. I thought maybe you were having an affair or something."

"An affair?"

He nods. "I was really upset about our relationship. Upset with you. He offered me another perspective. He helped me understand what you were going through."

"He told you about the..."

He nods. "But you've been clean since, right?"

I nod. We stare at each other. I can't believe Theo knew all this time. I loved Leo before, when all I knew was that he'd helped me get clean. But now, after knowing this, I'll be indebted to him for the rest of my life.

Theo's eyes leave mine when there's a knock at our door.

"You get it," he says with a grin.

"You," I fire back.

"I'm older and more tired."

"Liar. I'm older than you."

"Fine," he says and stands with an exaggerated groan, then reaches the door.

I hear it open, but I can't see who it is. I sit up, expecting to hear his voice, but I never do. Instead, Naomi and Jacob enter the room, followed by Theo.

"Sorry to barge in like this," Naomi says. "We just had something we wanted to discuss before dinner."

"It's okay." I sit up and lean against the headboard.

"I wish we had somewhere for you to sit," Theo says as he awkwardly stands behind them.

Jacob raises a hand. "It's fine. I'll kneel by the bed."

Naomi joins him at the foot, and Theo comes over to join me at the head.

"There's something I need to tell you," Jacob says, looking at me. "It's about Derek."

"I already know," I say and glance at Theo. He's not looking at me. He's still watching Jacob.

"I know you know he's Dominik, the man responsible for my father's death. But there's more."

I frown and look at Naomi. She nods.

"When I came back to the ship in Bratislava, I talked to the captain, Mr. Arany. He told me his sister had been raped many years ago by a boy named Dominik."

I inhale sharply, and everyone looks at me.

"I had to know if Derek was the same Dominik. So, I stole his wallet. In it, I found a picture of him when he was a boy back in Hungary." He holds up the picture for me to see. "I showed it to the captain, and he confirmed Derek is that same boy."

I swallow and look at Theo. This is his first time hearing this part. I can see the rage in his eyes.

"Captain Arany's sister killed herself after Derek went to America. The captain said she was never the same after what he did to her."

We all sit, looking down at the bed, nobody speaking. Finally, after what seems like ten but can't be more than a minute, I clear my throat.

"Why are you telling us this?"

Jacob looks at each of us, one by one. "Dominik is an evil man. He's responsible for two deaths that we know of and a rape. He's hurt people time and time again without any consequences. That has to stop."

I look at Naomi, but she's watching Jacob.

"What are you saying?" Naomi asks.

"I need to stop him," Jacob says. "*We* need to stop him."

Theo frowns. "How? Can we work with the police? Knowing this about the captain's sister should help. Maybe the captain knows someone?"

Jacob shakes his head. "No way. That'll never work. It's our word against his. Plus, the captain's sister is dead. There's no evidence he did what she said. Not to mention the statute of limitations."

I watch Jacob, trying to read his thoughts. "What are you saying?"

He looks at me gravely. "You know what I'm saying."

My left hand starts to tremor, and I cover it with my right.

He looks at each of us again. Finally, he says, "I've got a plan, and I need each of you. Will you help me?"

I look at Theo, and he stares back at me. I look at Naomi, and she has tears running down her cheeks. None of us speak, but Theo nods, then Naomi. My mind spins. I think of Derek and Brianna. I think of their kids. But then, I think of Jacob's father, Leo. I think about what he did for me. What he did for Theo and me. Without him, I might still be an addict. I could have lost everything. My husband. My family. Leo helped me more than I even knew.

I look at Leo's son and think about the captain's sister and what she must have endured. Before I can change my mind, I nod and agree. I'll help Jacob do whatever he needs to do.

PART II

Chapter 25
Peter Andrassy

Peter opens the exterior door to Szép Ilona's Bistro and waits patiently as two patrons exit. As he enters the building, his eyes focus on the blond behind the bar. She's helping a customer and doesn't see him. He stands admiring her. Nobody else in the room matters.

"Sir, are you lost?" a woman beside him asks. He turns to see Kata smiling from behind the host station.

He frowns as he looks at her. "Did you get demoted?"

She laughs. "Ildiko called out. I guess she's got a severe case of the 'I don't want to work tonight.'"

He smiles, and although Kata is a beautiful woman in her own right, he can't help shifting his attention back to the bartender.

"She told me, you know," Kata says.

He looks back at her. "Huh?"

"Zsuzsa...she told me the news." She shakes her head, a look of awe written on her face. "I'm so excited for you guys." Kata comes around the station and embraces him.

Peter grins as she steps back, but he can't help the butterflies that flutter in his stomach.

She eyes him closely. "What? Are you nervous?"

He chuckles. "Very."

She smiles. "You'll do great. You guys are going to be the best parents."

"You think?"

She nods. "I know it."

"Thank you."

Peter looks over and sees that the striking bartender's eyes are watching him. Kata sees it too and grabs him by the hand, tugging him in her direction. "Come on. I know you aren't here for me."

Peter follows as she leads him through the dining area and pats a seat at the bar. She looks at the bartender and grins. "I think this gentleman would like dinner. Would you mind serving him?"

The bartender wipes her hands on her apron, then looks at him, teasing him with her eyes. "First time here?"

He takes a seat and puts his elbows on the bar. "No, I've been here before."

She nods and doesn't bother asking him for his order as she fills a mug with Dreher beer and places it before him. "Well, welcome back." She smiles a dazzling smile that makes his heart skip. "We appreciate your patronage."

He grips the handle of the mug of beer, raises it to his lips, and takes a long drink. "You look lovely today."

She lowers her eyelashes. "Thank you, but my husband doesn't like men at the bar commenting on my looks." She raises her head, and a smile plays at the corners of her lips.

"Hmm. Is he the jealous type?"

"He can be."

"Hey, Zsuzsa," a man from the other side of the bar calls out, raising his glass. "Can I have another?"

She nods, but before she steps away from Peter, she gives him a wink.

Zsuzsa doesn't return for fifteen minutes, which is fine with Peter. He has nowhere he needs to be. He drinks his beer and watches her as she attends to other customers until she returns.

"Stroganoff?" she asks.

He nods, then shakes his head. "Actually, let's try something different. How about the chicken paprika?"

She frowns. "You've never had that before?"

He shrugs. "I noticed it at a table behind me. It looked good."

"Coming up," she says and walks back into the kitchen.

Peter feels a buzzing in his jacket and looks down. After he and Zsuzsa came back from New York, he was given a cell phone by the Hungarian National Police, his first. It had only rung twice since they had issued it, and he'd often forget he had it. He takes it out of his pocket and presses the answer button.

"Hello?"

"Peter?"

"Yes."

He presses his finger into his other ear to block out the noise. Between the poor reception and the restaurant commotion, he can barely hear the man on the other end of the line.

"We've got a situation. We need your help."

"What kind of situation?"

Detective Farkas, his boss in the Hungarian National Police's human trafficking task force, pauses on the other end of the line. "Detective Moricz has requested your help. Can you report to a cruise ship docked just below Freedom Bridge? He'll be there to meet you."

Peter frowns. Detective Moricz is the new head of the Major Crimes Unit in the National Police. Peter has never said more than a couple of words to him since he took over the job.

"Probably," Peter says.

"How soon can you be there?" Farkas asks.

"I'm in Buda. It'll take me about twenty minutes."

"I'll let him know."

Farkas ends the call, and Peter pulls the phone away from his ear and sees Zsuzsa standing before him.

"Who was that?" she asks.

Peter frowns. "Farkas. I have to go."

He sees the disappointment in her eyes. "How long will you be? Your food is almost ready."

He shakes his head and pushes away from the bar. "I guess I'm going to be hungry. The major crimes unit requested my help on a cruise ship on the river."

"A cruise ship. Why?"

He shrugs. "I guess I'll find out. Better not wait up for me tonight."

"That long?"

He raises his palm.

"I'll bring your food home. We can reheat it."

Chapter 26
Peter Andrassy

Peter exits the yellow tram line two and walks across the street toward the man standing beside the white Škoda with Hungarian National Police license plates. He's a large man with broad shoulders and a couple of days' stubble on his chin. A cigarette dangles from the side of his mouth as he sees Peter approach. He extends a hand. "Andrassy, thanks for coming. Sorry it's so late, but we could use your help on this one."

Peter grips his hand. "No problem. I was surprised to get the call. How can I help?"

Detective Moricz appraises him for a second, then takes a drag on his cigarette before dropping it and snuffing it out with the toe of his shoe. "You lived in America, right? You're American?"

Peter nods. "I lived in New York City for over twenty-five years. I was a detective there before I came back home to Hungary."

Moricz drops his eyes and nods before exhaling. "That's why I asked Farkas if I could borrow you. Our victim is American, and the FBI is headed over. I could use your help. My English isn't great."

Peter nods. He had assumed as much. Besides working independently as a private investigator, Peter works on contract for the National Police in their human trafficking task force. Receiving a call to visit a crime scene was nothing new. Being asked to assist the Major Crimes Unit is. Peter figured there had to be an American connection.

"What happened?" Peter asks.

Moricz turns away and begins walking down the set of stairs leading to the riverbank. He waves for Peter to follow. "A body was thrown overboard." Moricz gestures toward the river, but it's the word *body* that Peter notices most. The person must have been dead before hitting the water.

When they reach the bottom of the stairs, they turn and walk down a path toward several cruise ships docked on the bank. Moricz turns and walks down a ramp leading to one of them. Before entering the ship, they pass several police officers who nod with respect toward Moricz. As Moricz enters the lobby, a woman approaches. She looks familiar to Peter, but he can't remember ever talking to her before. There's a staircase on the right and a reception desk on the left with a cruise attendant standing behind it. The attendant watches them with curiosity. There's a hallway just beyond her leading to the ship's passenger cabins. The lights are dimmed, and Peter looks at his watch, noticing it's now officially the next day.

"Sir," the approaching detective says, keeping her voice low, glancing at Peter before returning her gaze to Moricz. "The captain and cruise director are waiting for you in the dining hall. It's just over here."

Moricz nods and goes with her as Peter follows. Peter had only been on one cruise ship before. He and his first wife, Karen, had spent seven days cruising around islands in the Caribbean. That ship was much larger than this. From what Peter could see, this ship had only three levels and was no wider than forty feet across.

The policewoman walks toward the stairs but doesn't go up. Instead, she pushes open one side of a large wooden door and holds it for Moricz and Peter. When Moricz and Peter round the corner of the glass wall, they see they've entered a large open room with fifty or more round tables and six chairs to a table. Each table is adorned with a crisp white tablecloth. A serving station is in the middle of the room. Two men occupy the table nearest the station. When they see Moricz, Peter, and the policewoman, they stand and wait as they approach. Moricz slows to allow the policewoman to lead out.

When she reaches the two men, she motions to the shorter of them while talking to Moricz. She speaks English. "Sir, this is Captain Arany and Cruise Director Wagner." She reverses her motion and the direction of her speech. "And this is Detective Moricz, head of the Major Crimes Unit of the Hungarian National Police, and Peter Andrassy."

"Arany," Moricz says, extending his hand. "*Magyar?*" (Hungarian?)

"*Igen*," Captain Arany says. (Yes)

Moricz nods, then shakes his hand before turning to the cruise director. "Nice to meet you," he says in heavily accented English.

The cruise director, a heavy-set, bald man in his early fifties, nods and shakes his hand. Peter follows suit and shakes both of their hands, and the captain invites them to sit while speaking English. His English is also heavily accented, but he's clearly more comfortable in the language than Detective Moricz.

"Thank you for coming. This has not happened in the past." He looks over at the cruise director. Director Wagner shakes his head.

"Director, where are you from?" Moricz asks.

"Vienna. Bécs," he says, using the Hungarian word for Vienna.

"*Beszél Magyarul*?" Moricz says, asking him if he speaks Hungarian.

Captain Arany shakes his head and answers for him in Hungarian. Peter sees the disappointment in Moricz's face. This conversation would have been easier for him in his native tongue.

"Okay," Moricz says, looking over at Peter. "Peter is American and Hungarian. He will ask questions."

Peter glances at Moricz, then back to the two men, hoping he's hidden his surprise. He was expecting to consult on this case. Not lead it. At this point, he has no idea what has happened and what they know. Captain Arany and Director Wagner sit back and turn their attention to Peter.

"I'm sorry," Peter says. "I was notified of this case but told very little about what happened. Can you enlighten me?"

Arany looks at Wagner and motions for him to answer. The cruise director is clearly a better English speaker. Peter thinks about the irony of this group. Here sit three native Hungarians speaking English because of one non-Hungarian speaker.

Wagner places his hand on the table and lightly pats it while speaking. "About an hour ago, while our post dinner entertainment was happening in the lounge, I got a call from Captain Arany. He told me there was an emergency and to meet him on the port side of the ship, middle level. I reminded him I was directing the entertainment, but he ordered me to turn it over to someone else and to come quickly."

He looks at the captain, who nods.

"I knew something was very wrong and went quickly. When I arrived, I found the captain and Director Novak waiting for me in the hall."

"Who is Director Novak?" Peter asks.

"He's in charge of hospitality on the ship."

Peter nods and motions for him to go on.

"The door to one stateroom was open, and they brought me inside." He looks at the captain, who drops his eyes and stares at the table.

Peter looks at the captain, then back to Wagner. "Why? What was inside?"

"A body was lying on the bed."

Peter frowns but doesn't prod him forward, patiently waiting for whatever the man might say next.

"A dead body," Captain Arany says without looking up.

Peter glances at him and then back to Wagner. "I understand the victim was thrown overboard and drowned."

"No," Wagner says and then stops. "I mean, yes, the body was thrown overboard, but the passenger was already dead."

Peter frowns. "How do you know that?"

Both the captain and cruise director stand. "Come," Wagner says. "We will show you."

Chapter 27
Peter Andrassy

Peter and Moricz follow Captain Arany and Director Wagner as they lead them out of the dining room and across the main reception area. They enter the hallway with dimmed lighting. The hall is lined with doors. Each has a gold-plated number. On the left are odd-numbered doors, and on the right, even. About halfway down the hall, Captain Arany stops and unlocks the door to room 349. He whispers something to Director Wagner, and Wagner nods and steps beyond the door in the hallway and motions for Peter and Moricz to enter.

The room is small, and Peter's eyes fix on the gray, lifeless body on the bed. The victim is lying on their back in water-soaked clothes. Peter looks at Moricz and sees a lack of surprise in his eyes. He's been here already. He's seen the victim. Captain Arany stands at the foot of the bed with Peter and Moricz beside him. Director Wagner has shut the door and remains in the hall.

Peter switches to Hungarian but doesn't address the captain. "Forensics has already been here?"

Moricz shakes his head. "Only me. I had the door locked. Nobody else has come in."

Peter nods and approaches the body and quickly notices why Wagner was so confident the victim was dead before hitting the water. Peter sees two stab wounds—one in the neck and one in the side. Whoever did this made sure the person was dead before pushing them off the boat. No simple task. The murderer must be strong. The wounds are deep and consistent with punctures rather than slashes. Whoever stabbed this person did it deliberately and with little fight.

Peter turns back to the two men. "Do we have the knife?"

Moricz shakes his head. "We think it was thrown in the river."

Peter bites his cheek and looks around the room. He notices a dark stain on the carpet and looks at Moricz. A message passes between them, and Peter motions for them to step to the side as he walks to the sliding glass door that opens onto the balcony. He steps out onto it and sees that the boat is docked between the Freedom and Chain Bridges. The lights have been turned off on both bridges, and the city is as quiet as he's ever heard. He looks across the river to the Buda side, then examines the railing between him and the water. He notices several flecks of dark blood and more on the balcony floor. Finally, he looks down into the dark water. Beside the boat, his eyes catch something floating in the water.

"Do you have a flashlight?" he asks.

"I do," Moricz says and hands one to Peter, joining him on the balcony.

Peter shines the light into the water and sees it's a paper.

Moricz turns around to the captain. "Do you have a pole with a net like they use to clean swimming pools?"

The captain thinks for a second and nods. He pulls out a radio and asks for the tool to be brought to the room. Less than a minute later, a crew member arrives with one. The captain hands it to Peter, and he leans out over the railing and catches the paper in the net and pulls it in. It's damaged, but in the light, they can see that it's a black-and-white picture of a boy with two older people. Probably family.

"Excuse me," Peter says to the captain as he pushes past him and enters the bathroom. He finds the hair dryer, dries the picture, and then rejoins them in the bedroom.

"You think that picture belonged to the victim?" Moricz asks.

Peter shrugs. "It's the Danube. There's all kinds of junk in it." He examines it more closely, then carefully puts it in his pocket and looks around the room.

"Whose room is this?"

"Nobody's," the captain says. "It's an extra."

Peter nods. "Is that why you brought the victim here?"

"Yes," says the captain. "We wanted to put the body somewhere that would cause the least alarm with the guests."

Peter nods. "How close was the body while in the water?"

"To this room?"

"Yes."

"Just outside of it."

"Where's the victim's spouse?"

Captain Arany frowns. "How did you know they were married?"

Peter points at the victim's hand.

The captain nods. "Director Novak is with them in their passenger cabin."

"How long was the cruise? Where did it start?" Moricz asks.

"Passau in Germany. Seven days total."

"How many passengers are on the ship?"

"Two hundred and forty-six persons. One hundred and ninety passengers and fifty-six crew."

Peter and Moricz look at each other, then Peter asks. "Did you know the victim before tonight?"

The captain frowns and looks Peter in the eye. "I make it my business to introduce myself to as many passengers as possible."

"What about this passenger? Did you introduce yourself?"

"Yes. We talked a couple of times."

"What about the victim's spouse?"

"Yes."

Peter rubs his beard. "Did you or your crew ever see any disagreements between the victim and another passenger?"

The captain frowns and shakes his head.

"Nothing? A week is a long time. Not even with the victim's spouse?"

The captain shakes his head and then stops.

Moricz sees it and presses him. "What? What is it?"

The captain hesitates. "It wasn't a fight or anything like that. It's nothing I would normally even think about. But one night, after we left Bratislava, one of my staff was walking down the hallway right out there when they heard raised voices. They stopped to listen."

He raises a hand. "Not to eavesdrop, more to just make sure there wasn't anything happening that might endanger a passenger. You follow me?"

Moricz and Peter nod.

"Anyway, she couldn't be sure, but she thinks it might have been coming from the victim's room."

"How would she know that?" Peter asks.

He shrugs. "You get to know people when you're around them for a week."

"But she doesn't know for certain?" Moricz says.

The captain shakes his head and motions all around. "These rooms are pretty small. It's hard to pinpoint the noise sometimes."

Peter eyes him. "Did the couple travel with anyone else?"

"What do you mean?"

"Maybe children or parents? Other family members?"

The captain shakes his head. "I don't know. But there were two other couples they were always with. They seemed to be friends, but I don't know if they were traveling together."

"Why do you say that?"

"Because they weren't leaving together."

Moricz frowns. "What do you mean?"

The captain shrugs. "The victim and spouse were scheduled to fly home tomorrow, along with another couple. One couple was staying on longer at a local hotel. They don't go home for another week." He looks down at his watch. "Actually, the car for the two couples flying home should be arriving soon."

"In the middle of the night?" Moricz asks.

"They had a very early flight. They arranged for a car to the airport."

Peter and Moricz look at each other, and Moricz dials a number into his cell phone while still talking to the captain. "Do you know where the flight was going?"

"Amsterdam, I think."

Someone answers Moricz's call. "Molnar? Listen, I can't explain right now, but I need to hold a plane at the airport. It can't leave until I can confirm certain people aren't on it." He looks up at the captain. "What are the names of the passengers?"

Chapter 28
Peter Andrassy

Peter, Moricz, and Captain Arany exit the room where the victim's body is being held, and Peter looks at Moricz. "What do you want to do now?"

Moricz looks down and rubs his forehead. "I think we should get the forensics team in here. Don't you?"

"Absolutely."

Moricz looks at the captain. "When will the passengers wake up?"

"We serve breakfast starting at six."

"That early?" Moricz says, frowning. "I thought these people were on vacation?"

"Old people on vacation," Captain Arany says with a shrug.

Moricz nods. "True. When does your staff wake?"

"Only ten work the night shift. The rest will get up around five."

"Can we get them up before then?"

"They won't like it."

Moricz nods. "Understood," he says but holds his gaze.

The captain frowns. "When?"

"How about four?"

Arany looks down at his watch. "That's two hours from now. Why do you need them?"

"We'd like to interview them. See if anyone saw anything."

Arany shrugs. "Whatever you need. You're the boss."

Moricz nods. "Send them into the dining room. We'll start with anyone on duty now. I'll need lists of all passengers and staff. I'd appreciate if the list includes job titles."

A man in a tie and dark jacket enters the hallway and walks toward them. In the low lighting, it's hard to see much about him. He appears to be in his late twenties with short dark hair.

"Detective Moricz," he says as he approaches. He's speaking English.

"Yes," Moricz says.

"My name is Special Agent Anderson with the Federal Bureau of Investigation of the United States of America. I'm told that an American citizen was killed on board tonight. I'm here to assist in your investigation."

Moricz nods, and the two men shake hands.

"We were expecting you. This is Peter Andrassy and Captain Arany. Peter works with me. Captain Arany is the ship's captain."

Agent Anderson hesitates, then says, "Nice to meet you both," in Hungarian and holds out his hand to Peter. Peter takes it and sees the other two men are as surprised as he is. It's extremely rare for an American with the last name of Anderson to speak Hungarian. Not only that, but although he has an accent, his grammar and pronunciation are technically on point.

"You speak Hungarian?" Peter says to him in Hungarian.

"Yes. I lived here for two years when I was younger, and I've been back for about six months." Anderson releases Peter's hand and shakes Arany's hand.

"Well," Moricz says, relief in his eyes. "Our victim is inside that room. We're about to bring in a forensics team. Our next step is to start interviewing staff and passengers."

"How did the passenger die?" Anderson asks.

Moricz looks at him soberly. "It appears he's been murdered. He has two stab wounds and was thrown overboard."

Anderson swallows. "And he's American?"

"Yes."

A silence falls over the group. Finally, Anderson says, "Well, I'm here to help you in your investigation. We understand the jurisdiction falls to you. If it's okay, I'd like to participate, especially when it comes to American citizens."

Moricz eyes him. "Good," he says and points to Peter. "Peter is also American. He works with us in the National Police, but he was a detective with the New York Police Department for twenty years. He was about to go interview the victim's wife. You can go with him."

Anderson nods and looks at Peter.

Peter returns his gaze but says nothing.

Moricz looks at Captain Arany. "Which room is she in?"

"Three nineteen," the captain says and points down the hall away from where they had come.

Peter thanks him and motions for Anderson to follow, then stops and turns back to Moricz. "I'd like to talk to the other Americans who were the victims' friends."

Moricz nods. "We'll find them and let you know when they're ready."

"Tell them as little as you can," Peter says.

Moricz eyes him and then nods before waving for Captain Arany to follow, and they walk back toward the center of the ship. Peter and Agent Anderson go in the opposite direction toward room 319. When they reach it, Peter looks at him and switches to English.

"I'm not sure what she knows."

Anderson nods and holds out his hands, palms up. "Understood. Like I said, I'm here to help. I'll stay quiet unless you speak to me."

Peter nods and knocks on the door. "How long have you been with the bureau?"

"Less than a year. Hungary is my first assignment following Quantico."

Peter hears footsteps behind the door, and when it opens, a man in a uniform similar to Captain Arany's looks at him. This must be Director Novak, the Slovenian head of hospitality. "Director Novak?"

"Yes?"

"Hello, my name is Peter Andrassy from the Hungarian National Police. This is Agent Anderson from the United States FBI. We're here to speak with Mrs. Costa. Is she available?"

He nods and steps to the side. "Yes, come in."

Peter and Anderson enter, and the room looks identical to the one Peter was in moments earlier, except for one difference—the body lying on this bed is alive. Mrs. Costa lies on the bed with her back resting against the headboard. Her arms are crossed, and so are her legs at the ankles. She's wearing a pair of light, comfortable pajamas. She holds a tissue to her nose. Her eyes are puffy.

"Hello, ma'am," Peter says.

She eyes him. Agent Anderson stands behind Peter, and Novak remains in the hallway by the closed door. "I'm sorry to be visiting you now. We'll be brief, but we think you might help us in our investigation."

She nods.

"My name—"

"I heard who you are, Peter. You're from the Hungarian National Police, and Agent Anderson is from the FBI. You don't need to repeat yourself."

Peter holds her gaze, trying not to show his surprise. "Okay. Do you mind if I sit down on the edge of the bed here and ask you a few questions?"

She angrily motions with her hand, then holds the tissue to her face and cries. "I'm sorry. I just..." She shakes her head and releases a sob.

Peter sits at the edge of the bed, and Anderson remains standing at the foot.

"Sir," Novak says, and Peter looks back at him. "I'll step out. Please call if you need me."

"Thank you."

When the door shuts, he turns back to the victim's wife. She's pulled herself together and looks down while holding the tissue to her nose. "Mrs. Costa, we understand how difficult this night must be for you. We're sure you're exhausted and need some rest. We'll be as brief as possible, but as I said before, we believe you may be able to help us determine what happened to your husband."

"You said that already."

"I'm sorry. You're aware that your husband was found overboard in the river and was retrieved?"

She nods but doesn't look up.

"You're also aware your husband was found to have two stab wounds, one in his neck and one in his side, and that he expired from the wounds?"

She looks up. "He didn't drown?"

Peter shakes his head. "We don't think so. The coroner will confirm, but we believe he was dead or near death when he hit the water."

She covers her mouth with the tissue.

"Mrs. Costa?"

She shakes her head. "Call me Naomi. He was stabbed?"

Peter nods.

"It wasn't an accident?"

Peter shakes his head and waits before speaking, allowing her to process the information. "Naomi, when was the last time you saw your husband?"

She lets her hand with the tissue fall to the bed and looks down at her lap. "Um, it was right after dinner."

Peter withdraws his notepad and makes a note. "Do you know about what time that was?"

She nods. "I think around ten thirty or eleven."

"Where were you when you last saw him?"

"We'd just finished dinner and were in the lounge. There was a program with Hungarian dancers and singers."

"And your husband came to the performance?"

She nods. "But he left during it."

"Where did he go?" Peter asks.

She shakes her head. "I'm not sure. He said he had to do something and left."

"And you don't know what it was that he had to do?"

She shakes her head.

"Was that common? Did he often leave to take care of business on his own?"

She shrugs. "Sometimes."

Peter bites his cheek and considers whether he wants to ask the next question. After a pause, he makes a note in his notepad and then looks her in the eyes. "Naomi, do you know who killed your husband?"

She looks at him and nods.

His eyes narrow. "Who?"

"Derek."

"Derek who?"

"Derek Murphy."

Peter watches her. "Who is Derek Murphy?"

She crosses her arms and rubs her triceps with her hands. "He's someone we met here on the cruise. He and his wife, Brianna, were friends we made. I think Jacob left the performance to meet with Derek."

Peter puts a hand on his knee and shifts his weight. His legs are off the side of the bed, and he has to twist to see her. "Why do you say that?"

"Because Derek left too."

"What do you mean? He was there during the performance and walked out?"

"Yes. He left only a few minutes after Jacob."

"Who else was with you?"

She looks up. "It was all of us. All six of us. Three couples. Then Jacob left, and a few minutes later, Derek."

"What are the names of the others in your group?"

"Me and Jacob, Brianna and Derek Murphy, and Melody and Theo Jones."

"And everyone was there at the performance?"

"Yes, we were all sitting together. There were a lot of people. The cruise director was the emcee."

Peter nods. "Did you notice anyone else leave?"

She shakes her head and then stops. "Nobody until Brianna and I."

"Brianna is Derek's wife?"

"Yes."

"Why did the two of you leave?"

"Brianna started to feel sick. Really sick. She was afraid she was going to throw up. She wanted to go back to her room, so I helped her back there."

Peter nods and makes a note in his notepad.

"Is she okay?"

Peter shakes his head. "I don't know. I haven't talked to her yet. What time was it when the two of you left the lounge?"

"I don't know. Close to eleven."

"After you left, where did you go?"

She looks across the room at the suitcase sitting below the TV. "After taking her to her room, I came back here to pack. We had an early flight." She looks down at her watch. "We were supposed to be going now. I was tired. I wanted to get a little sleep before the long day of travel home."

"Did you see anyone in the hallway as you came back here? How about Derek or Jacob?"

She shakes her head.

Peter nods and bites his lip. "One last question. You said you believed Derek Murphy killed your husband. Is there any particular reason besides their meeting? Any reason Derek would want to harm Jacob?"

Naomi hesitates. "Um...I don't know. There was something going on between them."

Peter frowns. "Going on?"

Naomi puts her right hand to her mouth and bites a nail. "Look, I'm sure you're going to hear about this. Jacob and I had a public argument. It wasn't a big deal. A couple days ago in Bratislava, he wanted to leave a walking tour early, and I kinda got mad at him." She looks over at Agent Anderson, then back to Peter. "Jacob wasn't acting like himself. He was different. He wouldn't tell me why. But I noticed it more when Derek was around. Anyway, he left after we got into an argument, and Derek followed him. Derek came back a few minutes later and said he hadn't found him."

"But you don't believe him?"

She shakes her head. "I don't know. I just know that Jacob continued to be upset for the rest of the day. But then the next day, he was better. I asked him if there was something going on between him and Derek, and he said yes. But he wouldn't tell me what it was. I didn't want to push him because I didn't want him to get mad again."

Chapter 29
Peter Andrassy

When Peter and Agent Anderson exit Naomi's room, they find Detective Moricz standing in the hallway waiting for them.

"How is she?" he asks in Hungarian.

Peter looks at Anderson, then back to Moricz. "Considering...she's holding up pretty well."

"Did she give you anything?"

"She thinks he was killed by a friend they met on the ship. Someone named Derek Murphy."

"He's one of the Americans in their friend group."

Peter nods.

Moricz looks down the hall toward the lobby. "That lines up with something else we've learned."

"Oh?"

Moricz turns back to Peter. "We've started interviewing some of the staff. A maid saw Derek leave room three forty-nine earlier tonight."

"Earlier?" Agent Anderson cuts in.

Both men look at him.

"Sorry."

Peter waves him off. "It's fine." He looks at Moricz. "How much earlier?"

"Right before the emergency overboard call."

Peter's eyes narrow. "Where is Derek now?"

"We found him in his room. We brought him to the dining room. I'd like you to interview him."

"Let's go," Peter says and turns toward the lobby, but Moricz reaches out and stops him.

"There's one other thing."

"What?"

"His wife is missing."

"What?" Anderson says.

Moricz nods. "The last time anyone saw her, she was leaving the lounge during the performance tonight."

Peter nods. "Mrs. Costa said she was feeling sick. She helped her back to her cabin. You say Derek was in there but Brianna wasn't?"

Moricz nods. "What time did Mrs. Costa take her to her room?"

"She thinks it was close to eleven."

"That's only minutes before the emergency call."

Peter and Anderson nod. All three men look at each other.

Finally, Moricz says, "Go talk to Derek. We'll work on interviewing the staff and finding Mrs. Murphy. Heads-up, he didn't want to go with us. He wanted to look for his wife. We had to force him."

Peter nods and starts down the hall with Anderson following, then stops and turns back. "Moricz?"

"Yeah?"

"What about the other two? Theo and Melody Jones."

"They're still in their room. We haven't talked to them yet."

Peter nods. "When you do, don't tell them anything."

Moricz frowns. "About the Murphys?"

"About anything."

Moricz shrugs. "Okay."

"Good. I'll interview them after Murphy."

Chapter 30

Peter Andrassy

When Peter and Agent Anderson walk into the dining room, they find Derek Murphy seated at the same table Captain Arany and Director Wagner had occupied earlier. Standing beside him are two uniformed Hungarian police officers. Peter nods to them, and they nod back as he approaches.

"Mr. Murphy," Peter says and extends his hand.

Derek starts to stand, but one of the officers pushes him back down. Derek looks up at him, then takes Peter's hand.

"My name is Peter Andrassy, and this is Agent Anderson of the FBI."

Anderson shakes Derek's hand, then both he and Peter sit at the table with Derek. Peter notices Derek's hands are shaking.

"Mr. Murphy, do you mind if I call you Derek?"

"No. Have you found my wife?"

Peter shakes his head. "We're looking for her."

Derek tries to stand again, and again, the officer pushes him back down. This time, Derek fights back, and both officers need to restrain him.

"Derek," Peter says, rising. "We're going to find her. The best thing you can do right now is help me by answering some questions. Can you do that?"

The two police officers hold on to him and watch Peter. Derek stops fighting, holds up his hands, and sits back down. The officers step back and watch Peter.

"Thank you," Peter says and retakes his seat. He takes out his notepad but keeps it close to his body, out of sight of Derek. "When was the last time you saw your wife?"

Derek leans forward and puts his forehead in both hands as his elbows rest on the table. "Earlier tonight. We were sitting in the lounge upstairs. Some Hungarian folk singers were performing."

Peter nods and makes a note. "Then what happened?"

"I left for a few minutes, and when I came back, everyone was gone."

"Everyone?"

Derek nods, still not looking at Peter.

"When you came back, nobody was in the room anymore?" Peter says.

"No," Derek growls in frustration and brings his head up. He uses his hands to emphasize the point. "Our group. Our friends. They were all gone."

Peter nods. "Okay. I understand. Who was in your group?"

Derek sighs and sits back in his chair, his aggravation obvious. "Theo, Melody, me, Brianna, Naomi, and Jacob. The six of us. We met Theo, Melody, Naomi, and Jacob on the cruise. They're from Arizona, just like us."

"They were all there when you left but missing when you came back?"

Derek nods.

Peter looks over at Agent Anderson, then back to Derek. He holds up his notepad and examines it closely. "Hmm, that's funny, because I have another witness who says Jacob left the lounge, and a few minutes later, you followed." Peter returns his eyes to Derek.

Derek looks away.

"Derek? Did you leave the lounge to meet Jacob?"

After several seconds, he looks back at Peter with a defiant face. "Maybe."

"Why?"

Derek doesn't answer.

Peter leans forward. "Look, you can be honest with me or not. Agent Anderson is here witnessing. I can be your friend or your enemy. But if you continue to lie to me, I'll consider you an enemy. Is that what you want?"

Derek returns his eyes to Peter. "I didn't kill Jacob."

"I didn't say you did."

The two men look at each other for a couple of seconds.

"Why did you leave to meet with Jacob?" Peter asks.

Derek bites his lip. "Theo gave me a note after Jacob left the lounge. It told me to go to room three forty-nine. Jacob wanted to talk to me alone."

Peter nods. "So, you went to the room?"

"Yes."

"Immediately?"

"Yes."

Peter makes a note. "What happened when you arrived?"

PART III

Chapter 31
Derek Murphy

Cruise Day 7 – Budapest, Hungary

I knock on the door to room 349, unsure what awaits me when the door opens. Today, as we rode the cable car down to the Chain Bridge from the castle, Jacob threatened me. He didn't come right out and say it, but his message was clear. He knows who I am.

What he doesn't understand is how strong my bond was with his father. I was first introduced to Leo Costa at an alumni function at Arizona State University. A first-generation Italian American, Leo made a fortune setting up telecommunication services in Europe, specifically Eastern Bloc countries. He became so adept at it that he went independent and provided his services to the highest bidder. Companies and countries paid him huge consulting fees. After his retirement, in an effort to give back, he sponsored students and former students who had entrepreneurial ambitions.

From our first meeting, Leo and I hit it off. It made sense, considering he had made all his money in telecommunications, and my business, Tela-Earth, was in that same industry. Then, when I shared my background and origin, he was all in. After only a couple of discussions, he was convinced Tela-Earth was going to revolutionize communication across countries, not just Europe. People in the United States would be able to speak with people in places like Germany for pennies or possibly nothing. The world was going to get smaller. No more hefty long-distance charges. Canadians could work with Australians as if they sat in the same office. We were going to revolutionize the industry and the world.

Leo wasn't just my biggest fan and greatest supporter but a dear friend. Anytime Tela-Earth needed additional funding, Leo was there. I hardly had to ask. He invested millions and persuaded some of his friends to invest as well. Without him, the business never would have become anything other than a dream.

For the first couple of years, Leo's money paid all the bills. With each investment, his ownership grew. After his final infusion, he owned 30 percent of the company. Tela-Earth was making progress building systems and testing theories but not yet selling products or services. Leo was fine with it. He was patient and encouraging. He was a silent partner; nobody knew of his involvement but me. He invested and consulted but left the day-to-day management and operations to me. His only ask was that I update him on progress every week over lunch. Friday afternoons were my favorite times of the week.

At the two-year mark, everything changed when we were approached by Konia. Konia was a large international player in tech and communications. They were well established in the industry, primarily in Europe. They had learned about our systems and pending patent applications through one of our investors, and it intrigued them. After a couple of meetings and a demonstration, they made an offer to purchase Tela-Earth for an amount of money that made my eyes bug out. We were going to be richer than I had ever dreamed.

Weeks later, we had a letter of intent, and the purchase process began. During our first lunch following the receipt of the signed LOI, Leo dropped a bombshell on me. He told me that he had not only given Tela-Earth all of his savings, but he had also mortgaged his home and liquidated his retirement accounts for our funding. He had nothing left to invest. He had bet everything, expecting to win, and he had. The sale of Tela-Earth would result in a tenfold profit on his investment. He was going to make not only himself wealthier but also his children and grandchildren.

But not long after signing the LOI with Konia, warning bells started ringing. Konia took forever to respond to requests, and things seemed to be moving increasingly slowly. After repeated attempts, they stopped responding. Our attorney eventually reached theirs and learned the deal was off. Konia was taking another path. Two weeks after that, we learned they had stolen our idea and were pushing ahead without us.

We consulted several attorneys and sued in international court, but the message was clear—we would never win. Konia had more money and power than we did. Even if we won a single case, they could bury us in legal fees. The war was theirs. They stole our idea, and there was nothing we could do about it.

I'll never forget my last meeting with Leo. We sat dejected in a Chili's in Phoenix, sharing a bowl of tortilla chips and salsa. I couldn't look at him. I was so ashamed. My heart and dreams were broken, and I had ruined his life.

"Look at me," Leo said, and I forced my eyes to meet his. "You're still young and brilliant. This is a setback. Don't let it define you. Go be better. Make something of yourself."

He was so insistent and encouraging that I suddenly had a glimmer of hope.

"What about you?" I asked. "You've lost millions. What about your home? Your retirement?"

He shook his head. "Eh, I'll be fine. I've made millions before, and I'll make millions again. It might just take me twenty or thirty years." He chuckled because we both knew the truth. He was sixty-seven years old and didn't have even half that time left. He should have been enjoying his retirement, not worrying about how he was going to pay for his next meal.

As we left the restaurant, he hugged me and gripped my hand. He stared into my eyes, and I had never seen him so stern. "Dominik," he said. "None of my family knows about you or Tela-Earth. They don't know about my investment. They don't know about my loss. If they find out..." He shook his head. "They're Italians from the East. They're...connected. Know what I mean?"

I nodded.

"I'll do everything to prevent it. I'll protect you. But if something happens to me, you need to disappear. Change your name. Move. Get away from here. You'll no longer be safe."

I looked at him, wide-eyed and shocked. I asked him to explain, but he wouldn't say anything more. We went our separate ways that night, and I couldn't stop seeing the intensity in his eyes. The next day, when I tried calling him, I couldn't reach him. After two more days, his wife finally answered. I didn't tell her my name, but I could tell from her tone that something had happened. He was dead. He had shot himself the morning after our meeting. Sitting in that Chili's, I didn't think I could feel any worse. I was wrong. My friend was dead, and I was to blame.

I hung up the phone and made plans. I was going to run. To leave Brianna and the girls. They were victims of my arrogance and stupidity, just like Leo. They would be better off without me. But the next morning, when I would have left, I looked Brianna in the eyes and couldn't do it. Although I believed she deserved someone better than me, I knew my life was nothing without her in it. She and the girls were my everything. I resolved that I was going to fight. No matter what it took, I was going to make something of myself.

The first step was honesty. I sat her down and told her everything about the company. I half expected her to leave. To turn her back. But she didn't. She hugged me and pledged to help me. We took what little money we had and moved into a rental apartment. I changed my name, and we got to work.

The door to room 349 opens, and Jacob stands in the entrance. "Thanks for coming," he says without a smile. He stands back, allowing me to enter. I don't bother asking what this is about. I walk to the bed and sit. He follows me and leans against the counter by the TV. He crosses his arms and looks me in the eye. "What's your name?"

I frown. "Derek Murphy."

"Your real name?" he says, glaring at me.

"Meszaros Dominik," I say without hesitation. I say it just like a Hungarian, surname first.

"Dominik," he says and nods. "You were the owner of Tela-Earth?"

I nod and see his father in his features. Leo was warning me about Jacob that night in the Chili's parking lot. He knew just how dangerous his son could be.

"Do you know who I am?" Jacob says, rubbing his lips with his index finger, his eyes never leaving mine.

"Yes, you're Leo's boy."

There's that smirk again. "Did you know the whole time? Did you plan this?"

"Plan what?"

"This," he says, motioning with his hand. "This trip. For us to be on the same cruise ship. Was this a game? Do you like to play games, Dominik?"

I shake my head.

He stares at me, and his jaw clenches. "When did you know?"

I consider lying but don't see the point. "Dinner in Passau."

He grins and then laughs. "Ha, day one."

I nod. "You told me your last name."

His expression changes, and his eyes smolder. "You killed Dad."

I frown. "No, I didn't."

"Oh, I don't mean you pulled the trigger. He did that. But you put the gun in his hand."

What do I say to that? I can't meet his gaze and look down. "I loved Leo."

He scoffs. "Some love. What did you do? How did you manipulate him into investing everything he had into that business? What lies did you tell him?"

I look back up. "I didn't tell him any lies."

He shakes his head. "You're lying right now."

I tell him about how we met and his father's involvement in the company. About how he invested everything he had without my knowledge. I told him about our final meeting and how I called and couldn't reach him, then learning he had taken his own life.

"I don't believe you," he says, but for the first time, I see a glimmer of doubt in his eyes.

"Believe me or not, that's what happened."

He shakes his head. "Why did you really leave Hungary?"

"What?" I ask, surprised by the sudden turn in the conversation.

"When you were a boy. Why did you really leave?"

I frown. I have no idea what he's talking about. "I told you, my mother arranged for us to leave. I didn't even know we were leaving. I thought we were vacationing."

He scoffs again. "You're such a liar. I can't believe anything you say."

"I swear. What? What have you heard?"

"I heard you raped a girl. Your mom saved you by getting you out. How many other lives have you ruined?"

I shake my head. "That's not true."

From the time he leaned against the counter, I could see he was holding something in the palm of his hand. Until now, he hasn't shown it to me. Now he holds it up. The light is dim in the room, so I have to squint to see it.

"Is this you?" he says firmly. He points to the boy in the picture.

I recognize it immediately. "Yes."

"These are your grandparents?"

"Yes."

He nods. "Do you remember Arany Reka?"

"Reka?" I whisper.

He nods.

"She was my girlfriend when I left Hungary. We grew up together."

He scoffs and points at me. "See? Right there. You told me you didn't have a girlfriend. You lied again." He shakes his head and opens the drawer beside him. He reaches inside, pulls out a gun, and aims it at my face. He reaches with his other hand and pulls a pillow from the counter and wraps it around the gun. "You know what I promised myself that day I walked into my parents' house and found my father covered in his own blood?"

I hold up my hands, my eyes wide.

"Do you?" he says in a menacing voice.

I shake my head.

"I promised myself I'd kill whoever was responsible."

We stare at each other. I consider pleading for my life. Telling him I wasn't responsible, that the executives at Konia were. But, once again, I catch a hint of his father's features. I see Leo in him, and I stop. I think about what Leo gave me. What he lost for me.

"Nothing?" he says. "You have nothing to say?"

I stare down the barrel of the concealed gun, and a calm washes over me. I shake my head and drop my hands. "Your father was an amazing man. From what I can see, you're a good man too. I can't undo what's been done, but if shooting me will ease your pain, I understand."

He stares at me, and I see the shock in his expression. His eyes fill with tears. "No," he yells. "Fight. Fight me."

I calmly shake my head.

"No," he says, standing before me and holding the gun to my head. "Did you rape her? Did you rape that girl?"

I stare at him for several seconds and then shake my head. "We were young. I thought I loved her. I did have sex with her. More than once. But I never raped her."

Tears roll down his face, and he wipes them with the back of his hand. "You swear it?" he says more softly

I nod. "I swear."

He looks at me, then the gun lowers, and he waves me away with his other hand. "Just leave. Get out."

I stare at him in shock, but after a moment, I stand and move toward the door. When I reach it, I turn back. He's pulled the chair from beneath the counter and sits with his back to me, looking out the window toward the water.

"Jacob," I say, but he doesn't turn. I watch him for several seconds, then open the door and leave.

Chapter 32
Brianna Murphy

Cruise Day 7 – Budapest, Hungary

We exit the dining room as a group after dinner and head up the stairs. Jacob and Naomi took some prodding. They claimed that because of their early-morning flight, they needed to get back to their room and pack. But I wouldn't let them. Tonight is our last night here, and I wanted us all together. Melody and Theo have the same flight, and they didn't try to separate from us.

I hold Derek's hand as we go up the stairs and enter the lounge. We find the last remaining spot with six seats and sit together at the back of the room. I gaze around, noticing that at least half of the boat is here. It's by far the most popular of the after-dinner performances. The cruise director stands beside the bar, messing with a microphone. An area has been cleared beside the bar for the performers to sing and dance. We're occupying the last seats in the room with the back of the boat behind us.

A man walks down the aisle. He's smiling broadly as he approaches our table.

"Arpad," Derek says when he reaches our table. "You serve up here too?"

He shrugs. "Not normally, but I love watching the dancers from our home."

"Do you have a girlfriend in the group?" Theo teases. "Anyone we should keep an eye on?"

Arpad blushes. "I wish. Can I get you drinks?"

Derek and Theo get beers. Jacob requests a Diet Coke, Melody a spritzer, and Naomi and I get tea. He smiles, tells us he'll return, and walks away. I look around at our group. These other two couples have become such close friends. Derek and I would have had a marvelous time on our own, but with them, it's been even better. At dinner, we talked about doing another cruise in a couple of years. I'd love to travel with them again. I wonder if we really will.

Although I enjoyed our time at dinner tonight, it was different. I wonder if it's because it's the last night. Everyone seemed a little preoccupied, as if they had a lot on their minds. The conversation didn't flow as usual. The Costas and Joneses were probably worrying about their day tomorrow. They fly to Amsterdam and then to Phoenix. It'll take all day, and they have to get up really early. Not only that, but Theo and Jacob said they have to be back at work the next day. Their trip is over. At least Derek and I have a few more days.

Budapest has been everything I hoped and more. I love it! We've only been here a day, but I told Derek we should buy a house here. He laughed and told me I was getting ahead of myself. He's probably right. But I can't help feeling excited every time I look at Derek. I love hearing him speak Hungarian and guide me around. He seems so comfortable. Like he's home. It's only too bad it's taken so long for us to get here. If I hadn't received that amazing offer on this cruise, we still probably wouldn't have come. I still can't figure out why they gave us a 50 percent discount. From what I've read, that's reserved for employees only. Maybe it's because Derek is a native Hungarian?

Cruise Director Wagner gets on the microphone and welcomes us all to the entertainment. He introduces the dancers—two beautiful women and two handsome men—and the musicians, a fiddle player and a piano player. After a short briefing on disembarkation, he turns the program over to a woman who is the director of the performance. She's in her mid-to-late forties with blond hair. She's a little on the heavier side, and I wonder if she used to be a performer. Her English is decent, and she lays out the program.

Arpad returns with our drinks and hands them out individually. He's especially helpful with mine, handing it to me and asking if he can do anything else for me. It's probably because it's so hot. But then, he didn't do that for Naomi, and she got the same thing.

He leaves, and we sit back and enjoy the show. The dancers wear elegant costumes with red, white, and green colors. Derek reminds me that those are the colors of the national flag. He says the outfits are traditional, and many women wore similar dresses during celebrations while he was growing up. The first musical number is fun and upbeat. The dancers are skilled and energetic.

When the first number ends, the director introduces a man who walks in from the back. He's wearing a dark suit and is quite handsome. He stands before us, and the piano begins to play. He has a rich baritone voice, and I'm entranced, even though I don't understand the words. Derek tells me it's a love song. When it ends, I notice Jacob is no longer sitting with us. He must have left during the performance. He probably slipped out the back.

The dancers return, and the next number is again energetic. I love watching the skirts of the women twirl and float. It looks fun. I lean over and tell Derek we should try it sometime. He smiles and shakes his head. When I turn my attention back to the dancers, I see Theo pass something to Derek from the corner of my eye. I glance at it, but the male dancers startle me by yelling something, and my attention turns back to them. They clap and yell as they dance, and I cheer along.

Moments later, Derek leans into my ear. "I've got to go to the bathroom. I'll be right back."

I nod, not taking my eyes off the dancers, and he slips out the back.

That number ends, and a woman in a beautiful white dress is introduced. She walks in with grace and dignity, and I can't help thinking she looks like a princess. I wonder if this is who Arpad was blushing about. She sings a haunting song. Again, I don't understand the words, but the feeling moves me. I imagine it's about a lover who got away. The emotion in her voice is incredibly powerful, and the crowd is silent. During the introduction, the director said the performers are from a playhouse in Pest, and I can see why. They do so much more than sing. They convey emotion.

Near the end of the song, something turns in my stomach, and I cover it with my hand. I feel my hand tremble, and my vision blurs.

Something's not right. The song ends, and the dancers return. One of the female dancers has a large bottle of wine and places it on her head. She begins to dance without holding it or spilling any. It's very impressive, and the crowd gets into the act, clapping and cheering along. I don't join in. With every passing second, I feel worse. My head spins, and I feel like I might lose my dinner.

Finally, I can't take it any longer and say to the rest of the table, "I'm not feeling very good. I'm going to go back to the room for a minute."

Naomi puts a hand on my shoulder. "Are you okay? You don't look well."

Theo and Melody look at me with concern.

"I'm fine," I say, shaking my head. "Maybe I just need to use the bathroom."

I slide out from the table and stand but nearly fall.

Naomi stands and grabs my arm. "I'm going to go with her," she says to Theo and Melody. "I'll be back in a couple minutes."

We exit through the back, and I'm glad she's with me. I lean on her, not feeling well at all. We walk through the dining room and then the lobby. When we reach my door, I thank her and tell her I'll be okay as I lean on the handle.

"Are you sure?" she asks. "Do you want me to come in with you?"

I shake my head. "Tell Derek when he gets back. Have him come."

She nods, and I go into the room and shut the door. Rather than go to the bathroom, I go to the bed and lie down. My head swirls, and my stomach groans. Was it something I ate? My vision darkens when I hear the door open. I don't have the strength to see who it is.

"Derek?" I say, looking up at the ceiling. "Honey, I'm not feeling well."

He doesn't answer. I turn my head to the side and look, but I don't see my husband. It's not Derek who entered the room.

Chapter 33
Melody Jones

Cruise Day 7 – Budapest, Hungary

I watch Brianna and Naomi leave the lounge and glance at Theo.

"She didn't look good." I have to say it much louder than I would like to be heard over the music. The Hungarian performers are near the bar, dancing and shouting. The woman who dances with the wine bottle on her head is now going around the room putting it on the heads of some of the audience members so they can take pictures.

Theo shakes his head. "What do you think is wrong with her?"

"I don't know." I look up and see the dancer walking toward us. I hate being the center of attention, especially when it's something embarrassing like balancing a wine bottle on my head. As she gets closer, I look for an exit plan, but I have none. I'm stuck.

She reaches me, and with a very heavy accent says, "You want to try?" She motions to the bottle.

I shake my head, but Theo already has his camera out and holds it up. "Come on, Mel. Do it."

"You try?" the dancer says again and motions to my head.

I see everyone watching me, and I can feel my cheeks getting hot. I nod in surrender and pinch my eyes shut.

She puts the bottle on my head and holds it while Theo encourages me to open my eyes. He takes several pictures. People clap and laugh at my embarrassment, and my cheeks feel like they're on fire. Finally, she takes the bottle off my head and motions to Theo. He shakes his head, but if I had to do it, he's doing it too.

"No," I say. "You're doing it." I nod at the dancer and point her over to him.

She laughs and follows my command.

He shakes his head and hands the camera to me, and I take several pictures, telling him to smile. I even get one with her in the photo.

She moves on and, thankfully, the attention goes with her.

Theo and I watch, and Theo claps several times when some of the audience really ham it up.

"Hey," I say, bumping him with my elbow. He looks at me. "Naomi hasn't come back. Jacob either."

Concern fills his eyes, and he looks down at his watch. He says exactly what I'm thinking: "Let's go."

We get up and exit the room, taking the stairs to the level below. We walk through the dining room and across the lobby. When we reach the hallway, it's quiet. Nobody's around. People are either asleep or in the lounge.

"What should we do?" Theo says.

"Let's go to our room," I say and pull him along. We reach our cabin across the hall from Jacob and Naomi's and enter. With the door shut, we look at each other.

"What do you think?" Theo says.

"Do you think he did it?" I ask.

Theo shrugs and goes back to the door but doesn't open it. He looks through the peephole.

"Can you see the room?" I ask.

He shakes his head. "I'm not sure. I think so. It's hard to tell."

"Is anyone out there?"

He shakes his head and then stops. "Wait." He sighs in frustration. "It's too hard to see who it is."

"Is it Jacob?"

"I don't know. I think so. It's a man. He's leaving the room. He went toward the lobby."

I step to him and push him aside so I can look through the peephole. "Do you think Naomi went back to the lounge?"

"I don't know," he says.

There's movement in the hall, but I can't make out anything about the person. I can't tell who it is. They enter room 349. At least, I think that's the room. I step away from the door and look at him. "Do you think he did it? Do you think Derek's dead?"

Theo looks at me and shrugs. "How will we know?" he whispers.

"Should we go back to the lounge? We were supposed to stay there."

He shakes his head. "We were supposed to stay to babysit Brianna. She left and went to her room. We're better off staying here."

Our eyes go back to the door when we hear shouting in the hallway. I look through the peephole again and see several bodies. I can't tell much about them other than they look like cruise staff. I put my hand on the door handle and open it, peering out. The hall is full of cruise staff, and the door to room 349 is open. A couple of men rush into the room, and other doors open along the hallway. Curious faces look out, trying to find out what's happening.

The woman from the front desk is standing in the hall and sees us. She raises her hands and speaks in a loud voice. "Folks. We've had an emergency. You're not in danger. Please reenter your rooms. We'll let you know when you can come out."

Nobody moves.

"Please," she says. "Go back to your cabins. Everything is fine."

An old woman steps into the hallway, trying to see into room 349, but the concierge stops her and guides her back to her room. "Ma'am, please. There's nothing to see here. Everything is fine."

I make eye contact with another woman across the hall. The concierge looks at us, and the woman shuts her door. I nod and shut ours, then look at Theo.

"I think he did it," I whisper. "I think Jacob killed Derek."

PART IV

Chapter 34
Peter Andrassy

Derek Murphy finishes his story and stares at Peter as they sit in the dining room of the ship. Peter's been watching Derek carefully, looking for any sign he might be lying. Peter glances at Agent Anderson and then back to Derek.

"So, after pulling a gun on you, Jacob let you go?"

Derek nods.

"After leaving the room, what did you do?"

Derek shrugs. "I went back to the lounge. I knew Brianna would wonder about me. But when I got there, everyone was gone."

"Everyone?" Peter asks. "The room was empty?"

"No," Derek says and glares at him. "Our group. Naomi, Theo, Melody, and Brianna. None of them were there."

"Did you see anyone on your way back to the lounge?"

Derek frowns. "I don't know."

"What about the concierge in the lobby? Was she there?"

He shrugs. "Probably."

"Anyone else you remember?"

Derek shakes his head

Peter makes a note in his notepad. "Did you notice anyone else who might have left the lounge while you were gone?"

Derek's tone shows his annoyance. "Like who?"

Peter shakes his head. "I don't know. I'm just wondering if you noticed anything out of the ordinary."

"No."

Peter nods. "When you reentered the lounge, did you come in the same way you left? From the back?"

Derek shakes his head. "No, I came in from the front."

"By the dancers?"

"I didn't go all the way. I looked past them, saw that everyone was gone, and left."

"Where did you go then?"

"Back to our room. I thought Brianna would be there."

"And was she?"

He shakes his head.

"So then what did you do?"

Derek sighs, turns his hand over, and begins picking at his calluses. "I sat in the room, thinking Brianna would come back, then I heard a bunch of commotion in the hallway. I opened the door and looked out and saw down the hall, near where Jacob and I had met, there were a lot of staff members. Something happened. They were rushing in and out of the room. So I walked down as far as I could before the director guy stopped me."

"Director guy?"

"Yeah, the one in charge of hospitality. The tall guy with dark hair. He's from Slovenia."

"Novak?"

"Yeah."

"What did he tell you?"

"That there was an accident, but everything was under control. But I knew what had happened."

Peter eyes him. "What happened?"

"Jacob shot himself."

Peter glances at Agent Anderson, then back to Derek. "You know that?"

Derek straightens a wrinkle in the tablecloth with his finger and doesn't look at Peter. "I shouldn't have left him," he says with a shake of his head. "He had the gun in his hand... I think looking for me was something that gave him purpose. He and Naomi weren't happy; that was obvious." Derek looks into Peter's eyes. "Jacob was troubled. When he let me go, he looked lost. Like he had nothing left. I could see the sorrow in his eyes." Derek's jaw goes tight. "His dad did the same thing. How could he do that to his family?"

Derek slaps the table. The officers standing behind him startle and grab him by the shoulders.

"It's okay," Peter says to them in Hungarian. "He's fine."

"No, I'm not," Derek says in Hungarian. "I need to find Brianna. You have to let me go."

Moricz enters the room and motions to Peter.

Peter stands, but Derek grabs his hand. There's pleading in his eyes. "Let me go find her."

Peter frees his hand. "Give me a minute. I'll be back."

Peter and Anderson follow Moricz out of the room, and they stop next to the staircase in the lobby.

"What did he say?" Moricz asks.

Peter tells him what Derek told them about Jacob. About going to room 349 and finding Jacob there. About their history with Jacob's father and Derek's company. About Jacob pulling a gun but then letting Derek go.

When Peter finishes, Moricz looks at Peter. "Do you believe him?"

Peter hesitates. "I don't know. He didn't seem to be lying."

Moricz looks at Anderson. "What about you?"

Anderson shakes his head. "I don't know. Was there a gun in the room?"

"We didn't find one."

"Hmm," Anderson says.

Both men look at him.

"What?" Moricz says.

"Well," Anderson says. "If you had a gun and someone came at you with a knife, wouldn't you defend yourself? Wouldn't you shoot?"

Moricz nods. "Good point." He looks at Peter. "Forensics finished a few minutes ago. They didn't find any trace of gunpowder. Even if he had missed his assailant, there would have been a gunshot hole somewhere. There would have been trace amounts of gunpowder." Moricz looks Peter in the eye. "We found fingerprints by the door and handle. I'm betting they belong to Derek and Jacob. Jacob was also seen leaving the room by a staff member."

"What are you saying?" Peter says as he watches him.

"I think you know what I'm saying." Moricz shakes his head. "I don't have a choice. I'm going to have to bring him in."

Peter nods. He expected it. "What about his wife? Have you found her?"

"Nobody's seen her. The last person was Mrs. Costa. We've got a team looking everywhere."

Peter bites his cheek. "Check pharmacies in your search."

"Pharmacies?"

"She left the lounge feeling sick. Maybe she went out looking for some relief."

Moricz nods and turns to leave, but Peter reaches out and grabs his arm. "Derek's real name is Meszaros Dominik. He's from Vác. See what else you can learn about his background. I don't know how, but that plays into all of this."

Moricz nods and reenters the dining room, leaving Peter and Anderson standing beside the staircase.

"I'm going to go with him," Anderson says.

Peter nods. "That's a good idea. You know what he told us. See what else you can learn about that."

Anderson nods.

"By the way, what's your first name? Or is it Agent?"

Anderson laughs. "Alan."

"Alan Anderson? I guess your parents were fans of alliteration."

He shrugs and smiles. "I guess so."

They hear shouting in the dining room, and they recognize Derek's voice. He's yelling at Moricz in Hungarian.

"I'd better go," Anderson says.

Peter nods. "Make some calls, would you? See if you can verify what Derek told us about his company and Jacob's father. Let's see if he's telling us the truth."

Anderson nods. "What are you going to do?"

Peter rubs his beard. "I'm going to go talk to the other couple. The Joneses. I want to see what they know."

Chapter 35
Peter Andrassy

Peter knocks on the door of room 356 and waits. He looks down at his Breitling Chronomat watch, the one given to him by his first wife, Karen, on their anniversary so long ago in New York City, and sees that it's almost 5:00 a.m. He's been on the boat for over four hours, and he never ate dinner. No wonder he feels so exhausted.

There's the sound of movement behind the door, then a tall bald man with a gray beard opens the door. His eyes are bloodshot, and the right side of his face is red. He's wearing a golf shirt and shorts, and both are wrinkled.

"Mr. Jones?" Peter asks.

The man nods.

"My name is Peter Andrassy. I'm an investigator with the Hungarian National Police. I need to talk to you and your wife for a few minutes."

"Now?" Theo says, glaring at him.

"I'm afraid so."

Theo sighs. "Can you give us a couple minutes?"

"Sure."

Theo shuts the door, and Peter looks up and down the hallway. A police officer sits on a chair several doors down. His job is to monitor both the Costas and Joneses' rooms. Peter looks at him and nods, and the officer nods back. The door opens, and Theo waves Peter in. The lights are now on in the cabin, and Theo shows Peter to a chair below the TV by the counter. The setup is the same as the other rooms he's been in, just reversed because it's on the other side of the hall. Mrs. Jones sits on the bed with her back against several pillows. She has the comforter pulled up, but Peter can see she's fully dressed. Probably wearing yesterday's clothes.

"Good morning," Peter says as he sits.

"Good morning," she responds.

"More like good night," Theo says as he lies on the bed beside her.

"I'm sorry to have to do this," Peter says. "But there's been an incident, and I need your help. We think you might be able to aid in our investigation."

Theo watches him. "Okay."

Peter pulls out his notepad and looks at them over the top of it. "Your name is Theo Jones, and yours is Melody Jones. Is that correct?"

"Yes," Melody says. "You said *incident*. What kind of incident?"

Peter watches them closely. He always loves it when an interrogation goes like this. Often, when a detective asks the questions, the interviewee is on guard. When it's reversed, he finds they typically are more relaxed and less guarded.

"A body was found floating in the river several hours ago."

Melody raises her hand to her mouth, and Theo frowns, but it's an act. Their surprise isn't genuine. They're putting on a show for him.

"What happened?" Melody asks.

"I was hoping you could tell me," Peter says.

Melody and Theo look at each other.

"Us?" Theo says. "Why us?"

Peter frowns. "Because I understand you knew the victim."

Again, Peter sees an act of surprise from both of them, but it's not genuine. They know something.

"We knew the victim? Who was he?" Theo says.

Peter notes the use of *he* in his question.

"He was from Arizona, just like you."

"Derek?" Melody asks.

Peter chooses not to confirm or deny the name. "Tell me, what do you know about Derek Murphy?"

Theo shrugs. "We met him on the cruise. He and Brianna are from the Phoenix area, just like us. We hung out with them quite a bit. Along with the Costas."

"Jacob and Naomi Costa?" Peter asks.

They nod.

"Do you know anyone who would want to hurt Derek Murphy?"

They look at each other and then shake their heads.

"No?" Peter says.

They shake their heads again, but their movements are rigid. Peter's glad he came to speak with them. He looks down at his notepad. "Well, we've had a report that Jacob Costa was furious with Derek

Murphy. Something to do with a business deal from many years before."

Again, their eyes go wide. These two think they're acting in a play. Their skills belong on a soap opera instead. They shake their heads.

"Hmm," Peter says. "I understand the six of you were in the lounge watching the performance when Jacob left, followed by Derek. Is that right?"

They nod.

"Do you know where they were going?"

They look at each other. "To the bathroom, maybe," Theo says, shrugging.

Melody nods.

"Then, Brianna and Naomi left?" Peter asks.

"Yes," Melody says. "Brianna was sick."

Peter makes a note. "What did you do then?"

"We stayed around for a few more minutes, then came back here. We had an early flight," Melody says.

Peter nods. "Did you see anyone on your way back here?"

"Jacob," Theo says.

Peter frowns. "Jacob?"

Theo nods. "Yeah, Jacob was coming out of his room. He said that he and Naomi were going to turn in for the night. He was headed back up to the lounge to tell us, but we caught him first."

Melody watches him.

"So, you left the lounge and saw Jacob on your way back here. Where exactly did you meet him?"

"In the hallway, just out there," Theo says, pointing.

Peter makes a note. "How did he seem?"

Theo frowns. "Fine. A little tired." He turns and looks at Melody, and she nods.

"Then what did you do?" Peter asks.

"We came back here," Melody says.

"We had to pack and get ready for bed. We had an early flight," Theo says.

"Anything else happen?"

Theo nods. "There was a lot of commotion out in the hall a few minutes later. Something was going on, but they wouldn't let us see what." Theo snaps his fingers. "That's probably when Derek..." He looks at Melody as if he's just thought of this.

"When Derek, what?" Peter asks.

"You know," Theo says. "When they found Derek."

Peter frowns at his notepad, then back at them. "Let's go back to when you saw Jacob. How did he look?"

"I told you," Theo says. "He looked tired."

"Did he look dead at all?" Peter asks, straight-faced.

Genuine surprise was now on both of their faces.

"What?" Theo says.

"Dead. Did Jacob look dead?"

Melody frowns. "What do you mean?"

Peter flips through his notepad. "Well, it was right before you said you saw him that he was found floating in the river. So, I'm just curious how he looked."

Both of their cheeks burn red. "Jacob...," Melody says.

Peter nods. "Jacob is dead. Not Derek. Derek is very much alive."

Theo becomes agitated, and his voice rises. "Jacob is dead?"

"Yes," Peter says, watching them carefully.

"That...," Theo says, then points at Peter. "Derek. He's the one who did it. Derek killed him. It was Derek." Theo looks at Melody. "Right? It had to be Derek," he says, shaking his head. She doesn't respond, and he looks back at Peter.

"Why are you so sure it's Derek?" Peter asks.

"Because Jacob left the lounge and then Derek. They were meeting. Then nobody saw them again before Jacob died. How did he die? He drowned?"

Peter glares at him. "You said they both went to the bathroom. Now you know they were meeting?"

Theo pauses, and Melody watches him.

Peter looks down at his notepad, then back at Theo. "You also said you saw Jacob after he had met Derek. You've got some holes in your story."

Theo stares back at him, not responding.

"So, which is it?" Peter says. "Did you see Jacob? Or didn't you?"

Theo looks at Melody. She looks at him with disgust and turns back to Peter. "We never saw Jacob. I don't know why Theo said that."

Peter nods. "So the last time you saw Jacob was in the lounge?"

"Right," she says.

Peter looks at Theo. "Why did you lie to me?"

Theo drops his gaze to his hands on his lap.

"Did you know that Jacob and Derek were supposed to meet?"

Theo looks at Melody, and she watches him. Finally, he nods.

"Why were they meeting?"

Theo looks away from Peter and stares at the wall. He sighs and shakes his head. He then tells Peter everything he knows about Jacob's father and Derek. About how Jacob had hired a private investigator and has been looking for Dominik for years.

"How did he learn Derek was Dominik while on the cruise?" Peter asks.

Theo continues to stare at the wall. "Derek was speaking Hungarian to Arpad one night at dinner. He heard him say the name Dominik."

Peter looks at Melody, and she nods. "Was Jacob going to kill Derek?"

Theo looks at Peter, tears in his eyes. He nods.

"With a gun?" Peter asks.

Theo says nothing and looks down. Peter looks at Melody, and she nods.

"How did he get the gun?"

Melody reaches out and puts a hand on her husband's shoulder. "We don't know."

"You don't know?" Peter asks.

Both of them shake their heads, but Theo still won't look up.

"Somehow, Jacob got a gun, and he was planning to have Derek come and meet him. He was going to shoot him," Melody says.

Theo looks up with tears on his cheeks. "He wasn't going to kill him. But then, when the captain told him what he did..." Theo shakes his head. "He just couldn't let that pass."

Peter leans forward in his seat. "What did he learn from the captain?"

Theo scoffs. "Derek was way more than a thief. He was a rapist. He raped the captain's sister when he was a boy. Before he left Hungary."

Peter watches him, then looks at Melody. She nods. Peter makes several notes in his notepad.

"Is Jacob really dead?" Theo asks.

Peter nods. "What was your role in all of this?"

Theo looks up at the ceiling and brushes the tears from his cheeks. "What do you mean?"

"Were you going to help Jacob kill Derek?"

Theo shakes his head.

"Listen," Peter says, leaning forward in his chair. "You've lied to me, and I can treat that as obstruction. I don't have to. But I want complete honesty moving forward. Are you with me?"

Theo looks at him and then turns to Melody. "Tell him," she says.

Theo sighs. "Jacob arranged a room for meeting Derek."

"Room three forty-nine?"

Theo nods. "I was supposed to give Derek a note to tell him while we were in the lounge."

"Did you give him the note?"

"Yes."

"What if Derek wouldn't go?" Peter asks.

"Then I'd get him to. I didn't know how. Luckily, it didn't come to that."

"Did Derek know who Jacob was?" Peter asks.

"What do you mean?" Melody says.

"Did Derek know Jacob was his former business partner's son?"

They shake their heads.

"I don't know," Theo says.

Peter nods. "So, after Derek left, did you do something to Brianna's drink? Did you put something in it?"

Both of their eyes widen with genuine surprise, and they shake their heads.

"Did Naomi?" Peter asks.

"I don't think so," Melody says. "I don't know how she could."

"What do you mean?" Peter asks.

"Well, Naomi was sitting at the table the whole time. There was never a time she had Brianna's tea."

Peter nods and looks down at his notepad, then back up. He already knows the answer to the question but asks it anyway. "How did Jacob get in the room? How did he get a key?"

"The captain," they say in unison.

Chapter 36
Peter Andrassy

After talking with Theo and Melody Jones, Peter left their cabin and returned to the lobby. It was 6:00 a.m., and after being up all night and not eating dinner, he was running on fumes. He talked to the officer who had introduced him and Moricz to Director Wagner and Captain Arany and confirmed that Moricz had taken Derek Murphy to the Hungarian National Police Headquarters for further questioning. He also confirmed they hadn't found Brianna Murphy yet and that Naomi Costa and the Joneses were being relocated to the Marriott only a few blocks away. Apparently, the US consulate and FBI had arranged it with the Hungarian National Police. Neither Naomi nor the Joneses could go home yet, but at least they were going to be comfortable.

Upon hearing this, Peter walked toward the ramp and told the officer he would go straight to the National Police Headquarters. But the officer called out to him and shook her head, waving him back. She told him that Moricz had forbidden it, saying he wanted Peter fresh for the day ahead. Moricz wanted him to go home immediately and not return until 3:00 p.m.

"Three?" Peter questioned, feeling that was oddly specific.

She shrugged. "That's what he said. He was very explicit."

Feeling conflicted because of Brianna Murphy but not wanting to anger Moricz, he simply said okay and headed back toward the ramp.

"There's a car waiting for you at the top of the stairs," the officer called after him. "The driver will take you home and pick you up again at three."

Peter turned back to her, raised an eyebrow, then chuckled and walked up the ramp and got in the car. After exchanging pleasantries with the driver and explaining where he lived, he sat back and thought.

Now, fifteen minutes later, he exits the car in Central Buda after the driver tells him he'll be back at three. Peter climbs the stairs of the apartment building where he and Zsuzsa live. Following their marriage a little over a month ago, and their honeymoon to New York City, they agreed to stay in Zsuzsa's apartment until they found a more permanent solution. Peter gave up his apartment in downtown Pest. It's a little inconvenient for him, because the National Police Headquarters are in Pest, but this apartment is only blocks away from Zsuzsa's work at Szép Ilona's. And it's easy for him to swing by the restaurant on nights she's working to have a meal and watch her work.

Peter opens the apartment complex door, rides up the elevator, and enters the apartment. When he walks through the door, he finds Zsuzsa sitting in the kitchen wearing a robe, fuzzy slippers, and sipping a cup of tea. She sees him and comes forward, greeting him with a kiss and sparkling eyes. No matter how many times she does it, he still can't believe a woman this beautiful is seemingly so in love with him.

"How are you?" she says, looking at him with concern.

"Exhausted. You're up early."

"I missed you. Come and sit at the table," she says, leading him to a chair. "Did you eat?"

He shakes his head.

"I'll warm your chicken paprika."

All he wants is his bed, but he allows her to guide him to a chair. She's probably right. He needs to eat something. It's been over fifteen hours since he had anything other than the beer at the restaurant.

When his food is warm, she brings it to him, along with a large glass of water.

"Thank you."

"Do you want to talk about it?" she asks as he picks up the fork and she sits across from him.

"Not really," he says with a mouthful of food.

"That bad?" she asks, picking up her teacup.

"No, I'm just tired of talking. You talk, I'll listen."

She smiles. "Every woman's dream. A handsome man who likes to listen to his wife talk."

He chuckles. "How was work? You told Kata, huh?"

She smiles. Before they came home from America, she had dropped a bombshell on him, telling him she thought she was pregnant. After they arrived back home, she went to the doctor and had it confirmed. That night, they discussed it, and she made him promise he wouldn't tell anyone until she was further along. Apparently, the same rule didn't apply to her.

"Oh, I know. But I had to tell her. We were talking and...I just couldn't stop myself. But she's the only one. I promise."

He chuckles and takes a drink of his water, then pauses. "That's why you're up so early."

"No," she says, smiling coyly.

"Yes. The ultrasound is today. What time?"

"Ten," she says with excitement.

Peter looks at his watch. That's in less than four hours. He finishes the rest of the plate in four mouthfuls and takes a drink before pushing back from the table. "I'm going to take a quick shower and then a nap before we go."

She reaches out for his hand across the table. "You don't have to go. Stay and get some sleep. There will be other chances. You've got a big day ahead. When do you have to go back?"

Peter looks at her. "You think I'd miss the opportunity to hear my child's heartbeat for the first time? If I were sleep-deprived and tortured, I'd still be there." He comes around the table and kisses her. "Wake me about twenty minutes before we have to leave. Okay?"

"Okay."

Chapter 37

Peter Andrassy

Peter climbs out of the car at the Hungarian National Police Headquarters in Pest and walks into the building. After taking a shower, he climbed into bed and slept for two hours before Zsuzsa had to wake him. They went together to her ultrasound appointment and heard their baby's heartbeat for the first time, immediately bringing him back to seventeen years earlier when he first heard the heartbeat of his first child, Catherine. So much in his life had changed since that moment. So much heartbreak.

Catherine was a beautiful baby, and Peter and his first wife, Karen, couldn't imagine loving anyone more. Catherine was the miracle baby they had tried so long to conceive. Their hearts broke when, just nine months later, she was diagnosed with brain cancer, and three years after that, when they finally laid her to rest in the Queens, New York, cemetery.

As Peter listened to the soft heartbeat of this new baby as the technician held the instrument to Zsuzsa's stomach, he couldn't stop the tears as they streamed down his face. He was going to be a father again. Never would he have imagined it those fourteen years ago in Queens. As the technician examined Zsuzsa, Peter had to stop himself from asking a million questions. Did everything look normal? Was the baby healthy? Was Zsuzsa okay? He refrained, as hard as it was. He knew it would be the doctor who would answer those questions.

Peter passes through security, showing his badge, rides the elevator up to his office floor, and enters. *Office* is a generous term. It's a cubicle in the center of a large room beside several more cubicles. The other members of the task force sit near him. He's the only consultant on the team. The rest are full-time detectives with the National Police. Director Farkas, his boss, has a small office fifteen feet away. Farkas sees him as he reaches his desk.

"I didn't expect to see you today," he says, exiting his office.

"Yeah, I came by on my way to talk with Moricz. I'll be going back to the boat soon."

"Sounds like quite a case. Good that you can assist."

Peter chuckles. "I don't think I had a choice."

Farkas grins. "True."

Detective Farkas is much younger than Peter but incredibly bright. In Peter's thirty years of police work, he's met no one more capable. Peter first met him on a human trafficking case Peter had accidentally walked into while working as a private investigator. That case led to his appointment as a consultant on the task force.

"I've got a few loose items I won't get to for a few days," Peter tells him.

Farkas waves a hand. "We'll pick up the slack for you. We're used to it."

Peter snorts, and they chat for a couple more minutes before he leaves and walks down the hall toward Moricz's office. He knocks on the door, and Moricz calls him in. Peter sits in the chair across from him and waits.

"Feeling rested?" Moricz asks.

"Yes," Peter lies. "Any update on Brianna Murphy?"

Moricz shakes his head. "Nothing. It's like she's vanished."

"I think I may know who took her."

Moricz rubs his forehead and stops. "Yeah?"

Peter nods. He tells him about his talk with Theo and Melody Jones.

"Captain Arany gave Jacob the key to cabin three forty-nine. He also told Jacob that Derek had raped his sister many years ago. Back when he was Meszaros Dominik. Before he left for America."

Moricz raises an eyebrow. "How do you know that?"

"That's what I was told by Theo and Melody."

"Do you believe it? Do you think Derek raped her?"

Peter shakes his head. "I don't know. I'd like to talk to Derek again. See if he can confirm what they told me. They weren't always truthful."

Moricz nods. "Derek's here in the building. I'll take you down to him." He pushes back from his desk, but Peter holds out a hand.

"There's more."

"What?"

Peter rubs his beard. "It was no coincidence that Derek and Brianna Murphy were on that ship."

"Huh?"

"Derek said they got an incredible discount to come on it. Something they couldn't refuse."

"Yeah."

"What if it were an employee discount?"

"You think it was the captain?" Moricz says.

Peter nods. "Captain Arany orchestrated this."

Moricz leans back in his chair and looks up at the ceiling. "Do you think he wanted the Costas and the Joneses on the same boat? Do you think it went that far?"

Peter shakes his head. "I don't know."

"Let's go talk to Derek," Moricz says, coming around the desk.

They walk down the hall and down the stairs to a room where Derek is being held.

"We haven't talked to him since we brought him in. He had some food and sleep. He should be in a better mood. He was furious when we brought him off the boat. We had to restrain him. He's a pretty strong guy."

Moricz opens the door, and Derek sits on a chair with his arms restrained behind him. He glares at them as they enter.

"Did you find my wife?" he asks in Hungarian.

Moricz and Peter sit down on chairs in front of him.

"No," Moricz says. "But we think we might know who took her."

"Someone took her?" Derek says. He's still far from pleasant.

"We think so," Moricz says.

"Who?"

Moricz looks at Peter, and Peter takes that as his cue.

"You told me you received a huge discount on this cruise. Can you tell me anything more about that?"

Derek glares at him. "So what?"

"Humor me," Peter says.

Derek shakes his head. "We've been getting mailers for the last year or so from the company. Somehow, we got on their list. Brianna has always wanted to come here, so we'd look at them but never thought we could afford it. Then we got an offer that seemed incredible."

"What was it?" Peter asks.

"Free airfare and fifty percent off the cruise. With our anniversary coming up next month, we thought we'd never get a better chance and booked it."

Peter nods and leans forward. "What do you know about Captain Arany?"

Derek frowns. "The captain?"

"Yeah."

Derek shuffles in the chair with his arms restrained behind him. "I talked to him a couple times. He grew up in Vác, just like me. We never knew each other."

"That's all?"

Derek shrugs.

"Do you know if he had a sister?"

"No."

"Did you have a girlfriend before you went to America?"

Derek's eyes go wide, and Peter can see the light bulb go off in his head. "Reka...," Derek says, and his mouth remains open.

"That was your girlfriend?"

Derek nods.

"What was her last name?"

"Arany," Derek says in wonder, then grits his teeth and unleashes a stream of obscenities. "He took Brianna. He has my wife."

Chapter 38
Peter Andrassy

Peter and Moricz exit the interview room and hurry down the hall, then back up the stairs before reaching Moricz's office. When they enter, Moricz picks up the phone. He calls someone and tells them he's leaving the office, then picks up a file and flips through it.

"What's that?" Peter asks.

Moricz keeps flipping until he finds the sheet he's looking for. His eyes scan the page, then he shows it to Peter. Peter sees it immediately. Captain Arany wasn't scheduled to be the captain on this voyage. He replaced the captain, who was scheduled but unable to work because of illness.

"He was sick?" Peter asks.

Moricz nods. "So was Brianna."

"Let's go," Peter says, and they walk out of the office with the file in hand.

They ride the elevator to the parking garage and get into Moricz's Škoda. Peter's not huge, but he is six foot two, and his frame doesn't fit easily. He looks over at Moricz as he fastens his seatbelt.

"Aren't you the head of the Major Crimes Unit? Shouldn't that mean you should have a nicer car?"

Moricz grunts and puts the car in reverse. "At least I have a car and a parking space." He pulls out of the garage and onto Teve Street as Peter flips through the file. "It looks like he lives in South Buda. Do you want to go there? Or the ship?"

"He's probably at his house. The ship is scheduled to reboard a new group tomorrow. I think he's off today."

"We could go by the ship on the way. Make sure," Peter says.

"Good point," Moricz says and turns onto Népfürdő Street and heads south.

Peter flips through the file, scanning the information. "He did grow up in Vác. Just like he told Derek."

Moricz nods. "The captain had a part to play in all this. There's not much doubt now."

"Do you think he killed Jacob?" Peter asks.

Moricz shakes his head. "I don't know why he would. Unless he was angry because Jacob didn't kill Derek."

"Derek could still have done it. He could have gone back," Peter says as Moricz stops at a red light along the river. "But I don't see why he would."

"Maybe Jacob was dead already when he left the room."

"Maybe," Peter says.

The light turns green, and Peter continues to read through the file as Moricz drives. When they reach the ship, Moricz parks, and they get out. They go down the ramp and find a cruise employee in the lobby. She confirms the captain has the day off, and Peter and

Moricz head back to the car. Moricz drives further south, crosses the river on Petőfi Bridge, and enters South Buda.

While driving, he reaches for something in his pocket and hands it to Peter. It's his phone. "Dial the office, would you?"

"Sure."

Peter dials the National Police Headquarters' main number and gets transferred over to the Major Crimes Unit. A female detective answers, and Peter hands the phone to Moricz.

"Detective Molnar? This is Moricz. Listen, I need officers dispatched to 4 Kászony Street. Tell them to go in quietly. Have them stay a block away until they see me. I don't want him to know we're coming."

Molnar says something on the other end of the line.

"No, I'm with Peter. We're going after Captain Arany. He's been withholding information, and we think he might have Mrs. Murphy."

He hangs up, and Peter has a map out and tells him to turn. They drive for another five minutes and pull up in front of a yellow house with a tile roof. There's a green fence in front of the house, and a well-maintained garden. They look around the neighborhood, checking for any other police cars, but don't see any.

"You want to wait?" Peter asks.

Moricz looks around, debating. "Let's just see if he's home," he says and climbs out of the car. Peter joins him at the gate, and they ring the bell. After several seconds, Moricz rings again, and nothing happens. Finally, the front door opens, and Captain Arany looks out at them, frowning. He walks to the gate, wearing a white tank top and a gold chain around his neck. He gives them a curious look.

"Sorry to bother you, captain," Moricz says. "We just had a couple of follow-up questions. They couldn't wait."

Arany opens the gate and shakes their hands. "No problem. Come on inside."

Peter and Moricz follow him inside the house, and he guides them to the kitchen. It's a well-kept home, but Peter sees immediately that the captain lives alone. It's plain. No woman lives here. Peter knows because when he moved back to Hungary, following the death of his first wife, he had an apartment of his own. It was decorated much like this house. Meaning there were no decorations. This house at least has a picture or two on the walls.

All three men sit at the kitchen table, which, unsurprisingly, is also plain. Nothing on the table but the dark oak surface. There aren't even cushions on the chairs.

"Do you want something to drink? Beer?" Arany asks.

"No, I'm fine," Moricz says.

Peter shakes his head as well.

"What can I help you with?" Arany asks.

Moricz looks at Peter.

"Well," Peter says. "We've been told Jacob Costa was meeting someone in room 349 last night when he was killed. We're still not sure how he got into the room. Do you have any ideas?"

Arany shakes his head, leaning back and crossing his powerful arms in the kitchen chair. "No. Maybe one of my staff let him in. Maybe he stole a key."

Peter looks at Moricz and then back to Arany. "Yeah, that could be. But then again, we were told you gave Jacob the key."

Arany frowns and shakes his head, but then stops as if he's just thought of something. He raises a finger. "You know. I think I did. I forgot about that. He told me he needed it for a confidential meeting. Every once in a while, we get requests like that from passengers. I try to accommodate when I can."

Peter and Moricz nod.

"Makes sense," Moricz says.

"Did you know he was meeting with Derek Murphy?" Peter asks.

The captain shakes his head.

"Did you know they knew each other from back home in Arizona?"

Arany shrugs. "No. But they were together a lot. It looked like they were all close friends. Is that who killed Mr. Costa? Was it Mr. Murphy?"

Peter shrugs. "We thought so, but the more we investigate, the less likely it seems."

"Really?" Arany says.

Moricz nods.

"Did you know that Derek Murphy's real name is Meszaros Dominik? He grew up in Vác, just like you."

"Really?" Arany says.

Peter and Moricz nod.

"Did you know him?" Peter asks.

Arany shakes his head, and Peter has to hand it to the guy. Not an ounce of nervousness. He's cool and confident.

"Hmm," Peter says and holds out the picture he found in the water last night so Arany can see it. "You remember when I found this picture? I didn't ask then, but I'm asking now. Do you recognize the people in this photograph?"

Arany studies it and then shakes his head.

"You're sure? That house is in the same neighborhood you grew up in. You're sure you've never seen those people?"

Arany shakes his head. "I don't know them."

"I didn't ask that," Peter says. "I asked if you had ever seen them before."

Arany leans forward in his chair, and his voice becomes hard. "I've never seen those people. I don't know them."

Peter looks him in the eye. "I think you're lying to us. Do you know why I think that?"

Arany stares at him but doesn't answer.

"Because I was told you believe Derek raped your sister. Or should I say Dominik."

Arany scoffs and leans back in his chair again. "That's a lie."

"Is it?" Moricz cuts in. "We checked your employment records. Derek and his wife were given a big discount on the voyage. It was an employee discount. Do you know who the employee was?"

Arany glares at him.

"You. Now, how would Derek and Brianna get your employee discount unless you knew them?"

The phone rings and startles all of them. Arany stands. "I've got to answer it," he says over his shoulder as he leaves the room and walks down the hall. Peter and Moricz look at each other, and Peter points at the phone on the counter in the kitchen. It has an answering machine attached. Arany doesn't want it picking up. He doesn't want Peter and Moricz to overhear his conversation. Moricz nods, and they both withdraw their guns and follow Arany down the hall. The bedroom door is cracked open, and Peter looks through. Arany stands beside the bed holding the phone. His voice is low, almost a whisper, but Peter can just make out the words.

"I can't go to Vác," he says. "You'll have to go without me."

He hangs up the phone and then reaches into his nightstand and withdraws a gun. Peter pushes the door open, and it crashes against the dresser along the wall. Arany spins around and holds up his gun as both officers enter the room, aiming theirs on him.

"You've got nowhere to go," Moricz yells. "The house is surrounded."

Arany doesn't react, keeping his gun pointed at Moricz.

"Drop the gun," Peter says. "Let's just talk."

Arany glances at him but doesn't move his aim from Moricz.

"Put the gun down," Peter yells.

Arany ignores him and pulls the trigger. Instinctively, Peter and Moricz open fire on him. Two bullets strike him in the chest, and he falls back against the wall. His eyes go wide, and he drops the gun and slumps to the ground, knocking over the nightstand. Peter turns away from him and looks at Moricz. Relieved to see the bullet missed. Moricz is unharmed.

Chapter 39

Peter Andrassy

Peter and Detective Moricz stand outside Captain Arany's house, leaning against Detective Moricz's white Škoda. After shooting Captain Arany, officers entered the house and found them. Moricz and Peter did a quick search of the house, and then Moricz called in a forensics team. They didn't find any evidence that Brianna Murphy had ever been there, and Arany wouldn't be answering any more questions.

"Who do you think was on the phone?" Peter asks.

Moricz shakes his head as he takes a drag on his cigarette and blows out a puff of smoke. "Yeah, I've been thinking about that."

"He must have been working with someone," Peter says.

Moricz nods and pulls out his phone and dials a number. Peter watches as he asks for the Major Crimes Unit and then waits on hold.

"Phone records?" Peter asks.

Moricz nods and flicks his cigarette, then snuffs it out with his shoe.

"Detective Molnar, this is Detective Moricz again. Listen, I need you to do something for me." He nods and looks down at his shoes. "Yeah, he pulled a gun on us. Anyway, I need you to gather phone records for the house. He took a phone call before we shot him. It sounded like it might have been someone who had been working with him. An accomplice."

Molnar says something on the other end of the line, but Peter can't hear it.

"Right. Pull all the phone records, but look specifically for a call." Moricz raises his left arm so he can see his watch. "At around six tonight. It was the last call received on that line."

Peter has a thought, taps Moricz on the shoulder, and motions for the phone. Moricz gives it to him, and Peter puts the phone to his ear. "Molnar, this is Peter."

"Hi, Peter."

"Hey, do you have a list of all the employees on the cruise ship? Everyone who worked on the voyage?"

"Yes. I have one right here on my computer," she says.

"Good. Does it have the countries each crew member is from?"

Peter hears several keystrokes in the background.

"No, I don't see that listed."

"Hmm," Peter says. "Do they have surnames?"

"Yes."

"Look at the surnames. How many are Hungarian?"

"Uh, give me a second."

Again, he hears keystrokes on a keyboard, then several clicks of a mouse. "I can see three right away."

"Good," Peter says. "Who are they?"

"Captain Arany."

"Yes."

"Barta Arpad."

"Okay."

"And Meszaros Edit."

The last one stops Peter short. "Meszaros? That's her surname?"

"Yes. But I saw something else that had a Feher Edit. Not Meszaros. Must be a different woman."

Peter shakes his head. "No, I think that's the same person. Do you have her address? Do you know where she lives?"

"It has her address on this list. She's downtown. Right in the center of Pest."

"Perfect. What's that address?"

She reads it out to him, and he jots it down on his notepad.

"Molnar," Peter says. "Send several units right now. I think she's got Mrs. Murphy. We're in Buda. We'll get there as soon as we can."

"Should I have them wait to go in?"

"No. Send them in as soon as possible. Mrs. Murphy's in great danger."

Peter ends the call and climbs into the car. Moricz heard the conversation and already started it. "She's in Pest," Peter says as he slams the door. "I just hope we can make it in time."

PART V

Chapter 40
Brianna Murphy

Cruise Day 8 – Budapest, Hungary

My eyes flutter open, and I jerk back as an enormous mouth with a pink tongue and sharp white teeth pants in my face. I can't move. My arms are restrained behind my back, and my legs are tied together. The face, complete with whiskers and a powerful jaw, watches me, inches from my own. Its eyes are dark and trained on me. I take a deep breath, preparing to scream, when a woman's voice stops me.

"Oh, I wouldn't," she says as I turn my head to look at her. She's seated on a chair in front of me. The gigantic dog is on one side, and she's on the other. My back is propped against a heating unit with my hands tied to it. A plastic sheet is spread out beneath me. I don't recognize the room. It's nothing like the cabins on the ship. "Attila gets furious whenever he hears a woman scream. If you want to keep that pretty face of yours, I'd suggest you keep your voice nice and low."

I look at her, then back at the massive dog's snout panting in my face. I can hardly believe it's a dog. It looks more like a bear. My eyes go back to her. "Who's Attila?" I whisper.

"This is Attila," she says and rubs the top of his head. "Do you know your history? Have you heard of Attila the Hun? You should have. You're married to a Hungarian, after all."

I try to shake my head, but any movement sends lightning bolts through my skull. I feel weak. My head is in a fog. "No," I croak.

She clicks her tongue. "What a shame. Attila the Hun lived over a thousand years ago and was known as one of the most ruthless killers in history. He was so bloodthirsty that he killed his own brother to become the undisputed ruler of the Huns. He was known for torturing and mutilating his enemies." She leans forward and rubs behind his ears. "It's a perfect name for you, isn't it?" she says to the dog in a baby voice, then looks at me. "He was trained to be just like his namesake."

I look at her and start to cry, and Attila's mouth curls back in a snarl as he bares his teeth.

"Oh," she says. "He doesn't like crying either. I should have mentioned that."

I take several deep breaths, forcing myself to stop. I can feel my whole body trembling. I'm shivering, but it's not cold.

"I need to go to the bathroom," I whisper.

"So go. You have plastic under you." She laughs at the face I make.

"Where am I?" I whisper.

"You're in Budapest. Pest, more specifically. Close to the boat we came in on."

My mouth feels dry. I need water.

"What did you do to me?"

She winks. "Drugged you. But I shouldn't take all the credit. I had help."

I frown. My whole body is shaking, and I can feel my bladder losing control. I'm still wearing the dress I wore to dinner and the performance in the lounge. After several seconds, I look at her. "Where's Derek?"

Her eyebrows lower, and I see anger flash in her eyes. "That's not his name. His name is Dominik." She crosses her legs and puts her chin in her hand. She's wearing a short skirt that highlights her shapely legs. The anger vanishes as quickly as it came. "He's alive, unfortunately. He shouldn't be. He wasn't supposed to be. But some people can't be trusted to do their jobs. And that's why you're here." She looks up at the ceiling, then back at me. "The cops have him at the police headquarters. With any luck, he'll be released soon, and you'll be bait."

Bait? What does she mean by that? I think back to last night. At least, I think it was last night. Jacob left the lounge during the performance, and so did Derek. I got sick, and Naomi helped me to my room. While lying on the bed, the door opened. I thought it was Derek. But it wasn't. It was the captain. Before I knew it, I passed out.

She watches me as tears stream down my face, but I don't make a sound. "Oh, honey. I didn't want to do this to you. You weren't supposed to be part of it. Believe me. It's Dad we wanted."

I frown, not comprehending. Who's Dad?

"Dad. My dad," she says, pointing to herself. "He's the one who should be here. Not you."

I stare at her.

She smiles. "You don't see it?" She lifts her head from her hand and moves her face back and forth, giving me different angles. "Can you see the resemblance?"

What is she talking about?

She recrosses her legs and holds her hands in her lap as she leans toward me. "I've always wondered what he told you. Did he tell you he was a virgin? Did you believe him?"

I don't answer. I can't. I only stare at her.

She laughs. "He did, didn't he? And you believed him?"

I don't respond.

"Nope," she says and shakes her head. "You weren't his first." She puts her hand over her open mouth in mock surprise. "He even had sex before he went to America." She pauses and looks up at the ceiling. "I wonder how many girls he had before you?"

My chest burns with rage. "Shut up," I shout and instantly regret it. Attila's hair bristles, and he snarls and bares his teeth. Spit splashes on my face, but I'm powerless to wipe it away.

She clicks her tongue again and shakes her head. "I told you, Attila doesn't like that."

"I don't care what Attila likes," I whisper.

She laughs. "You have fight. No wonder Dad likes you."

I look at her, and I can see it now. She has the same hazel eyes as my husband. The same lips.

"Why?" I ask.

"Why what?" she asks in a patronizing tone.

"Why are you doing this?"

She looks coldly into my eyes. "It's Dad you should ask. But since he's not here, I'll tell you. I'll tell you everything." She picks a cup of water off the floor and takes a drink, then puts it back down. My eyes follow it. "Oh, do you want some?" she says, pointing to the cup. She shakes her head and looks down at my midsection. "You'll just pee yourself again. I might be a maid, but I don't want to clean it up if I don't have to." She leans back in her chair. "You can't imagine how often I've cleaned up pee. It's disgusting. People are disgusting." She clasps her hands in front of her and says, "Anyway, where was I?" She taps her finger to her lips. "Oh, yes. By the way, what do you think of my English? It's good, huh?"

I frown. Yes, very. On the ship, when she introduced herself, she had a heavy Hungarian accent. So heavy, I could barely understand her. Her vocabulary was also extremely limited. Now, she speaks with almost no accent. She sounds almost American.

"Do I sound like an Arizonan? I should after spending four years there."

I stare at her. She lived in Arizona?

"I went there after Mom died. Cancer," she says with a pout. "Even though Dad never came back to Hungary, I thought I could find him and introduce myself. I guess people might say I've got daddy issues, huh? I applied to so many American schools but only considered one. I went to ASU, just like you. But school was always secondary to finding him. I didn't know where he was or what he was doing, but I knew his name and thought I could easily locate him." She shakes her head. "It took me a while. Much longer than I would have thought. Phoenix is a big city. But I finally found him. I couldn't believe he had four daughters. Five, if you include me." She stops and looks to the side. "And why shouldn't you include me? I'm his oldest."

Attila relaxes and lies down beside me with his head on my thigh. He's listening to her but watching me.

"Anyway," she says and waves her hand. "So, I finally find Meszaros Dominik. I knew his name from Mom. She always thought he'd come back. She loved him." She shakes her head. "Stupid woman. Can you believe she waited fifteen years for him to come back? He broke her heart."

She pauses and looks at me, but I say nothing.

"Well, after I find him, I start checking into him. I find he has this business and even a house and a family. I'd go there a lot, you know? I'd park out front and watch the house. Did you ever see me? I swear, you did. You looked right at me a couple times."

I don't answer.

"No?" she says.

"No."

"Hmm. When you checked in on the boat, and I brought the luggage, I worried you'd recognize me, but he answered the door. Do you remember?"

I nod.

"It was so crazy seeing him up close like that. He didn't know me..." She waves a hand. "Anyway, my story. So, I'd come by every few days and park outside your house and watch you. I kept telling myself to go to the door and introduce myself, but I just couldn't. What do they say in America? I was a scared cat?"

"Scaredy-cat," I say.

"That's it," she says, snapping her fingers. "I'd see you and him and my sisters. Once, I even spoke to your oldest daughter. But I didn't tell her who I was."

She stands and starts pacing back and forth. "So, this goes on for months, then one day, when I've psyched myself up enough, I go to the house and knock on the door, but nobody comes. I leave and come back the next day, and again, nobody answers. I go around the back and enter the house through the sliding door. I look around and see everything is gone. You guys left without a trace." She shakes her head. "I was so mad. I went to Dad's office, but that was empty too." She stops pacing and looks at me. "So I realized somehow he knew about me. He knew and was so ashamed that he moved all of you away to avoid me. He disappeared because of me."

She walks back to her chair, lifts the cup, and takes another drink. "Do you know what that feels like? I was so hurt. I came back here and tried to forget about him, but the more I thought about Mom and him, the madder I got. I told my uncle about what he did to me. I told him everything." She brushes back her hair. "He never liked Dad anyway. He was convinced Mom was raped by him." She waves a hand. "Maybe I told him that. I don't remember. Anyway, we started working to find him and get our revenge."

"How did you find him?"

She smiles. "You're not the only pretty one who can get men to do things."

I frown at her, and she laughs.

"I had a boyfriend at ASU. I promised him I'd come back if he found Dad." She puts on a pouty face. "I guess I'll have to finally go back and give him what he wants. But not until I'm done with you two." She turns away and gazes over at the far wall. "Speaking of," she says and looks at the clock. "I need to call someone."

She walks across to the kitchen counter, picks up the phone, and dials. She turns to look at me, then he answers.

"Uncle, it's me," she says in Hungarian. At least, I think that's what she says. I recognize the word for *uncle*. He speaks to her on the other end of the line, and her face falls. She turns back to look at me with the phone still pressed to her ear. After several seconds, she pulls the phone away and stares at it, then hangs it up and walks back to me. She puts her finger on her chin as she stares at me. Something's changed.

Attila raises his head and looks away from me to her, sensing the change.

Her face is flushed, upset. She says something in Hungarian and shakes her head before walking back to the kitchen and pulling a butcher knife from a drawer. She turns back and begins walking toward me with a menacing look on her face. I can see in her eyes what she's planning, and I can't help the scream I let slip.

Attila jumps to his feet, leans down, and wraps his mouth around my thigh. I scream again and realize I'm never leaving this apartment alive.

PART VI

Chapter 41
Peter Andrassy

As Peter and Moricz drive over Petőfi Bridge on the way back to Pest with the siren blasting, Moricz's phone rings. Rather than answer while driving, he hands it to Peter.

"Detective Moricz's phone, this is Peter."

"Peter, this is Detective Molnar."

"Yeah, we're getting close. We're only a couple minutes away."

"Okay. We're here, but Edit is gone. It looks like she knew we were coming. She left."

Peter lowers the phone and speaks to Moricz. "She got away," he says, then raises the phone again. "What about Mrs. Murphy? Was she there?"

"Yes."

"Is she still there now?"

"Yes, but...well, you'll see when you get here."

Peter wonders what that means as he watches pedestrians pass as they walk along the sidewalks. It's a beautiful early evening, and the sun is setting over the Buda hills. The traffic is light, considering it's Budapest, and the sun will be down in the next fifteen or twenty minutes. A woman crossing the street in front of them catches his attention, and he gets an idea.

"Molnar," Peter says. "Look around the apartment. Do you see anything missing? Anything she might be carrying. Maybe a suitcase? Anything?"

"Uh...I don't know."

"Look for a missing jacket. Something that might help us recognize her."

"Okay," Molnar says as she breathes into the phone while walking around.

"Actually," Peter says. "What about a picture? Can you find a picture of her? Anything that could tell us what she looks like?"

Molnar remains quiet on the other end of the line as she searches. Finally, she says, "Got one. I think this is her. She has long dark hair. She's pretty. She's hugging a dog."

This piques Peter's interest. "What kind of dog?"

"It's big. I think it's a rottweiler, maybe. It's got black-and-brown fur."

"Molnar," Peter says. "Is the dog in the apartment?"

"No."

"Can you find dog dishes and food?"

"Yes, there's one on the floor."

"Okay, listen carefully. Get everyone out looking for the woman. Share the photo with the public-transportation office. Share the photo with the team and the local police. Get the word out to every cop in the city. We've got to find her before she disappears."

Peter ends the call, turns off the siren, and looks at Moricz.

"We're looking for a woman with a rottweiler, huh?" Moricz says.

Peter nods. "That's her building," he says, pointing up ahead. Several police cars are parked in front.

"Where do you think she'd go?" Moricz asks.

Peter shakes his head. "If I had to guess, I'd say east."

"Why?"

"Because it's the opposite direction from the ship. Maybe psychologically, she thinks the ship is where it began. It's where we'd be looking." Peter shrugs. "But I'm no psychologist."

"Good enough for me," Moricz says.

"Hey," Peter says, smiling. "We've got a one-in-four chance."

Moricz turns east, and they drive for several blocks, seeing multiple women walking with dogs. None of them with a rottweiler until the tenth.

"Is that her?" Moricz asks, pointing.

Peter shakes his head. "Too young. That girl's a teen."

They keep driving, expanding their radius. After ten more minutes, and with the streetlights now on, they see a girl in a jacket with a large rottweiler on a leash. She's headed east.

"That could be her," Peter says.

Moricz pulls the car to the side of the road, and they get out and approach. The girl wears a jacket with a hood. They can't see her face or her hair.

"Edit," Peter says from several steps behind.

She doesn't respond and keeps walking.

"Meszaros Edit, is that you?"

The girl doesn't turn, but the dog does. It's powerfully built and has a huge mouth. Something seems off about it.

"Call for backup," Peter whispers to Moricz.

Moricz takes out his phone and begins dialing as he walks.

The girl picks up her pace but still hasn't turned.

"Molnar," Moricz says into the phone. "Send a team of officers to," he looks around, trying to find a street sign and stops, lowering the phone. "Keep going, Peter. I'll catch up."

Peter keeps trailing her, and after several seconds, she finally turns. She's lovely, with dark-brunette hair and light eyes. She makes eye contact with him, then turns forward and starts to run, surprising the dog. Peter gives chase, feeling his knees groan as he keeps pace but not getting too close, knowing she might have a gun and not wanting to tangle with the dog.

She turns south on the next side street, and Peter follows. It's a narrow alley, and halfway up, Edit pauses long enough to unleash her dog. She screams something at it and points at Peter.

"Oh, no," Peter says as the dog bounds toward him, snarling. It's fast and quickly gaining ground. There's no way he's going to outrun it. As the dog approaches, he balls up his fist and prepares for a fight he doesn't want. The dog leaps at him, and he moves to the side at the last moment, striking down with his elbow. The dog smashes to the asphalt but spins and comes at him, mouth wide. Peter puts up a forearm to shield himself and feels the dog's teeth rip into his flesh. Its canines are so long, he feels them wrap around the radius bone in his arm. Peter cries out in pain and punches the dog in the side. The dog releases and comes at him again. Peter kicks but misses and falls to the ground. The dog jumps on top of him, biting and snarling. Peter screams and rolls onto the dog, pressing his weight into it. He sees a flash of red in the fur and grabs the collar.

"Peter," he hears Moricz say, running up.

"I'm all right," Peters yells to him and holds the collar with two hands while the dog thrashes against him. "Go after her."

Moricz stares at him, wide-eyed, then continues up the alley.

Peter grips the collar tight, knowing that if the dog gets loose again, he may not be capable of holding him back.

Chapter 42

Peter Andrassy

Peter had to hold the dog back for only a couple of minutes before reinforcements arrived. Another officer took a turn, and Peter was transferred to paramedics who put him in an ambulance. The bites to his forearm, shoulder, and leg were of varying depth but all extremely painful. All were bleeding, and he had several scratches from the fall and wrestling the dog.

When Peter arrived at the hospital, they took him to the emergency room and asked him several questions, including who he'd like them to contact. He gave them Zsuzsa's name and number as they put an IV in his arm and began giving him painkillers to make him more comfortable. After talking with a doctor and getting a rabies shot, they pulled the curtain closed, and he lay back in the bed. Exhaustion overcome him, and he fell asleep in less than a minute.

Now, he opens his eyes and sees he's still in the same room, but he isn't alone. Zsuzsa sits beside his bed in a chair. She's reading a magazine and looks up when he shifts his leg. She stands and comes to him, leaning down and kissing his lips.

"What's wrong with you?" she asks.

"What?"

"A dog? Now you fight a dog? Wasn't getting shot in New York enough? I'm tiring of finding you in hospitals."

He looks down and sees his arm is wrapped, and a bandage is on his shoulder and leg. He looks back up into her eyes. "Big dog," he says.

She smiles and shakes her head. "Did the girl get away?"

Peter shifts in the bed, and his body, not just his arm and shoulder, scream at him. He's sore all over. "I don't know. I hope not."

The curtain parts, and a nurse enters. "How are you feeling? You were tired."

Peter nods and looks at his watch. He was asleep for four hours. It's almost midnight.

"The doctor will be along in just a minute. Your X-rays look good. You didn't break anything. I think she'll let you go home."

"Okay," Peter says and looks at Zsuzsa. She smiles at him, but it's forced.

"Can I get you anything?" the nurse asks.

"No, I'm fine," Peter says, and she leaves the room. He looks back at Zsuzsa. She's still standing at his bed, holding his hand. "Are you all right?"

She looks at him and nods, but her eyes fill with tears.

"What is it?"

She shakes her head and wipes at the corners of her eyes with the back of her hand.

"It's really not that bad," Peter says. "I'll be fine in a couple days. I'm sorry I scared you."

She sighs and shakes her head and reaches for a tissue and dabs at her eyes.

"Zsuzsa," he says. "What is it? What's going on?"

She shakes her head. "We can talk about it later."

"No, what is it? What's wrong?"

She holds a tissue to her nose. "I got a call from the doctor today."

"Oh," he says, and feels a stab deep inside.

"They moved up my appointment to review the ultrasound results. They want me to come in again in two days."

Peter stares at her in shock. "Did they tell you anything?" His eyes look down at her middle.

She shakes her head. "It was the scheduler. She wouldn't say anything else. She said the doctor reviewed my ultrasound results and needed to change my appointment."

Peter reaches for her, and she leans down to him. He kisses her and looks into her eyes. "It may be nothing. It's your first time being pregnant. They probably just want to talk to you."

Her eyes fill with tears again, and he reaches up to touch her cheek.

"Whatever it is, we'll get through it together. It's going to be okay."

She wipes the tears from her eyes, takes a deep breath, and nods as the curtain to the makeshift "room" opens and Moricz sticks his head in. "Oh, I'm sorry," he says when he sees Zsuzsa standing with her back to him.

"It's fine," Peter says, waving him in.

"You sure?"

"Absolutely," Peter says.

Zsuzsa pulls herself together and turns around and extends her hand to him. "Detective Moricz? I'm Andrassy Zsuzsa, Peter's wife."

Moricz takes her hand and nods. "Nice to meet you, Zsuzsa. You can call me Bence." He sees the tissue in her hand and her puffy eyes. "I know this won't come as much consolation, but your husband is like nobody I've ever worked with."

She smiles. "Oh, I know."

He grins and looks at Peter.

"Did you get her?" Peter asks.

Moricz nods. "She's at headquarters now. She was a pretty good runner. I kept her in my sight long enough to get some help."

Giving up cigarettes would help with his cardiovascular endurance, but Peter doesn't think now is the time to point that out.

"Good," Peter says. "I can't wait to talk to her."

Moricz nods. "You can talk to her tomorrow. Tonight, go home with your lovely wife."

Moricz turns to leave, but Peter calls him back.

"What about Mrs. Murphy?"

Moricz's face falls, and he shakes his head.

"She killed her?"

Moricz nods. "Be happy you didn't see it. The dog got to her too."

Chapter 43
Peter Andrassy

Peter hobbles into Moricz's office in the Hungarian National Police Headquarters and tells him good morning. Moricz looks away from his computer.

"How are you feeling?" he asks, looking at Peter's bandaged arm in a sling.

"Like I fought a lion," Peter says. "If people ask, can we tell them that?"

Moricz chuckles. "That dog was as big as a lion. Seems accurate to me."

"Where are we with things?" Peter asks as he sits across the desk from Moricz.

Moricz turns in his chair to face him. "Edit opened up and talked last night after we offered her a deal. You won't believe it, but she's Mr. Murphy's daughter."

"What?" Peter says.

Moricz nods and expels a quick laugh. "Yeah, I couldn't believe it either. I guess Dominik had a girlfriend before he left the country. The girlfriend was pregnant, and Edit is that daughter. She's got a lot of hatred for him. He wrote letters to her mom saying he was going to come back, but he never did. I guess he broke her heart. Then Edit went to America after her mom died, and he disappeared before she could introduce herself. She thinks he knew and rejected her."

"Wow, do you think that's true?"

Moricz shrugs. "I'd like to see if we can get Dominik to agree to a paternity test. That might help us know how much of her story is true."

"What about Mrs. Murphy? Did she say anything about that?"

He nods. "She admitted to killing her."

"And Jacob Costa?"

Moricz shakes his head. "She said she didn't do it."

"Really?"

Moricz nods.

"Does she know who did?"

Again, Moricz shakes his head.

Peter rubs his beard. "What about the captain? What was her relationship to him?"

Moricz leans back in his chair. "He was her uncle. Her mom's brother. He helped her in all of this."

"What about him? Could he have been the one who killed Mr. Costa?"

Moricz shakes his head. "She says no. She says he was helping her kidnap Mrs. Murphy at the time. They were at Edit's apartment with Mrs. Murphy when he got the call about Mr. Costa."

Peter frowns. "It had to be one of the others in the group of friends then. Maybe Derek really did it?"

"Maybe. We're running out of time. We've either got to charge him or let him go. Maybe you can go talk to him again. See if he's changed his story at all."

Peter nods and gingerly rises from his chair and turns toward the door. "Does he know?"

"Know what?"

"Know about his wife? Or that he has another daughter?"

Moricz shakes his head. "We haven't told him anything."

Peter exits the room and walks down the hall, knowing he would rather fight the dog again than deliver this news. He takes the elevator to the room Derek is being held in. When he opens the door, Derek looks up from the book he's reading.

"What happened to you?"

Peter sighs. "I fought a lion. What are you reading?" Peter sits across the table from him.

Derek turns the book around so he can see. It's in Hungarian but an American story, *The Adventures of Tom Sawyer*. Peter notices Derek's hands are still handcuffed at the wrists, but at least now, they aren't restrained behind his back. His behavior must be improving.

"I've got some news for you," Peter says.

Derek drops the book and looks at him anxiously. "Did you find my wife?"

Peter nods, and Derek blows out a breath of relief. "Where was she?"

"She was kidnapped."

"By who?"

"By your daughter."

Derek screws up his face in confusion. "What? My daughter?"

Peter nods. "Did you know your girlfriend was pregnant when you left Hungary?"

Derek shakes his head. "Reka?"

"Was that your girlfriend's name?"

Derek nods.

"She had a daughter. Did she ever tell you?"

"No."

"Well, this woman claims to be your daughter. We'd like you to agree to a paternity test to find out."

Derek stares at him. "What would you need?"

Peter shrugs. "It's pretty simple. We'd take a cheek swab and test your DNA against hers."

"That's it?"

"That's it."

Derek shrugs. "Sure. Is Brianna okay? When can I see her?"

Peter watches him. Unfortunately, in his life, he's delivered a lot of bad news. It never gets easier. The only thing he's learned is that there's no advantage to stalling. It's like a Band-Aid. Best just to rip it off. "Brianna's dead."

Derek stares at him, not comprehending. Peter watches as he processes the information. First, his eyes go wide, then his jaw clenches, and he closes his fists. "How?"

"She was killed during the abduction."

"How?" Derek screams and rises from his seat, knocking over the chair.

Peter doesn't respond.

Derek goes to the door and tries to open it. It won't budge. Derek pounds on the door, the metal handcuffs clicking on the metal frame. A guard sees him and opens the door. Derek tries to push past, shoving him. The guard wraps him in a bear hug and forces him back inside the room. Another officer joins him as Derek screams and kicks, fighting to get loose. The officers force him to the ground and put him on his chest and restrain his legs. One officer straddles his back as he fights.

"Derek," Peter says in English. "They're going to taze you. Stop fighting."

Derek cries out, and the officer uses a taser on him. His body goes rigid, and they unlock his handcuffs, pull his arms behind his back, and relock them. They leave him lying on the floor on his stomach, moaning, and looking away from Peter. The guards look to Peter for instruction, and he tells them they can leave. They close the door but remain outside the room.

Peter sits in his chair, watching the man's heart break. Derek's face is turned away from him, and Peter thinks back to when officers showed up at his door in Manhattan and told him his first wife, Karen, had been found. She was missing, just like Derek's. And just like Derek, the result was the same.

After several minutes, Peter finally speaks to him. "Derek, who killed Jacob?"

Derek doesn't move. He's no longer moaning, but his face remains turned away from Peter.

"I don't believe you killed Jacob. I believe what you told me before. Help me. Give me something to use. If you don't, they're going to charge you."

Derek lifts his head and turns so he can see Peter. "Go ahead. Charge me. What do I care now?" Anger and hate burn in his eyes.

Peter watches him, and after several seconds, he says, "My wife was murdered."

Derek stares at him.

"She was killed by someone I knew. Several years before that, my only daughter died of cancer."

Derek continues to stare at him while lying on his stomach on the floor of the interrogation room.

"The thing about grief is that it hits everyone differently. No two situations are alike. Nobody knew what I was going through, and nobody will know what you're going through. After Karen died, I considered ending my life. I was so tortured with pain. My last resort was coming back here. I had to get away from everything that reminded me of them."

He watches Derek and sees he has his attention.

"When I got here, I was going through the motions. I was brokenhearted and grasping for anything that might numb the pain. I threw myself into my work, thinking the busier I was, the less I'd think about what I'd lost. Then you know what happened?"

Derek doesn't respond, just watches him.

"Fate stepped in. I met someone while working. She changed everything for me. I had something to look forward to. My life had purpose again." Peter leans forward in his chair. "Listen, you're going to go through hell. But you already have purpose. You have four beautiful daughters at home who've lost a mother, and they don't even know it. Don't make them lose a father too."

Derek stares at him. "Naomi," he says.

"What about her?" Peter asks.

"After I left the room with Jacob, I saw Naomi in the hallway. I don't know why or how, but I think she's the one who killed Jacob."

Chapter 44
Peter Andrassy

Peter exits the room, goes up the elevator, and walks down the hall to Moricz's office. When he reaches it, he sees Moricz is busy in a meeting. Not wanting to interrupt, Peter walks past the office, but Moricz sees him and calls out. Peter turns back and recognizes Agent Anderson of the FBI.

"Peter," Moricz says. "Agent Anderson came by. He's got something to tell us."

Anderson stands from the chair and looks at Peter, extending his hand but then letting it drop. "What happened to you?"

"I fought a lion," Peter says and points for him to take the far seat while Peter takes the nearest one. "What do you have for us?"

Anderson looks him over questioningly, but after seeing he's going to get no more explanation, he looks at Moricz and switches to Hungarian for Moricz's benefit. "We started looking into all the Americans. We checked their backgrounds, criminal histories, everything."

"Good," Peter says.

"Well, there wasn't much of anything. We ran a deep background check on Theo and Melody Jones. No criminal backgrounds, other than some minor traffic incidents. Theo's an executive with a mortgage company, and she runs her own bakery. They have several kids, and one passed away years ago. I couldn't find any link between them and the Murphys."

"Okay," Peter says.

"Next came the Costas. Again, no criminal background for either of them, and Jacob worked as a mortgage executive, just like Theo but for a different company. Naomi works as a real estate agent. They also have a handful of grown kids."

"Sounds like a dead end," Moricz says.

Anderson holds up a finger. "So then we switched tactics. We started checking Derek's story. You know, Peter. The one he told us."

Peter nods.

"Well, it turns out, he did have a company called Tela-Earth. It went bankrupt, just like he said, and Jacob's father was a heavy investor in it. All of that was true."

Peter and Moricz watch him carefully.

"Just like Derek said, his real name is Meszaros Dominik. When he changed his name, he moved all of his bank accounts to his new name, except one. That one remained under the name of Dominik." He reaches out and hands a sheet of paper to both men.

"What am I looking at?" Moricz asks.

"That's the bank account ledger. You can see a monthly deposit and corresponding withdrawal."

"Yeah," Peter says.

"I checked into the withdrawals. They were a monthly automated check made out to Jacob Costa."

Peter and Moricz look up, frowning. Anderson nods. "Derek's been paying Jacob Costa every month since his father died."

"Why?" Peter asks.

Agent Anderson shakes his head. "I don't know."

Moricz frowns. "Was it court-ordered? Because of the company?"

Anderson shakes his head. "Nope. There was no legal reason."

Peter and Moricz sit back in their chairs, considering this.

"And there's more," Anderson says, handing them another sheet of paper. They look down at it. It's a life insurance benefit form for Jacob Costa. "Jacob got a new life insurance policy at the same time as these payments started. From what I can see, the payments paid the premium and left some extra money each month."

Moricz looks up, confused. "So? You think they were related? Derek was somehow paying for Jacob's life insurance? Why?"

Anderson shakes his head.

Peter looks at the sheet more closely and sees something at the bottom. "Naomi Costa was the beneficiary."

"Huh?" Moricz says.

"Naomi Costa was the beneficiary," Peter says, pointing to the line at the bottom. "She benefited if Jacob died."

"How much is this policy worth?" Moricz asks.

"Three million dollars," Anderson says, then slides one more sheet of paper over to them. "Look at that. It's a bank account owned by Naomi Costa. Look at the deposit amounts."

Peter and Moricz examine the sheet.

"The same amount of money as the checks from Derek," Moricz says.

Anderson nods.

Peter sits back and rubs his beard. "Derek knew who Jacob was before they came on the cruise. But so did Naomi."

Anderson and Moricz nod.

"Which means Derek also knew Mrs. Costa."

"Could be," Moricz says.

"I'd like to go talk to Mrs. Costa again," Peter says.

Agent Anderson gets up from his chair. "I'll come with you."

Chapter 45
Peter Andrassy

Peter knocks on the door of the royal suite inside the Marriott Hotel in Budapest and gives Agent Anderson a look as he stands beside him. Neither man says anything, waiting for the resident to open the door. After several seconds, the door opens, and Naomi Costa stands in the doorframe.

She stares at them for a moment, then recognition fills her eyes. "Hello, Peter," she says, holding out her hand. He takes it, and she turns to Anderson. "I'm sorry, I don't remember your name."

"Agent Anderson, ma'am."

"Oh, that's right. Well, come in," she says with a sweep of her hand, and both men enter as she shuts the door. The suite is at the top of the building, near the major shopping street in Budapest on the Pest side of the river. The drapes are pulled back from the large window, and there's a panoramic view of the city with the river and Buda hills in the distance. "Isn't this room beautiful?" she says, pointing for them to sit on the couch while she takes the chair across from them. The room is a grand living room with two couches, chairs, a coffee table, end tables, and a huge TV. There are several closed doors behind Naomi, and Peter wonders how many bedrooms are in this suite.

"It sure is," Peter says, taking several steps to the large window and looking out at the view before sitting beside Anderson on the couch.

"Are you responsible for this?" she asks Agent Anderson.

He shakes his head. "I think it was the embassy. They handled all your arrangements."

She nods. "Well, will you thank them for me? Everything that has happened with Jacob and Derek...I can't tell you how hard this has been."

Peter nods. "I'm sure."

"So," she says. "What brings you here? Do you have an update for me?"

Peter nods. "We do."

"I understand Derek is still being held by the police in your head-quarters?"

"He is."

"Good." She shakes her head and holds a hand to her lips, as if fighting back tears. "I still can't believe he'd kill my husband."

Peter nods. "Neither can we."

She frowns. "I know. He seemed like such a good man. He and Brianna were so good together. How's she doing with all this? I haven't seen her at the hotel."

Peter's a little surprised she doesn't know. But, then again, why would she?

"Well," Peter says, avoiding the question. "We've found some recent evidence we wanted to talk to you about."

"Okay," she says, then holds up her hand. "I'm sorry. How rude of me. Can I get you two anything? Something to drink?"

They shake their heads.

"You're sure?"

They nod.

"Okay, anyway," she says, waving a hand. "What were you saying about recent evidence?"

"Right," Peter says, reaching into his jacket and pulling out a clear plastic bag with a knife inside it. She stares at it as he holds it up to her.

"What's that?" she asks, flushed.

"It's a knife, ma'am. Your husband's. We took it from the river only a few minutes ago."

She stares at Peter, then at Agent Anderson. "That's not Jacob's knife."

Peter frowns. "It's not?"

She shakes her head. "No. He doesn't carry a knife."

"Hmm," Peter says, examining it in the bag. "I wonder why it's engraved to him, then."

"What?" she says.

He stands and goes to her, showing the name of Jacob Costa on the handle of the knife.

She stares at it, then looks up at him. "I'm sorry, but you've got to tell me what this means."

Peter watches her carefully, then goes and sits back down beside Anderson. "It was pretty lucky, really. The scuba divers found the knife wedged between several rocks in the river. I didn't think there was a chance we'd find the murder weapon."

She watches him but says nothing.

"Did you know fingerprints can still be taken from a knife that's been in water for days?"

She frowns, and color drains from her face.

Peter nods. "I'd heard that but wasn't sure of it. Well, turns out, this knife had fingerprints, and guess whose were on it?"

"Derek's?" she says.

Peter shakes his head.

"Jacob's?"

"Yes. And one other person's."

She shakes her head.

"Yours."

"Are you accusing me of something?" she says, bristling.

"Should I be?"

She scoffs. "So, what? That means nothing. I'm his wife."

"True," Peter says and looks at Anderson. "She has a point."

He nods but says nothing, and Peter turns back to Naomi.

"But, then again, you didn't recognize the knife. Or, at least, claimed not to, and we know you handled it."

"So?"

"So, it seems like you might be trying to cover something up."

She shakes her head. "I want you to leave. I want you to leave right now," she says, pointing to the door.

"But there's more," Peter says.

Her face falls.

"Don't you want to hear the rest?"

She doesn't respond.

"We have a witness who watched you leave room three forty-nine."

"What? Who?"

Peter smiles. "We also have your fingerprints in the room."

Naomi shakes her head. "That's impossible."

Peter smiles. "Why, because you wiped the fingerprints clean on the door handle?"

Naomi doesn't respond.

"But you forgot the chair Jacob was sitting in."

PART VII

Chapter 46
Naomi Costa

Cruise Day 7 – Budapest, Hungary

I close the door to Brianna and Derek's room as Brianna enters and look up the hallway. It's empty. Nobody around. It's not surprising. More than half the ship are still upstairs in the lounge watching the dancers. I walk up the hall and stop in front of room 349. It's quiet, and then I hear Derek's voice. I can't make out the words, but he's close to the door. The handle turns, and I dash around the corner by my room. Derek exits room 349 and walks up the hallway toward the lobby. I don't think he saw me. I open our cabin door and enter, seeing Jacob's suitcase on the bed. He started packing before going to dinner. It's wide open, and the knife he bought on that trip to Cancun several years ago sits on his book. I pick it up and examine it, holding it by the handle.

He was supposed to kill Derek. I knew he wouldn't. I knew he didn't have it in him. I married a coward. He always said if he ever found Dominik, he'd kill him. He couldn't even do it after learning about Dominik's rape of the captain's sister. Even then, he wasn't man enough.

When he told Theo, Melody, and me he was going to kill Derek, I almost believed him. He seemed genuine. When the captain gave him a gun, I knew my opportunity to be rid of my husband had finally come. Jacob would shoot Derek and then bring the gun back with him to our room. The captain would come later to pick it up and dispose of it.

That was the plan. What they didn't know was that I had my own plan. I was going to tell the police about it, and Jacob would go to prison for the rest of his life. The captain would be in trouble too. Well, now that's over. Just another thing Jacob couldn't follow through with.

I stare at the blade and get another idea. I'm going to do it. If he couldn't come through, he'll pay for it with his life.

I hide the blade in my trousers under my shirt and exit the room. The hall is still clear, and I take several steps to room 349 and try the door. It's not locked. It opens, and I see Jacob sitting in a chair looking out at the river. It's completely dark in the room, and I can only make out his silhouette. I close the door behind me and creep forward. He hasn't even moved. I pull the knife from my back and, before I can change my mind, grip the back of the seat and thrust the knife into his side. He jerks, and I withdraw it and plunge it into his neck. He jumps from the chair and runs forward out the open sliding door and falls off the balcony into the water below. He never turned around. He never saw it was me. I wonder if he knew.

I edge toward the balcony but stop. What if someone sees me? The blade is still in my hand. I look around, wondering where I should put it, then get an idea. I lean forward and throw it as far into the water as possible, then turn and go to the door. I look out the peephole, checking the hallway. It's still empty. I open the door, wipe the handle with a towel I take from the bathroom, duck around the corner, and reenter our room. I rush to the bed and sit down, breathing heavily. I hear a commotion in the hallway and go to the door, looking out the peephole. People rush by in staff uniforms. My heart pounds as I watch them go by. Several doors open now, including Theo and Melody's. Melody steps out into the hall, but a staff member stops her and forces her back into the room.

I go back to the bed, push Jacob's suitcase to the floor, and lie on his side of the bed. He's gone. I'm finally rid of him. I can finally breathe.

PART VIII

Chapter 47

Peter Andrassy

Peter unlocks the door and enters the room where Derek Murphy is being held. Derek sits with his arms and legs restrained with shackles. He has his book on the table, and he's leaning over it. He looks up as Peter walks toward him. Peter motions for him to scoot away from the table, and Derek complies. Peter goes to a knee so he can reach Derek's ankles and unlock the shackles.

"Could you turn for me?" Peter asks as he straightens.

Derek stares at him, then turns in his seat so Peter can reach his back. Peter unlocks the restraints around his wrists, puts them on the table, then sits down across from him.

"You're free to go."

Derek raises an eyebrow. "What happened?"

"You were right. It was Naomi," Peter says. "We found the knife in the river. It was lucky, really. Her fingerprints were still on it. Without that and the fingerprints in the room, I don't think we would have been able to prove it was her."

"Where is she now?"

"She's here. The FBI will take her back to the States soon."

Derek watches him. "So, I can just leave?"

Peter nods. "There's something else you should know."

Derek sighs. "Peter, I can't take any more."

"We got the results from the paternity test back."

Derek looks up.

"Do you want to know?"

Derek shrugs. "I guess."

"She's your daughter."

Derek turns away, looks at the wall, and nods.

"Would you like to see her?" Peter asks.

Derek looks at him. "Are you kidding? You want me to see the woman who killed my wife?"

"She's not just the woman who killed your wife. She's your daughter."

"No, she's not. I don't care what some stupid paternity test says. I have four real daughters back home. She's nothing to me."

Peter watches him for several seconds, then says, "Speaking of, the flight you and Brianna were scheduled on is in two days. We might be able to get you out sooner. Would you like us to try?"

Derek looks down and shakes his head. "No, it's fine. I'll go on that flight."

Peter nods.

"What about my hotel?" Derek asks. "Do I still have a room at the Hilton up by Fisherman's Bastion?"

"Did you pay for it beforehand?"

Derek nods.

"By now, they probably thought you weren't coming. But they'll have to give you a room if you go there. Do you want us to see what we can do?"

"If you wouldn't mind."

"No problem. We'll even give you a ride up there."

Peter stands and goes to the door, but Derek doesn't join him. He's looking down at his feet.

"Peter?"

"Yeah?"

"Do my girls know?"

Peter shakes his head, but Derek's head is still down. He doesn't see it. "No."

Derek looks up. "I have to tell them, huh?"

Peter watches him, not knowing what to say.

"Should I call them? Or wait until I get home?"

Peter shakes his head. "Derek, I'm afraid that's something you'll have to decide."

Derek stares at him.

"But if it were me, I'd call them. They deserve to know, and I wouldn't want to carry that burden the entire way home."

Derek swallows. "Can I call them from here?"

Peter nods.

"Will you sit with me when I do it?"

"Of course."

Chapter 48
Peter Andrassy

Peter and Zsuzsa sit in the doctor's office waiting to be seen. After arriving, Zsuzsa filled out a clipboard of documents, then handed it back to the receptionist and took a seat beside Peter. Peter holds a magazine in his hands, flipping pages. He hasn't a clue what's on them. His thoughts are with Zsuzsa and the baby.

Several weeks ago, when Zsuzsa had told him she was pregnant, he was thrilled and a little skeptical. He and Karen had tried for years before it finally happened. After Zsuzsa went to the doctor and it was confirmed, he felt a mix of excitement and anxiety. When Catherine was born, and he held her for the first time, he felt an incredible love he had never experienced. There were all kinds of benchmark moments, like the first time she called him Dadda or when she took her first steps. But along with those sweet memories come the incredibly painful ones too. Like when she was diagnosed with cancer. When the cancer had gone into remission, and when it came back. And the most painful of all, when she took her final breath on that fateful day many years ago. He knows as well as anyone the joy and pain children can inflict on their parents.

"Mrs. Andrassy?" a woman calls as she pushes open the door behind the check-in desk.

"Yes," Zsuzsa says and stands as Peter joins her.

The woman smiles and holds the door for them as they walk down the hallway. She asks Zsuzsa to stop at a scale to take her weight, then leads her to an examination room. She has Zsuzsa sit on the examination table while Peter sits on the chair along the wall. The woman puts a cuff around her arm and begins taking her blood pressure.

"How are you feeling?" she asks as she pumps the ball.

"Great!"

"No pain?"

"No. I'm sleepier than normal. But other than that, doing good."

"Have you had any morning sickness?"

Zsuzsa shrugs. "Only a couple times. I've been lucky so far."

The woman smiles. "Great. The doctor will be with you in just a moment."

She leaves the room, shutting the door behind her.

Peter and Zsuzsa look at each other. Peter stands and kisses her. "It'll be okay."

She nods, and the door to the examination room opens. Peter returns to his seat.

The doctor smiles at Zsuzsa after entering the room. "Hi, Zsuzsa. How are you feeling?"

"Great," she says.

The doctor looks at Peter and holds out her hand. "Mr. Andrassy, I'm Dr. Takács. I think we've met once before."

Peter nods and takes her hand, then she turns back to Zsuzsa. "Thanks for coming in today. I wanted to see you because there's something important we need to discuss."

Zsuzsa nods.

The doctor looks her over. "You look great. Everything about you seems perfect. I have no concerns after looking at the ultrasound."

Zsuzsa lets out a breath in relief. "Oh, good."

The doctor watches her. "But your baby..."

Zsuzsa's face falls.

"There is a problem. Now, I have to preface this by saying it's possible that the ultrasound is wrong. You're still early in your pregnancy, and it could be a false positive. We'd like to order a more in-depth ultrasound to see if we can learn more."

"What's wrong with the baby?" Zsuzsa asks.

The doctor watches her. "Your baby appears to have a heart defect."

Tears form in Zsuzsa's eyes, and the doctor hands her a box of tissues.

"But you said it isn't certain," Peter says, and the doctor looks at him.

"Correct. At this stage, we aren't certain. It's possible that the report from the ultrasound is wrong."

"How likely is that?" Peter asks.

"I don't know, exactly. But I'd say that about sixty percent turn out to be correct. Meaning there is a heart defect. These can also vary in severity. Some require what we'd call minor surgery after birth.

Some are more major. And others would require a heart transplant, if that's an option."

"So what now?" Zsuzsa asks, wiping her eyes.

The doctor turns back to Zsuzsa and puts her hand on her knee. "Let's get you scheduled for the other ultrasound, then I'll have you back to discuss the results, and we can talk more when we know more."

Zsuzsa nods and thanks her, and the doctor says the nurse will return to schedule the appointment. The doctor leaves, and Peter goes to Zsuzsa. He wraps her in his arms as she cries. The nurse opens the door, and he steps back. The nurse waits as Zsuzsa wipes her eyes. They discuss their schedules and plan the ultrasound for next week. Peter takes Zsuzsa's hand, and they walk out of the office and down the hall. When they reach the elevator, they look at each other.

"I love you," Zsuzsa says.

"I love you too."

Chapter 49
Derek Murphy

I exit the bus and check the map again to get my bearings. It's been thirty years since I've been here, and although many things look familiar, some things have changed. Like the trees, I don't remember there being so many. But maybe that's because I live in Arizona, where trees are a rarity. I walk along Kosdi Street, and it takes me back almost forty years. I was eight years old, and my friend Lajos and I were throwing rocks. We didn't have many targets and quickly turned our attention to the metal shed across the street. That is, until Mr. Németh came out and shooed us away. I look across the street and see the shed is still there, although I thought it was green. This one is painted gray. I wonder if it's the same one or if they knocked down the old one and rebuilt it. Back then, Kosdi Street was a dirt road. Now, it's a paved road with a lot of traffic. Cars are whizzing by, and I have to stay on the side of the road to avoid them.

I walk along for about five minutes and reach a small side street called Basa köz and stop. I check the map and look around. I think this is it. It's a dirt road, and on my right, there's a new house. It's a beautiful home surrounded by a custom iron fence. This was a field when I was a boy. It was part of my grandfather's property. Beside it, there's another house. It's a two-story home with a large covered patio and burned orange brick. I continue past it, feeling my excitement grow as my memory clears. Further up the road, I see the outline of a roof, and a feeling of familiarity washes over me.

I reach the outside of the home and look past the gate. There wasn't a gate thirty years ago, and the brick has been painted, but it's my house. My childhood home. The house I grew up in. Large power lines run overhead just to the side of the property. Those weren't here before. I look more closely at the gate beside me. Two mason pillars are on either side and look a little worse for wear. I run my hand along its rough edges. I remember my grandfather talking about putting a gate in front of the house. Is this his gate? Did he build it?

There's a mailbox in the center of one of the pillars with a name written on a piece of tape stuck to the outside. *Sandor család* (San-dor family). It's peeling at the edges, and I help it by grabbing an edge and peeling it back. There's a name stenciled into the metal, and I hold my breath when I read it. *Mészáros család.* I stare at it for several seconds, then replace the tape, but it won't stick. I give up and rub my palm along one pillar, thinking of my grandparents. Did they put these pillars in together? Did my grandfather do it alone because I wasn't here to help him?

I pull my backpack from my shoulders and get my wallet from the largest compartment. I step across the street and pull out the picture and hold it up. It's old and faded, but I can still see the similarities between the house in the photo and the house standing before me. I stare at my grandparents in the picture. Grandpa died many years ago. But Grandma, she lived well into her eighties. I should have come back. I could have seen her.

I stare at the house and wonder what my life would have been like if I had stayed here. If I hadn't gone to America. What would I be doing now? Would I have married Reka? She died several years back. Would I be a widower just like I am now?

I spend ten more minutes looking at the house and remembering my childhood before I replace the photo and walk away. I walk back to the bus stop and look across the street. There's a go-kart track. This wasn't here thirty years ago. I wonder how old it is. I walk across the street and stick my face against the chain-link fence, watching as two teenage boys race around the course. It looks like fun. I walk over to the small shack and ask if I can try it. The man tells me the price, and I hand over the forint. He opens the gate, and I step inside. He gives me a helmet and sits me down on the go-kart and explains the operation.

"Only one rule," he says, holding up a finger. "No bumping other cars."

"Okay," I say, and he waves a flag and has me join the race. I drive the first lap timidly, getting used to the controls. By the second lap, I'm gaining on the teenage boys. By the third lap, I've caught them, and I'm staying close, looking for an opportunity to pass. The second kart turns wide, and I go to the inside and pass him easily. He honks his horn in anger, and it makes me smile. I'm sandwiched between them now, looking for an opportunity to take the lead.

We come around a tight corner, and the lead car goes a little wide, and although there's enough room to pass, he sees me coming and corrects. Our wheels touch, and the momentum bumps him into the tires lined up on the outside of the course. He catches air and smashes into the fence, skidding to a stop. The course operator comes out yelling and blowing his whistle. I keep driving, pressing the pedal to the floor. The boy in the other cart stops, and I finish the course in first place.

I pull into the pit and turn off the go-kart as the operator and two teenage boys approach.

"Hey, I told you no bumping other karts," the operator yells at me.

"I didn't," I say as I take off my helmet.

"What do you call that?" he says, pointing to the kart leaning against the fence. One of the tires is off, and the frame has a dent.

I point at the boy. "He turned into me. I was trying to pass, and he wouldn't let me. It was his fault."

The boy throws down the gloves he's holding and comes forward. He's taller than I am, but I outweigh him by thirty pounds. He looks like he's going to take a swing, and I stare at him, daring him to do it. The operator reaches out and holds him back.

"Get outta here," the operator says, pointing to the exit. "Don't come back."

I glare at all of them. "I won't," I say and drop my helmet on the cart. I kick a tire on my way out.

I cross the street, wait for the bus to come, and climb aboard. Still smarting from the encounter, I take a seat next to an old lady. My frustration and anger cause my hands to shake, and she notices. She turns and glances at me, and I jerk slightly. She looks just like my grandmother. Complete with the large bag she holds on her lap and simple farm dress. She glances down at my hands, then back up into my eyes. She watches me with concern, and I can't meet her gaze. I look out the window as the bus makes its way back to Budapest. There's something else I need to do. I don't want to, but I know I can't go home before I do.

Chapter 50
Peter Andrassy

Peter sits at his desk at the Hungarian National Police Headquarters and makes notes in a file. Now that the case of Jacob Costa has been solved, he's returned to the human trafficking work he was doing before the case. A young girl went missing in Csepel, and the circumstances remind him of another case from several months ago. He pulled the other file and now has both open on his desk as Farkas leans over the cubicle wall.

"Peter?"

"Yeah?"

"Have a second?"

He motions with his finger for Peter to follow. They don't go to Farkas's office. Instead, Farkas leads him to a small conference room used only for team meetings. There's a table with six chairs, a large whiteboard, and windows facing the northern end of the city. One seat around the table is already occupied. Detective Moricz watches them walk in and stands to shake their hands.

"Thanks for coming, Peter," Moricz says.

Peter looks at Farkas, but he only sits and motions for Peter to do the same. Once they're all seated, Moricz and Farkas look at each other.

"You want to go?" Farkas asks.

Moricz shakes his head. "No, he's been working with you. It's your meeting."

Farkas nods and looks at Peter. "Once again, Peter, your work on the American case was exemplary. You're a real asset to the National Police."

"Thank you," Peter says. "I'll be sure to send my doctor bills to you."

Farkas smiles. "Moricz came to me with a proposal, and we wanted to bring it to you. It's your decision. No pressure either way."

"Okay."

"Moricz wants to offer you a permanent job with the Major Crimes Unit. He'd like you to go full time as a detective."

Peter looks at Moricz, who nods.

"I'd like to keep you with the human trafficking task force but can only keep you on as a consultant. We don't have funding for a full-time detective role."

Peter eyes them both.

"What do you say? What are your thoughts?"

Peter takes several seconds. "I enjoyed my time on the Costa case. I could do without any more death on the Danube. And, maybe not the dog part."

They all laugh.

"But I'm not looking for a full-time job. I still like some of the PI cases I work, and I appreciate the flexibility the consultant role gives me. If my only option is to go full time or not, I'll stay not."

Moricz nods. "I was afraid you'd say that. So, I have another thought."

"Okay."

"What if you consult for both? You help in the Major Crimes Unit when we need it and remain a consultant with the human trafficking task force."

Peter nods, considering it.

"What do you think of that?" Moricz asks Farkas.

"I'd rather keep Peter with us, but I can see where you'd need him, and if Peter wants to do it, I'd support it."

They both look at Peter.

"Seems like I'd need a raise," Peter says.

Moricz chuckles. "I think we can find some money in our budget."

Peter rubs his beard. "And I don't want to lose any of my flexibility."

They both nod.

"Let's try it, then," Peter says.

"Great," Moricz says and springs out of his chair to give Peter a handshake.

After they exit the room and Peter goes back to his desk, he finds someone sitting in his chair.

"Derek?" Peter says.

"Hi, Peter."

"What brings you here?"

"I wondered if I could still take you up on your offer."

"Okay," Peter says, unsure what that offer might be.

"I'd like to meet Edit."

Peter smiles. "Absolutely. Come with me."

Peter walks him down to the jail, and they go through security and enter one of the consultation rooms. "Take a seat. I'll get her and be right back."

"Peter," Derek says as Peter starts to close the door. "Will you stay in the room with me?"

Peter watches him, then nods. "I'd be happy to."

"Thanks."

Five minutes later, Peter guides Edit into the room. She's wearing a prisoner uniform and has her feet and wrists shackled. She and Derek look at each other, and Peter guides her across the table to a chair, then sits beside Derek.

For several seconds, Derek and Edit stare at each other.

"I don't know what to say," Derek finally says and looks at Peter.

Peter remains silent, and Derek looks back at Edit.

Again, they sit silently staring at each other.

Finally, Derek says, "Why? Why Brianna?"

Edit shrugs. "She wasn't supposed to be involved."

Derek frowns. "Then why kill her?" His voice rises with anger.

Edit glares at him. "Because I couldn't get to you. Jacob was supposed to kill you, and when he didn't, we took Brianna as leverage."

"Leverage? For what?"

"For you..."

"I did nothing to you."

Edit scoffs and looks away. "She didn't deserve it. But you did. After my uncle was killed, I had no choice. I had to kill Brianna. At least her death hurt you."

Derek shakes his head. "You're crazy."

She shrugs.

"Plus, I deserved it? How did I deserve it?"

She shakes her head, and tears form in her eyes. "You were so ashamed of me, you disappeared. You turned your back on your own daughter. You knew I was there and just disappeared."

Derek shakes his head. "Where? In Arizona? I didn't know you were there. I didn't even know you existed."

"Liar," Edit screams, and tears spill onto her cheeks. "I saw the letters. I saw the letters you wrote to Mom. You said you would come back. She believed you. You broke her heart."

Derek stares at her for several seconds, then shakes his head. "Did you read them? Did you see anywhere in them where I referenced you? Anywhere I talked about you? No, because I didn't know about you. Reka never told me she was pregnant. I didn't know you existed until now."

Edit shakes her head. "I don't believe you. Everything you say is a lie."

"You've got a lot of room to judge me; you killed my wife."

"You broke my mother's heart," Edit fires back. "You abandoned me."

Derek clenches his fists and starts to stand, but Peter puts a hand on his knee and looks at him. Derek looks away from Edit to Peter and forces himself to calm. After several seconds, his breathing slows, and he puts a palm on his forehead. "Look, I didn't come here to argue with you. I'll never forgive you for what you did to my wife, but I recognize how it might have looked to you. But there's something you need to understand: when I left Hungary, I thought it was a vacation. I thought I'd be back in a couple weeks. I didn't know Reka was pregnant. I loved her as much as a juvenile fifteen-year-old boy can. When I wrote those letters and said I'd come back, I meant it. But as time went by and I got more comfortable in America, I had a life there. I fell in love again. I had a family and a career. My life was there."

Edit glares at him, but his message seems to have landed. There's not the same amount of venom in her eyes.

"You may never understand. And I'm sorry I wasn't in your life. But what you did..." Derek stops and looks at his hands, then back up into her eyes. "You belong in here for good."

Chapter 51

Peter Andrassy

Peter exits the yellow tram at Móricz Zsigmond Square in Southern Buda and walks along Karinthy Frigyes Way for several blocks until reaching a small park outside some large apartment buildings built during the communist rule. He looks at a park bench and sees who he came to visit. His friend, Lantos Tamás, sits alone, a cigarette dangling from his mouth.

Tom, as Peter likes to call him, has been his close friend for a couple of years now. They met at the screening of an American film here in Budapest. There weren't even Hungarian subtitles. Tom had learned English while living in London before the start of World War II. He moved back to Budapest before the war started and then couldn't leave. Now, he enjoys practicing his English with Peter.

"I thought I might find you here," Peter says as he approaches.

Tom looks over his shoulder and breathes out a puff of smoke. He watches as Peter sits beside him. "I wondered if I might see you today," Tom says.

"Missed me, huh?" Peter asks.

"Ha, no. I was actually wondering if you'd found out yet."

Peter eyes him. "Found out what?"

"About me and Zsuzsa," Tom says. "Did she finally tell you?"

Peter smiles. "Tell me what?"

Tom puts a hand on his shoulder. "I'm sorry, Peter. She's decided to leave you for me. She just couldn't resist anymore."

Peter chuckles. "Well, I knew it couldn't last forever. I thought it would be more than a few months, but I guess it was inevitable."

Tom finally smiles. "How is that gorgeous wife of yours anyway?"

"Honestly, things could be better."

Tom frowns and takes a drag on his cigarette before letting out the smoke. "What's wrong?"

"She's pregnant."

Tom's face nearly splits with a grin. "You're kidding. That's great." He fishes his pack of cigarettes from his pocket and hands one to Peter. "Join me for a celebratory smoke."

Peter shakes his head and holds up his hands. "You know I don't smoke."

"Just one," Tom says, forcing a cigarette into his hand.

Peter sighs and takes it, putting it in his mouth and grabbing Tom's lighter and lighting it. He takes a breath and chokes, coughing.

"Ha ha," Tom says, patting him on the back. "Congratulations, my boy. I'm so happy for you two."

Peter gets his coughing under control and holds the cigarette, knowing he won't take another drag. They fall silent, Tom periodically smoking, while Peter holds his, hoping it burns out quickly.

"So, you said things could be better. Has she been sick?"

Peter shakes his head. "No."

"Moody?"

"Not more than usual." Peter grins.

"What, then?"

Peter drops the cigarette and smashes it out with his foot. "When she had her first ultrasound, they found a heart defect."

Tom frowns. "In her?"

"No. The baby."

Tom looks at him gravely. "Oh."

"Yeah."

"What did the doctor say?"

"She wants her to go in again for another ultrasound. She said it's possible it could be a misdiagnosis."

"And what if it's not?" Tom asks.

Peter shakes his head. "Anywhere from a minor surgery at birth to fatal."

Tom turns away from him and looks out over the park. There's a group of people playing tennis, and he watches them for several seconds. He turns back to Peter. "How are you feeling?"

Peter shrugs. "I'm worried about Zsuzsa. She was so excited about being pregnant. If we lose the baby..." Peter shakes his head. "I don't know what that will do to her."

Tom drops his cigarette and turns toward Peter. "I didn't ask about Zsuzsa. I asked about you. How are you feeling?" Tom points at his chest.

They stare at each other for several seconds before Peter has to look away. Peter shakes his head. "I don't think I can do it again. I can't lose another child."

Tom nods, and the two men sit silently, staring at the ground.

"What if it's me?" Peter asks after several seconds.

"What? What's you?"

Peter shrugs. "What if it's me that causes this? My genes. Something about me."

Tom glares at him. "What, are you stupid?"

Peter looks back at him.

"You really have a high opinion of yourself, don't you?"

Peter frowns. "You're supposed to be my friend."

"I am your friend. That's why I can call you stupid."

Peter looks away from him.

"Listen to me. That's why you came, isn't it?"

Tom leans toward him, staring, and Peter finally looks at him and nods.

"Your daughter died from cancer. Your baby has a possible heart defect. Neither is linked. It's nothing you did. God's not punishing you. Bad things happen to good people. You're one of those good people." Tom raises his sleeve to reveal the numbered tattoo he received in the concentration camp so many years ago. "Do you hear me?"

Peter looks at him and nods, and Tom puts a hand on his shoulder. "I hope it's a girl."

Peter looks at him warily. "Why?"

Tom shakes his head wistfully. "Because, I'd like to live in a world with more Zsuzsas running around."

Chapter 52
Derek Murphy

Cruise Day 11 – Phoenix, Arizona

I get my bag down from the overhead storage, wait my turn in line, and walk off the plane. I follow the signs to baggage claim and stop in front of the doors that separate ticketed passengers from the rest of the airport. I look out and see my daughters lined up, waiting for me. Calling them from Hungary and telling them their mother had died was an experience I wouldn't wish on my worst enemy. It was beyond awful. But now, standing here, I'm glad I went through it. If I had to tell them now, in person, I'd never have left the plane. They would have had to carry me off.

I take a deep breath and walk out the doors. They see me, and my oldest, Allison, runs forward with her sisters trailing behind. I set down my bag and wrap her in my arms. We say nothing. After several seconds, her sister Leslie hugs me, then Tina, and finally Wendy. When I release Wendy, I look at them as they stare at me with tears running down their cheeks.

"Let's get the bags," I say and motion them forward.

Allison helps me with mine, and Wendy holds my hand. We walk to the baggage claim and wait with the other passengers. I see the first bag, and it's a pink suitcase. It's Brianna's. I point to it, and Leslie steps forward and retrieves it. Another of Brianna's bags comes out, but mine never does. Finally, the conveyor belt stops running, and we're left alone at the baggage claim.

I grit my teeth. "I guess they lost my bag."

I walk to the airline baggage office. A woman with bright lipstick sits behind the desk.

"I just came in on a flight from Amsterdam. My bag never came out."

The woman looks at me. "Do you have your claim receipt?"

I reach into my pockets but can't find it. "No. I must have lost it."

She rolls her eyes. "Sir, we give those to you for a reason."

Her flippant attitude is more than I can take, and I unleash a barrage on her. I feel myself losing control as I yell at her.

A man comes out of the office. "Sir."

"What?" I yell.

"Calm down. We'll find your bag."

A door opens behind me, and I see it's my daughter Leslie. She comes to me, grabs my hand, and starts pulling me back. "Dad, it's okay."

"No, it's not," I say to her and turn back to the man. "You lost my bag and blame me for it?" I scowl at the woman.

The man holds up his hand. "What does it look like?"

I tell him, and he returns to his office to make a call. He comes out a minute later. "We've found your bag. An agent is bringing it around. Wait outside, and we'll have it here shortly."

"Good," I say. "Thank you." I scowl at the woman behind the desk one more time and follow Leslie out of the room.

My girls are standing together when we exit, and I see the concern in their eyes. Tina comes forward and rubs my arm. "It's okay, Dad. It's just a bag."

I look at her and nod. This isn't like me. I've never yelled at an airport employee. Never. I can feel my nerves fraying.

After a couple of minutes, the agent comes with my bag, and we leave. The drive home takes twenty minutes, and when we pull up to the house, I notice pink ribbons tied around trees, bushes, and light poles. There's a sign in the front welcoming us home. As I pull into the driveway, I turn to Allison, who sits beside me in the front seat. "Was this you?"

She nods. "All of us. We had to do something."

I force a smile. "Your mom would have loved it."

I look in the rearview mirror and see all of my girls crying, and I come to a realization. I'm inadequate. I don't know how to take away the hurt. I don't know what to say or what to do. Why couldn't it have been me rather than Brianna?

We exit the car and bring the bags inside. I have my backpack draped over my shoulder and hold one of Brianna's bags. "Girls," I say, gathering them around me. "It's been a really long couple of weeks and a long flight home. I want to talk to you, but I need a minute. I'm going to go take a shower, then maybe we can go to dinner and talk."

They nod, brushing back tears, and I go up the stairs feeling as if the house is going to collapse all around me. I enter our master bedroom, set down my bag, and put Brianna's on the bed. I enter the bathroom and turn on the water but don't remove my clothes or enter the shower. Instead, I go back to Brianna's side of the bed and open her bag. She packed my toiletries. I pull them out, sit on the bed, and look around. I look at the closet and see Brianna's clothes hanging there. I look in the bathroom and see her sink. I look in her bag and see the book she was reading and pick it up. It's the same one she was reading on the plane. There's a bookmark on page 179. She still has over a hundred pages to read. I stare down at the bookmark, and something breaks inside me. Tears well up in my eyes and spill onto the pages. A flood of emotion overwhelms me, and I fall to my knees beside our bed.

I sob like I've never cried before. The ache and hurt overwhelm me and come pouring out. How can I do it? How can I live without her? How could she leave me? I drop my head onto the bed and feel overwhelmed with grief. I feel completely alone when I sense hands on my shoulders. I look up through the tears to see my daughters surrounding me. They're crying just like me. We've all lost her. I reach out and hug these beautiful girls, who remind me so much of their mother, and realize I don't have to help them through this, they're going to help me.

Afterword

*All of us on the final night in
Budapest*

In August 2025, my wife, Brooke, and I embarked on a European river cruise that started in Passau, Germany, and finished in Budapest, Hungary. We had talked about doing a river cruise for many years but never had. Mostly because of cost. In 2025, we celebrated our twenty-fifth wedding anniversary and finally pulled the trigger. I only wish we had received a 50 percent discount like Derek and Brianna.

On the first day of the cruise, while touring Passau, we ran into two other couples who were from our same state back home. As we talked, we learned we had a lot in common and became fast friends.

Our vacation was even better because of them. Their names are Jeremy and Nancy Coccimiglio and Tom and Michelle Gledhill. For the rest of the cruise, we spent a lot of time together, including every meal. Sometimes we were assigned to different walking-tour groups, but we ignored that to stay together.

Our ship captain, server, and maid were all Hungarian. It was fun for me to speak Hungarian with them. Our cruise ported in Passau, Germany; Linz, Austria; Krems, Austria; Bratislava, Slovakia; and Budapest, Hungary, just like in this book. At the time, I had finished writing *Freeing Nicole* and was waiting for it to be published. I had a plan for my next book, but plans change.

At dinner one night—I think we might have been in Vienna—I told the group I had a new idea for a book inspired by this cruise. I was pleased to see how excited they all were about it. For the rest of the trip, the idea kept rolling around in my mind. On the flight home, I knew I had to write it.

So many of the story beats in this book came from actual events. No, there weren't any murders. But the cruise followed the same itinerary in real life. I took a lot of liberties with each character, but Brianna is loosely based on my wife, Brooke. I'm Derek. Jeremy is Jacob, and Nancy is Naomi. Just to be clear, Nancy is definitely not a killer... Tom is Theo, and Michelle is Melody. Just like in the book, the six of us officially met at the same hiking spot beneath the castle in Passau. And just like in the book, Nancy admitted later to having overheard us talking at breakfast and knowing we were neighbors back home.

We experienced all the excursions detailed in the book, although, just like in the book, Brooke and I visited the art museum and Elisabeth museum alone in Vienna, while the other two couples rode bikes along the river and came across a group of nudists. We heard all about it at dinner.

In Budapest, after the walking tour, I served as our guide, taking them to all the places I described in the book. You'll notice on the book's cover there's a torn photo of three couples standing in front of Matthias Church in Budapest. That's us. It's a real picture we took together. It poured rain later that day, just like in the book. And, after dinner, Brooke and I watched the Hungarian performers in the ship's lounge and even balanced the wine bottle on our heads to take pictures. The other two couples didn't join us. They had an early flight. We even went upstairs to the top deck afterward, which is where I got the idea for the first chapter.

Brooke and I extended our stay in Budapest for several more days, touring around and even going to some spots I had never been to before, while also staying at the Hilton up by Fisherman's Bastion. We never made it out to Vác, although I've been there several times before. I included the go-karts because I used to drive them as often as I could in that exact spot in Vác.

If you've read some of my other books before, you know I'm a music lover. I listen to music when I write, when I work, when I exercise, and whenever I'm in the shower. I have a huge playlist of songs, thousands of titles deep. I like to listen to it all—country, rock, rap, and instrumental music, especially soundtracks—while I write. One day, as I was writing this book, I was in the shower and listening to my playlist when an old song by Tim McGraw came on, "Can't Be Really Gone." It's a song about a man who was left by his wife. The moment I heard it, I knew how I wanted to end this book. I wanted Derek back home, seeing all his wife's things, and believing she couldn't really be gone.

I hope you enjoyed reading this book as much as I did writing it. It felt like I was back on vacation again, which was fantastic. I would highly recommend it to anyone. We can't wait to go on another. Maybe for our thirtieth?

I've said it before, and I'll never stop saying it. Thank you to all my readers for giving my work a shot. If this is your first Peter book, I have five others. This one picked up where *9-1-1* left off. If you've read them all, thank you! I love Peter, and as I've said in the past, I'll keep writing him as long as people keep reading about him.

My next book will be back to Hank and Joyce. I'll give myself a month or two to rest, then start back up. I don't have a title yet, but look for it to be published in the fall of 2026.

D.J. Maughan

Also by D.J. Maughan

D.J. Maughan novels by date of publication

Vanished From Budapest – published December 9, 2022. Peter Andrassy novel one. Psychological thriller. Standalone.

The Villains Mask – published March 15, 2023. Prequel to Vanished from Budapest. Short story. Standalone.

Pursuit of Demons – published March 17, 2023. Peter Andrassy novel two. Book one of the Vanished series.

Revealing the Shadows – published July 23, 2023. Peter Andrassy novel three. Book two of the Vanished series.

Chasing the Wicked – published November 22, 2023. Peter Andrassy novel four. Book three of the Vanished series.

One Desperate Life – published April 26, 2024. Standalone gripping thriller.

Idaho Fall – published October 1, 2024. Hank and Joyce novel one. Standalone twisty whodunit.

The First Five Peter Andrassy Thrillers box set – published October 12, 2024. Available in eBook only through Amazon.

9-1-1 – published March 27, 2025. Peter Andrassy novel five. Crime thriller. Standalone.

Trick or Death – published October 1, 2025. Hank and Joyce short story. Standalone.

Freeing Nicole – published October 1, 2025. Hank and Joyce novel two. Standalone twisty whodunit.

Death on the Danube – published March 19, 2026. Peter Andrassy novel six. Psychological thriller. Standalone

About the author

D.J. at Szepilona's Bisztro

D.J. Maughan is an avid reader, event manager, father, husband, public speaker, and award-winning author. No surprise that he writes in the Thriller/Mystery genre, that's what he loves to read. He craves the unexpected and strives to provide that to his readers. He seeks inspiration everywhere, especially while studying and visiting diverse places and cultures. Whether jumping from a cliff in Hawaii or hiking the Plitvica Lakes in Croatia, he's in heaven as long as his wife and four sons are at his side.

Signup for my newsletter for a couple of free short stories and updates on my writing and publishing djmaughan.com

Acknowledgements

Thank you to my beta readers. Your insights helped shape this novel. Brooke Maughan, Lupe Merino, Rachel Browning, Paul Gyorke, Jessica Earles, Dawn Resue, Katie Jablonka, Kelsey Housman, Erin Sterett, Hannah Exey, Heather Kerber, Raeann Wolfley, Jennifer Harper, Laurie Clark, Luke Barber, Jerry Paskett, Jeremy Coccimiglio.

A big thank you to my editor, Jonathan Starke. I also want to thank Amanda Cox, my cover designer. I appreciate your help and kindness. Finally, thank you to my son, Wally. He named the novel.